Fatal Fiction

Kym Roberts

LYRICAL UNDERGROUND
Kensington Publishing Corp.
www.kensingtonbooks.com

LYRICAL UNDERGROUND BOOKS are published by

Kensington Publishing Corp.
119 West 40th Street
New York, NY 10018

All Kensington titles, imprints, and distributed lines are available at special quantity discounts for bulk purchases for sales promotion, premiums, fundraising, educational, or institutional use.

Special book excerpts or customized printings can also be created to fit specific needs. For details, write or phone the office of the Kensington Sales Manager: Kensington Publishing Corp., 119 West 40th Street, New York, NY 10018. Attn. Sales Department. Phone: 1-800-221-2647.

Lyrical Underground and Lyrical Underground logo Reg. US Pat. & TM Off.

First Electronic Edition: December 2016
eISBN-13: 978-1-60183-731-8
eISBN-10: 1-60183-731-3

First Print Edition: December 2016
ISBN-13: 978-1-60183-732-5
ISBN-10: 1-60183-732-1

Printed in the United States of America

For my kids—
You are my world

ACKNOWLEDGMENTS

I'd like to thank the members of Chick Swagger for their constant support—you ladies are the best! To the Chick Swagger Sirens for their supply of "inspiration"; you make my writing world ROCK! (You know exactly what I'm talking about—and who). To my family, for your love, support, and patience during the dinners and weekends without me while I write the night away, I couldn't do it without you.

Thank you to my agent, Kim Lionetti, who continued to push me to write my best and finally got my work out there to the readers. Martin Biro, my editor, you are awesome! Even if you marked up my manuscript with all kinds of color and notes and suggestions and no-no-nos! It wouldn't have worked any other way—plus you gave it a GREAT TITLE—thank you!

I love you all.

Chapter One

L ife has a way of putting some people in the wrong place at the wrong time. Take me, for example. I happen to be one of those unlucky souls who finds themselves in bad situations more often than not. My parents should have tattooed a bull's-eye of doom on my forehead at birth. My luck can be *that* bad, and today was proving how rotten my karma could be.

The cab ride to town cost thirty-eight dollars. I had forty-five dollars in my purse. There was one credit card in my matching leather wallet, but I'd charged it to the max when I'd purchased my plane ticket that morning. I'm sorry to say that tipping the cabby hurt—a lot. And my driver was less than happy with his two-dollar tip. He pulled away from the curb spitting gravel and dust all over my black dress, causing me to sputter and choke as dirt filled the dry, hot air. I turned away, hoping I still looked my best, and faced my childhood playground. The family business I swore I'd never come back to, yet here I was—standing in front of the biggest eyesore in town, while the rest of the shops looked like picturesque postcards.

Back when I was a kid, the store was kind of quaint. The Book Barn had been a blast from the past: a faded red dairy barn with the washed-out logo, "Livery & Feed Stable" painted across the face of the second-story hayloft door. It had fit in perfectly with the rest of the town's Wild West atmosphere. My parents had displayed the books in the old stable stalls, separating the categories and creating havens for me to disappear in for hours. The second-story hayloft was a thing of awe—a never-ending library of used books overlooking the center of the barn. The entire building had been decorated with antique western gear and paraphernalia. It was historic and allowed visitors to imagine what it must have been like for a cowboy who drifted into town. His first stop would be at the stable, where he'd drop off his horse for the night before crossing the dirt road to wet his whistle in the saloon.

The saloon, however, hadn't served drinks since the Prohibition era. It was now a salon that produced trademarked big Texas hairstyles and offered manis and pedis instead of shots of rotgut whiskey. No doubt they also had a tanning bed inside from the look of the leathery hide of the blonde currently exiting the store while talking on her cell phone.

My skin would never need a tanning bed, my ethnicity giving my complexion a naturally golden tone that had been the envy of every girl on the cheer squad in high school. But if I stayed in town too long, I'd have to revert back to my teen years and make an appointment for a hot oil treatment at the Beaus and Beauties salon to keep my brown curls from turning brittle in the dry Texas heat.

I turned my attention back to The Book Barn. Its newly remodeled exterior was an eye-catching monstrosity in a bright shade of fuchsia with glowing white trim. The fresh coat of paint erased all remnants of the stable's original logo and punctuated the store's new name, The Book Barn *Princess*. What made it unique was the cute— or tacky—armadillo that formed the letter *i* as it stood on its hind legs with a tiara dotting the letter, almost like a suspended halo. In effect, the new design ruined the Old West image the town had held for decades.

There was absolutely nothing picturesque about the store's current color, which was brighter than the pink purse draped across my chest. It was horrible, in a girlie kind of way . . . and part of me melted. My dad had remodeled the family bookstore in my favorite color—despite the fact that the business was centrally located in the heart of downtown Hazel Rock, Texas, population 2,093, where the new color stuck out like a displaced neon sign in the middle of the Wild West show.

And he'd named it after me.

My eyes moistened. After a dozen-and-a-half-years, my dad was trying to make amends to his "little princess."

Then I remembered the cab ride that had cleaned out my wallet and allowed the pain from the past to close the door on my heart.

Pink won't erase the past, Daddy.

I ignored the speculative looks from two more blondes with big hair exiting the salon and stomped to the front door. I would've slammed the front door wide open and let it bang against the wall, but Dad had installed automatic doors that glided open with a soft swish. A little buzzer, low and unobtrusive, sounded as I stepped inside—nothing like the slap of my boots as I crossed the freshly stained concrete floor. The voice of a popular country singer who'd made it big on one of those reality TV talent search programs streamed through the store's deserted sales floor. Not a soul wandered through the rows of new and used books for sale.

Obviously some things never changed.

"Are you hiding from me? 'Cause if you brought me down here to make a laughingstock out of me, I will make sure you regret it . . . *Daddy.*" My tone wasn't pleasant. If anything, it was downright threatening.

I knew I shouldn't talk to my father that way, and part of me felt bad. The other part, the living-in-reality part, only remembered the pain I'd experienced during my junior year of high school and I couldn't let it slide. I leaned over the bright white counter, cluttered with princess knickknacks for sale in every shade of pink imaginable, expecting to find him cowering down behind it.

It was as empty as the dry creek bed I'd passed on the way into town.

I turned toward the back of the store, still stomping, making my way through the aisles of books that made me want to stop and browse. I resisted the temptation and headed for the storeroom, calling throughout the cavernous space on my way. "If you had Marlene call me so you could finally sell this place, why are you hiding?" My voice carried through the store, punctuating the fact that I was alone.

But I wasn't. I couldn't be. The store was open for business, a coffeepot was on behind the counter, and the place was filled with the aroma of my father's favorite vice: rich, dark Colombian coffee beans.

I yanked back the soft pink velvet curtain hanging across the doorway to the stockroom, the material heavy and luxurious in my hand, and got the shock of my life. Marlene Duncan, the Realtor who'd contacted me and convinced me to fly down and get my daddy out of the financial mess he'd created with the tacky remodel, was in front of me—wearing the pink bejeweled belt I'd cherished in high school.

But it wasn't around her waist. It was tightened around her neck and she was deader than a doornail.

Chapter Two

I stood frozen to my spot. Unable to believe I was in my hometown looking at the body of the woman who'd been the only one able to convince me to return to Hazel Rock in over twelve years. A woman who had spoken with so much life and animation on the phone less than six hours before was now dead.

That's when I heard it. The sound of paper tearing. The slow, painful rip of someone maliciously destroying the work that had poured from an author's heart and soul. I looked up at the loft. A book slammed to the floor somewhere above me.

My feet thawed faster than an ice cube in July. I ran for the front of the store. The bell dinged, the doors swished, and I was down the two steps on the porch before I could scream. I did what came naturally—I ran for the salon across the street and burst through the door.

Six pairs of eyes turned and looked at me.

"Charli Rae Warren, is that you? There is no way I could ever forget those curls."

Trying to calm myself, I pulled my purse up on my shoulder and gulped the fresh scent of perm and fingernail polish. I swung around to the voice I should have recognized but didn't. The redhead with a pair of scissors in her hand looked vaguely familiar, but I didn't remember anyone with that vibrant hair color or that smile. Then I took another breath and realized her hair was probably chemically treated. I squinted, as if that would help me figure out who she was—but it wasn't helping in my current state.

"Welcome home, Princess."

"No one calls me Princess anymore. It's just Charli." I breathed, still unable to place her despite her bright smile. "Can I use your phone?"

She continued as if I hadn't said anything. "I didn't have red hair in high school. It was boring brown." She turned and started cutting the hair of the older woman in the chair in front of her. "Is that all you need, a phone? Or do you need to get your hair done?"

Unable to process a word she said, I dug in my purse for my cell. The woman I apparently should have recognized rambled on about me finally coming home to visit as I pulled my phone from my purse and dialed 911 with shaking hands.

I turned away and waited for the dispatcher to answer as my breathing slowed down. I stared out the front window toward the big pink barn. A deep voice answered my call and I found myself trying to convince the male dispatcher that there really was a dead body in the storage room across the street while keeping my voice low enough so the beauty shop occupants wouldn't hear about my gruesome discovery. The last thing I wanted to do was break the news of someone's death.

"Did Bobby Ray put you up to this? That guy is a regular prankster," the dispatcher said.

I lost it. The composure I'd struggled to maintain flew out the window and my angry tongue took over. About the time I blurted out my fourth expletive, he finally got a clue that I was telling the truth and that a killer could still be in the store. It was either that or he believed I was crazier than a two-headed sow eating out of a trough for one. He cleared his throat and advised me the sheriff would be "en route." He further directed me not to leave the salon. I was to sit and wait right where I was.

Considering my legs were wobbling like a newborn filly's, I didn't argue . . . much. I plopped down in an empty chair and briefly closed my eyes as I hung up the phone. That's when I realized the background noise had disappeared. Voices were silent. Scissors weren't snipping, and the juiciest gossip that had hit this town in more than a decade was forming into front-page news right before the beauty crew's very eyes. I peeked through the slit of my left eyelid at the six women staring in my direction. They couldn't possibly have heard my conversation, but they definitely caught my cussing.

Suddenly the identity of the stunning redhead standing with her scissors frozen in midair hit me. It was the current faint smile she wore, the calm one that had lost some of its sparkle, kind of like Mona Lisa; she saw everything but gave nothing away. That coupled with the constant jibber-jabbering she'd done when I ran in knocked my memory into gear.

"Scarlet." My voice sounded a little breathless as I said her name. She had been the principal's assistant back in high school, the girl with the overbearing glasses, an IQ of about 180, who could talk your ear off about nothing and not hear a word you said in return. Scarlet Jenkins, little Miss Bookworm had transformed. She still wore glasses, but they were in vogue and trendy, and her hair was a gorgeous auburn with soft, short curls around her face that complimented her alabaster complexion, the exact opposite of my biracial heritage. Her sense of style was right out of a fashion magazine. She was beautiful, with curves I didn't have.

Then she smiled that five-hundred-watt smile again, the one she'd given me when I first walked in. The one I definitely wouldn't have forgotten if she'd used it back in high school, which she hadn't.

"You remembered! So are you in town to say good-bye to the store? It's a little different than what it used to be." The woman in the chair getting her hair cut snorted, but Scarlet continued. "I know it was probably a shock when you saw it. It pretty much shocks everyone, but people like to take their pictures in front of it, and for the most part it's been a good draw for tourists. Some of the locals grumble and complain . . ." The woman in the chair snorted again and I wondered if I should know her, but my brain was focused on one thing:

Marlene was dead.

"Get her a cup of coffee, Joellen." Scarlet patted the bony shoulder of the older woman in her chair, who was eyeing me like a serial killer incarnate. Scarlet put her scissors down at her station and approached me while the blonde, Joellen, who'd been doing her own nails when I walked in, glanced down at her work and then jumped up and went into the back room.

Searching my face, Scarlet saw something. What, I'm not sure, but she suddenly turned toward the hairdresser applying the perm solution on her customer's hair. "Aubrey said she didn't go in to work at The Barn until after school, right, Mary?"

The beautician didn't look up from the bottle she was squirting on her customer's curlers. Her scratchy voice fit the wrinkles on her face, despite the fact that she couldn't have been more than forty.

"Yes, she said she had a test this morning and she had a term paper to work on before she went to work at four."

Scarlet turned back to me, studying my expression, which I desperately tried to keep neutral . . . I failed. She saw what the other women didn't and knew something was seriously wrong. The conclusion she came to, however, was awry. She pulled me into an embrace that felt awkward and comforting at the same time. Standing almost a head taller, I bent over to return it like we were long-lost buddies. That's when she whispered in my ear, "Is something wrong with your daddy? Do I need to go over to The Barn with you?"

"No!"

My panicked outburst caused Mary's customer to jump. The hairdresser just rolled her eyes and continued wrapping a piece of the woman's hair in foil.

Scarlet pulled me close once more, her voice too low for the others to hear. "OMW. Charli, it's okay. Everything will be okay." Her voice hitched with emotion and she patted my back.

After I'd unleashed enough filth out of my mouth to fill the county sewage plant, Scarlet was using an acronym for "*Oh my word.*" I cringed as she continued. "Don't you worry. Marlene will help make sure the sale of the store goes through. She's the best real estate woman this side of Abilene. She'll take care of you."

Nodding, I didn't say a word. Scarlet had obviously drawn the conclusion that something horrible had happened to my dad, and for some reason, I was content to let her believe it . . . for now.

Then I remembered how Scarlet talked and talked while I sat in the principal's office as a kid. At the time I'd thought she was trying to get me to confess my sins, but all she did was fill the void my silence left. Just like she was doing now, and there was no way I was going to break the news to anyone that Marlene was the one who was dead. That the woman who had been a Realtor in Hazel Rock for as long as I could remember had been murdered in The Book Barn . . . Princess.

I stared at the tiara on the front of the building. The new look was everything my mom would have hated, everything I might have loved as a teenager still trying to figure out my style. Or at least everything my dad would have thought I'd like.

Joellen came out of the back room with a steaming cup of coffee and I took it, attempting to smile at the young woman and grateful for something to do with my hands while Scarlet rambled on about Texas pecan coffee, which you could only find in the Lone Star State. I thought about telling her, "It's available on Amazon," but kept my mouth shut and took a sip. If I was going to be stuck waiting for the county sheriff, who I'd been avoiding most of my life, while listening to Scarlet, I was going to do my best to get my thoughts in order. This fiasco was costing me a day's wages, a plane ticket, and cab fare my dad obviously wasn't going to reimburse me for. Even though Marlene had promised he would.

And the fact that I was worrying about money when poor Marlene was lying on the floor across the street in need of a makeover, a manicure, and a beating heart, made me feel about as low as cow manure smeared between the sole and heel of a cowboy boot.

Closing my eyes, I took another drink of the steaming brew, aware that even my lips were trembling. A glance at the clock told me it'd been seven minutes since I'd dialed 911. Scarlet continued talking through it all. She was currently touching on the subject of family plots in the town's cemetery while I convinced myself the killer had snuck out the back door and was long gone.

A police cruiser pulled up and parked two stores down. I watched a cop I didn't recognize cautiously enter The Book Barn with his gun drawn. He didn't wear the standard issue cowboy hat, and his uniform fit snuggly across a broad chest and chiseled physique.

All the women stopped what they were doing to watch the cop, who definitely wasn't the old-as-dirt sheriff I remembered, and then they turned to look at me. Waiting for me to answer the questions they weren't asking. Everyone, that is, except Scarlet. She'd returned to her customer and was cutting her hair as if nothing was wrong. Her sniffle proved otherwise.

I took a gulp of the hot pecan coffee and concentrated on the burn that would scar my esophagus for life as I waited for the cop to exit the store, preferably in one piece.

It took him five minutes to come out. Five minutes that went by without a word from the women in the salon, at least nothing past a whisper as everyone excluding Scarlet and her customer, who I remembered owned the quilt shop in town, huddled at the front window. When the officer finally did step outside, the women ran to their separate stations as if they hadn't been plastered to the picture window waiting to see what would happen next.

They struggled for topics to talk about. Mary was rambling on about the new patch her doctor had given her to help her quit smoking, while Joellen tried to show Scarlet's customer the design she'd painted on her fingernails and the older woman "oohed" and "ahhed" about her skill. From where I sat, it looked as if at least two of them were smudged beyond repair.

Thanks to a stern look from Scarlet, not one of them said a word to me or quizzed me about what was happening, even though I knew they wanted to. Another cruiser pulled up outside and the sheriff gave the arriving deputy instructions about taping off the crime scene as he pointed around the perimeter of the store.

He spoke into his shoulder mic a few times but never let his gaze stray from the salon for too long. When he finally crossed the street, I got a better look at the man with skin almost as dark as mine. He had large brown eyes accentuated by a row of dark curly lashes and his thick, dark hair was cut short like a military man's.

I'd always been a sucker for tall, dark, and dangerous, but that uniform was the last thing I wanted to see on my bedroom floor. He caught my assessment as he walked in the door and returned it.

"You must be Charli Rae Warren." He looked around the beauty shop as Scarlet went over and shook his hand. Then he nodded hello to Joellen, who was back at her table doing something to her nails. He tipped his chin to Mrs. Walker in Scarlet's chair, then Mary and her customer. I didn't catch the last woman's name as I watched him amble toward me.

"You must be Sheriff . . ." My voice trailed off. He certainly wasn't the sheriff I was expecting. The man I'd known my whole life should be in his seventies, if not older, and would be spouting verses from the good book by now, just like he had every time I'd sneezed the wrong way as a teenager. No, this sheriff was my age and very attractive. If I was in to the type of guy who wore a uniform and a gun. Which, again, I reminded myself, I wasn't.

"Espinosa. Mateo Espinosa, ma'am." He held out his hand to shake mine and I nearly spilled my coffee all over my lap. He steadied the cup and shook my hand without batting an eye. "You called 911?"

"Yes, sir." I looked at the other women, who leaned forward to get the details so they could spread them through the county gossip channels. Scarlet interrupted, thank God.

"Mateo, Charli grew up here. She came back to sign off on the sale of The Book Barn Princess, but . . ."

Sheriff Mateo nodded his head in understanding, but his eyebrow lifted in my direction. I didn't take that as a good sign.

I gulped down the last of the still steaming coffee and suffered through the trail it blazed down my throat. I stared at my cup while trying to figure out a way to talk to him without everyone and their sister getting the scoop before the sheriff could notify Marlene's family. Fortunately, he was one step ahead of me.

"Ms. Warren and I need to speak in the back room for a minute or two, if that's all right with you, Scarlet?" He didn't wait for a response, and the next thing I knew, I was following his orders and standing in a break room with a table, a refrigerator, and a microwave while being crowded by the new—to me—sheriff.

"Why don't you tell me what happened, Ms. Warren?" He pulled a notepad from his shirt pocket.

"It's Marlene Duncan. She's dead . . . on the floor in the back room of The Book Barn."

He nodded and looked toward the door. "When did you find her?"

I removed my phone from my purse and glanced at the time. "Nineteen minutes ago. I walked in and there she was."

After giving what I thought was a pretty good account of what had happened, Sheriff Espinosa said, "Why don't you start from the beginning." It wasn't a question.

"I'd rather not." I glanced at the curtain, pretty sure one of the women had strayed closer to get an earful.

He looked at the swaying curtain and nodded in understanding. "I need to get your formal statement. Would you be more comfortable in my patrol car?"

"I don't think I can make it," I confessed.

"I'll help you," he insisted.

"I need more time to rest."

"If you don't come with me, I'll have to make you," he warned.

My hands suddenly stopped shaking. "What the Sam Houston for?" That's the way a good girl from Texas avoids using a four-letter word. Sheriff Espinosa was lucky I remembered how to hold my tongue.

His jaw tightened. "There's a dead woman in your father's store. Right now you're the only lead I have. Time is critical in a homicide investigation."

I'd already told him everything I knew. Now, it was time for me to get the heck out of Dodge—or rather Hazel Rock—so he could do his job and I could calm my nerves. "I called you. I told you everything. What more can I possibly do?"

"You may have more information . . ." I shook my head, but he continued, "That you don't even realize will help the case." He looked at my purse draped across my body as if it could hold a gun the size Dirty Harry carried.

Granted, we were in Texas, but I'd just arrived from the airport. Stopping to buy a gun hadn't been on my agenda. "It's not big enough to hold any weapons," I said, answering his unspoken question.

"Ma'am, can we go have a seat in my car so I can get your statement?"

"Fine." Then I decided to take my final stand, digging the heels of my boots into the floor. "Why don't you understand that I don't want to go near the store?"

"I understand completely, ma'am. You won't have to see Marlene."

I didn't give up. I knew what he was saying wasn't true. "What about when they take her body out of the store?"

His jaw tightened, again. I suspected he wanted to force me to comply with his demands, but he wasn't willing to use actual force. Yet.

Taking hold of my arm, he walked me over to the far wall and pulled a chair out from under the table. I plopped my butt in the seat a little harder than necessary.

"Have you talked to Bobby Ray?" he asked.

I froze before managing to say, "No. Have you?"

He shook his head, pulled out another chair, and sat down in front of me. "He wouldn't answer his phone."

"He wasn't there and I just kind of forgot about everything when I found Marlene behind the curtain. Is he at the diner?" It was too late for his morning breakfast, but maybe Dad had started eating lunch there too.

"Stay here," the sheriff ordered.

I leaned back, thankful for the physical reprieve. "I'm not going anywhere." I was doing my darnedest to hide the wobble in my legs, but I wasn't about to admit that to the bossy man in front of me.

He looked at my vibrating legs and then my hands before starting back toward the front of the beauty shop. Pushing through my embarrassment, I remembered what made me run from the building—aside from the dead body, that is. "Did you find anyone upstairs?"

He turned back toward me as he reached the doorway. "No, just Marlene." His frown became a determined straight line and he puffed out his chest. Taking in my short dress and boots, I got the impression he was trying to determine if I was in danger, or a danger to the women in the beauty shop.

"I've been cooperating completely," I reminded him. He obviously didn't know what I was like when I didn't cooperate. "Besides, I couldn't make it three feet right now." I was really regretting skipping breakfast and not grabbing something to eat at the airport.

"Don't move. I'll be back as soon as I talk to some of the others," he instructed. I nodded and he left the break room.

Scarlet's voice carried through the swinging door. "Mateo, what in the Sam Hill is going on?" She didn't wait for an answer, just plowed on with more questions. "Is it Bobby Ray? Who's going to tell Marlene? She's going to be heartbroken, but she'll do right by his daughter and take care of her." There was a long pause before she added, "We have a right to know what's going on in our town."

"Ladies, as soon as I can give you the facts, I will. Until then, if you could make sure Ms. Warren is comfortable, I would be in your debt. I'll need everyone to stay in the salon until I come back. Now, if you'll excuse me for a moment . . ."

The facts. I wanted to laugh, except it might sound hysterical if I did. Because the real truth was in the sheriff's actions. He had a job to do. He didn't trust me but didn't completely believe I was guilty either. So, to cover all his bases, handsome Sheriff Mateo Espinosa had left me in the company of the best interrogators the world had to offer—the ladies of Beaus and Beauties hair salon.

If I survived until he returned it'd be a miracle.

Chapter Three

It'd been almost three hours since I'd found Marlene's body, which was now zipped up tight in a black bag and being wheeled to the rear of an unmarked black minivan. I'd made it through the worst of the women's questions without disclosing who'd died. They'd moved me back up to the front of the salon, where the barrage of inquiries and demands came nonstop.

The man pushing the gurney with Marlene's body wore a nondescript white button-down shirt with black slacks. He opened the rear lift gate to the van and loaded the gurney like an ambulance driver, the legs folding up as he pushed it against the vehicle. Then he got in the driver's seat and drove away at the speed of a funeral procession.

The mood in the salon fit the somber atmosphere of a wake.

The crowd inside and out had diminished throughout the afternoon; the heat of the sun kept many people from gathering. Each woman who'd left the salon spent some time talking to the sheriff while sitting in his patrol car, no doubt telling him what kind of crazy woman I was.

At the moment only Scarlet, her younger sister Joellen, and Mary, the hairdresser with the raspy voice, remained, all three shedding tears as the vehicle drove down the street. I felt the lump in my throat return, sad for them and the woman who'd died too soon.

After combing the town for more witnesses and taking numerous statements outside and inside his patrol car, Sheriff Espinoza seemed to have the scene organized to his standards and finally returned. He broke his silence as he closed up his pocket-size pad of paper. "Why don't we go back over to the shop so you can walk me through what happened."

Again he wasn't asking me a question; he was doing that polite suggestion/order thing he liked to do so much. I nodded in agreement this time, too exhausted to argue. The last thing I wanted to do was return to the crime scene, but he seemed determined, so I pulled myself out of the chair and stood on wobbly legs. When this was over, the first thing I was going to do was wolf down a large burger and fries with an extra-large Coke.

Scarlet hugged me a little less awkwardly this time and Joellen rubbed my back. Mary turned away and went into the break room, ignoring me as if this whole affair was my fault. The sheriff grabbed my arm, but I wasn't sure if he was trying to help me or keep me from running away. Which was ridiculous because I wasn't sure where I was going to go after we were done. My return flight was just an old pipe dream at this point and I didn't have enough money to stay at the B&B in town. I was praying my dad would return at some point and give me the financial remedy I'd been promised. Sooner rather than later would be nice.

We made it across the street with a few glares and whispers from the mini-crowd gathered outside of the crime scene tape. There were faces I recognized and others that were strangers. Based on some of their expressions, I was lucky not to be stoned or pulled away and hanged without a trial. Firsthand knowledge of the way rumors could poison a community's viewpoint caused me to move closer to the sheriff.

He looked at me from out of the corner of his eye and I gave him a forced smile that probably looked more like constipation.

Crossing the threshold of The Book Barn Princess, the doors swished open and the buzzer sounded as I tried to slow my erratic breathing. I wasn't quite sure why the trek from the salon to the bookstore seemed to be so difficult for me. It wasn't as if I ran this time. Yet one minute I was relatively calm and the next my breathing was racing, my blood pounding through my ears, and my chest heaving as if I'd just finished a marathon. Not that I'd ever run more than a mile—which nearly killed me every time I did it—but I imagined it would feel similar to the boulder currently pressing on my lungs.

"Did it bother you that Marlene convinced your father to sell the family business?" the sheriff asked.

"What?" Surely I hadn't heard him correctly. We stopped in front of the antique register that was lost in all the girlie junk cluttering the counter.

The sheriff stared at me, waiting.

I stared right back. Dad was selling the business because he was in debt. At least that's what Marlene had said on the phone. It was the only reason I'd agreed to sign on the dotted line. But if that wasn't the case, why was he selling the dream he'd shared with my mom? And why would Marlene lie to me?

The sheriff dropped another bombshell. "Witnesses heard you threaten your father as you walked in."

Before I had time to respond, the door swished behind us and we turned in unison. I was hoping it was my father, maybe out of breath because he'd been down at the diner and finally seen that something was amiss at the store. The sheriff was looking for something more sinister as his hand touched the weapon on his hip.

"Sheriff, what's going on?" Another taut masculine voice echoed through the bookstore and made this day officially the worst of my life. My heart stopped its frantic beat and felt like it'd never beat again.

The last thing I heard before the world faded to black was, "Holy mother. You're back."

"You're damned lucky I was there to catch her."

"You're damned lucky you did."

"You both can stick it where the sun don't shine and get away from me," I croaked.

My ex–high school sweetheart, Cade Calloway, and Sheriff Espinosa were hovering over me like two bickering mother hens.

"Are you pregnant? Do you need an ambulance?" Espinosa asked.

I balked and shuddered at the sheriff's insinuation. "What?" I screeched, then cleared my throat and asked again. "What would give you that idea?"

"You fainted," he stated.

"I passed out from lack of food, seeing my first dead body, and being accused of murder." I sat up and batted his hand away.

"Your blood sugar is low, isn't it?" Cade said accusingly and then handed me a glass of iced tea and a cookie.

I accepted the drink and the snack without a word. He was right, but I wasn't about to admit it as I sipped the heavenly sweet brew I hadn't tasted in more than a dozen years. Texas sweet tea is sugar heaven in liquid form.

"You were fine until Cade walked in the door." The sheriff eyed my ex.

"Yeah, well, he triggered everything and made it all real." I yanked my dress down as far as I could, then looked at Cade. My heart skipped another beat. "Where did you get the tea?" I asked.

"Your dad created a little teahouse over there when he remodeled the store." He nodded in the direction of one of the larger side stalls I'd missed earlier. White lace table cloths draped several small, round tables, each one adorned with centerpieces of wild flowers in mismatched antique milk jugs and vases. Old and rusted tin food advertisements decorated the stable walls. It was exactly the way I'd described my idea to my dad back in high school. And it was the only place in the entire store that didn't need to be toned down.

I turned away, took a bite of cookie, and followed it up with another sip of tea, then looked at the sheriff, purposely getting lost in his eyes. They were gorgeous and nothing about them reminded me of the past.

I wondered how well he knew Marlene. Probably better than I had. To me, Marlene was the Realtor in the company jacket who always had a smile on her face. We'd never really spoken beyond me ringing up a book for her in this very store or waving good morning to her when Cade picked me up for school in his vintage Camaro. I looked at Cade, a grim expression marring his face.

Sheriff Espinosa got back to the business at hand. "We were going to walk through the store so you could show me how you found Ms. Duncan. If you can stand, we can move to a more comfortable area until you're ready."

Cade took my tea and I pulled my purse off, lifting it over my head. I stood up and they both reached for an elbow. I'd like to say I turned away their assistance, but I didn't. My blood sugar was low, I hadn't eaten all day, and the last time I'd fainted from blood sugar issues I was sixteen and working the register behind the counter.

Once I was on my feet, I made sure my dress was still in place and shook off both of their hands before reaching for my tea.

"It's good to see you, Charli." Our fingers touched and Cade used that mischievous smile that I'd loved when I was younger. Even now, it had the power to make me wonder what if. . .

My spine stiffened. "'Holy mother, you're back,' doesn't sound happy to see me." I took another gulp of tea and thought a strong glass of Amaretto Sour would have been better, but the sweet tea would do the trick—just as Cade knew it would.

He had the good manners to look embarrassed. Of course he would. He was a Calloway through and through, part of the political machine that had run the town and county for decades. The strong family ties were evident in his square jaw, tall frame, and hazel eyes. If anything, my high school boyfriend was taller and better-looking than the last time I'd seen him.

Which was disappointing. I'd secretly hoped he'd turned round through the middle and lost his hair. No such luck.

I changed the subject. "Have you seen my dad?"

"No, not for a couple days. He told me he was selling the business last Tuesday, when we were having breakfast at the diner. He didn't tell me you were coming back to town."

"Why did you come back?" The sheriff had pulled out his little notebook and was writing quickly across the pages as Cade took my elbow and led me to the tea area.

It was spooky how familiar the room felt. Every small detail sank into my psyche, bringing me back to the time when I'd sat on the floor with colored pencils scattered around me and I'd drawn my vision for my father to see. From the lace napkins with the store's initials embroidered at the corner to the wire-back chair I sat in and the deer antlers attached to the wall—a sanded-down version of a coatrack.

"Ms. Warren?" The sheriff's pen stood poised to write on his pad of paper.

"I told you: I needed to sign the papers so my dad could sell the store." I laid my purse at my feet and took a healthy gulp of tea and another bite of a delicious sugar cookie with frosting.

"Couldn't that be done by fax or mail?" he persisted.

I wouldn't admit I'd asked the same question. I swallowed the tasty bite of sugary goodness and replied, "Marlene called me yesterday and said there was a buyer lined up, but they needed the papers signed today or the buyer would back out. She said my dad would pay for my airline ticket and expenses. All I had to do was show up."

"And you came?" He sounded skeptical.

"It worked with my schedule." More like it was the saving grace in my schedule, but neither one of them needed to know what I would have faced if I'd stayed in Denver.

"So your father didn't call you?" Espinosa looked up from his pad.

"No. Marlene said he'd meet me at the airport. When no one showed, I took a cab."

"When was the last time you spoke to your father?"

I didn't hesitate because I had nothing to hide. "When I was eighteen."

Cade inhaled rather sharply. Obviously, he hadn't known how bad my relationship with my dad had been since I'd left town. The sheriff just stared and waited for me to finish.

I ignored his attempt to get me to explain my estranged relationship with my father and waited for his next question.

"Who's buying The Book Barn?"

Surprisingly, Cade corrected the sheriff before I could. "It's The Book Barn *Princess*."

For some reason his butting in and using my nickname grated on my last nerve. I turned away from him, kicking my purse and blocking him out in the process. "I don't know and I don't care. I came to sign on the dotted line and leave."

I *really* needed to leave.

"Because staying would mean you'd have to face things," Cade interjected.

"What things?" Espinosa quickly asked.

"No*thing*." I refused to look at Cade. I knew my tone got under his skin by the sound of air flowing through his nostrils. I chose to ignore it and focused on the curious glint my response created in Sheriff Espinosa's eyes.

He looked back and forth between us, waiting for one of us to say something. Cade clearly wanted to argue but wisely kept his mouth shut. The fact that my lips were pressed so tightly together they were barely visible may have had something to do with his decision.

The sheriff continued with his questions. "What time did you arrive at the store?"

"Around one o'clock," I responded.

"Was there anyone in the store at that time?" His question sounded accusatory, as if maybe I was hiding something . . . or someone.

"No, it was empty . . . or so I thought, but then I heard someone moving around upstairs." I glanced at Cade. His arms were folded neatly across his chest, as if he were the one who needed answers.

"Your father wasn't here?" The sheriff's tone continued to be accusatory and I didn't like it one bit. I wasn't covering for anyone, especially my own father.

"I already told you, he wasn't."

"You and your father are estranged?"

"That's an understatement."

Then his questions went in a direction that made me even more uncomfortable. Back to the subject that had left me flat on my back: "Were you against selling the store?"

"I wasn't happy about it. The store was my mom's dream, but Marlene explained how bad things were."

"Did that make you angry with her?"

"I wasn't happy. Period. The last thing I wanted to do this weekend was come back to Hazel Rock." Actually, there was something I was avoiding even more than my hometown, but that was information neither one of them needed to know.

Then the sheriff let loose with something almost as shocking as a heifer birthing three calves. Heifers don't have calves, let alone three. "How did you feel about Marlene dating your dad?"

"Excuse me?"

He didn't even blink an eye as I nearly missed setting my glass of tea on the table. "Are you telling me you didn't know your father was going to marry Ms. Duncan?" he asked.

"No!"

He nodded and jotted something down on his notepad. I hoped it said *find another suspect*. But I knew bad karma was stuck to me like the stank of an angry skunk.

"Have you ever seen the belt that was around Ms. Duncan's neck before?"

"Yes," I admitted, not wanting to explain but certainly not about to lie.

His eyebrow arched once more. An expression that said: *Don't hold back information from the police, Charli.*

I sighed and confessed the whole truth, knowing I was neck deep in the Rio Brazos without a leg to stand on. "That was my belt. I made it in high school."

It was Cade's turn to suck in some air. He knew exactly what belt we were talking about and apparently hadn't heard how Marlene died. Now he knew. Marlene had died with the same belt he'd taken off my body and playfully wrapped around my wrists the last time I'd seen him. The playing had stopped right then and there. It was a memory I'd tried to forget.

Something brushed up against my leg. Like a cat, only harder. Much harder.

I squawked and scooted my chair back, then stared at the image painted on the front of The Barn that had come to life at my feet. Black, beady eyes blinked back at me. Long, pointy ears twitched. Sitting on its hindquarters, with its front claws hanging down against its vulnerable hairy underbelly, a pink armadillo stared up at me like a dog begging for a treat.

My purse lay at my feet, on its side with the contents spilling out for everyone to see. I scooted away from the rodent, willing to sacrifice my last five dollars to the weirdest creature I'd ever seen . . . in a bookstore.

"What is that?" I asked.

"That's Princess," Cade and Sheriff Espinosa said in unison.

"Why is it pink?"

"A freak of nature, we think. Possibly a crossbreed between two different types of armadillo," Cade explained.

The sheriff stuffed his notepad and pen into his shirt pocket, then pulled a pair of rubber gloves from his back pocket.

It was about that moment I realized the pink armadillo had added something else to the mix of papers, tampons, dollar bills, and lipstick spilling out of my purse.

"Don't move," the sheriff ordered.

I wasn't going to argue with him. Cade, on the other hand, ignored him completely. He moved behind me and rested his hands on my shoulders. I wanted to wrench myself away, but instead I let myself enjoy his steadying touch.

Sheriff Espinosa examined the contents of my purse up close and personal. I had no doubt he was cataloging the brand of my feminine hygiene products along with the logo of my Bobby V. Merrill Elementary School pen. The item that interested him the most, however, was the yellow and black scarf laying over the top of my purse. The one item I didn't recognize but instinctively knew spelled trouble.

"That's not mine," I blurted out.

Cade squeezed my shoulders, his fingers digging in sternly. "Don't say another word, Charli."

"You're right. It's not yours. There's only one person in this town who wears a Yellow Jacket Realty scarf." The sheriff's brow didn't arch this time. If anything, it lowered and became deadly serious as he rose to his full height. "The woman who planned to marry *your* daddy and died on the floor in the back room of *your* store with *your* belt around her neck. The woman who was going to sell the business you *begged* your daddy not to sell."

"There's been a big misunderstanding, Mateo," Cade said.

The sheriff interrupted. "Ms. Warren, could you stand up please?" Once again his question didn't sound like a request.

My tongue started tripping all over itself. "Wh–wh–what for?"

Cade's fingers slipped away and I suddenly felt very alone, until he stepped in front of me, protecting me from the long arm of the law that wanted to reach out and snatch me out of the chair where I'd parked my behind.

"Mateo—" Cade started.

The sheriff didn't let him finish, "I'll kindly ask you to step aside, Cade."

"*Sheriff.*" Cade's voice was deeper, darker, almost threatening.

But there was a new sheriff in town. One that didn't answer to the Calloway name.

"*Mayor*, the last thing you need is an obstruction-of-justice charge before the upcoming election." Both men stared at each other.

I looked around the two of them, expecting to see Cade's father in all his haughty, southern man-in-charge glory walking into the store, but the sheriff wasn't looking at a senior version of Cade. He was looking directly into the eyes of my ex-boyfriend. The new political leader in town, who caved faster than his daddy ever would have. Cade stepped to the side so I could get a front-row view of the law-man unsnapping his handcuffs from the belt on his hip.

"Ms. Warren, you're under arrest for investigation of the murder of Marlene Duncan."

I blinked and stood up, looking from the man with the gorgeous brown eyes to the other man, who'd started to take a stand a dozen years too late. Only the sheriff met my gaze. Cade turned on his heel and beat feet to the front of the store.

As I turned around and placed my hands behind my back, metal bracelets clanked on my wrists and I heard the buzzer at the door announce Cade's departure. Once again, Cade Calloway had walked out on me in my time of need. Only this time it wasn't his daddy's election at stake. This time it was his own.

That action alone seemed to satisfy the little rodent I'd forgotten all about. I looked down at Princess, who blinked at each one of us and then waddled toward the stairs, the pale pink leather plates of her shell waving good-bye with her every movement. I watched her jump for each step, which seemed to take an incredible amount of effort, yet she never tired and continued her way up the steps to the loft above. That little ball of energy had just sealed my fate with her innocent stare and so-ugly-she-was-cute smile.

But I wasn't fooled. By dropping that scarf on my purse, she'd set me up for a fall better than any man in town ever could. And this time I couldn't run away.

On the bright side, I had a place to stay for the night. The town jail cell couldn't be *that* bad, could it?

Chapter Four

A lot of people say, "Don't count your chickens before they're hatched." In my case, I shouldn't have expected any of the stupid birds to survive. Hazel Rock, Texas, didn't have a jail. The jail cell I'd been threatened with as a teenager was gone, a thing of the past like the crotchety old sheriff who'd held that threat over my head. The new sheriff transported me to the new county jail twenty miles away, where I was asked to give up everything in my possession—my purse, my phone, my jewelry, the laces from my boots . . . even my socks. That's when the sheriff with the dreamy eyes abandoned me. He left me with a young female deputy who wasn't interested in me at all, or at least that was the impression I got from her unsympathetic response to my request to sit with her outside the glass cage. I was a murderer in her eyes who belonged on the inside.

She fingerprinted and photographed me with a nasty gray towel around my neck that reeked of body odor. My objections were once again met with that same dull look, her eyelids half closed, as if I was keeping her from her nap. Her brown hair was pulled back in a loose braid that tucked underneath itself at the back of her neck. She was polite enough, just not willing—or maybe incapable—of showing compassion for someone like me—an inmate totally out of her element in the filthy detention center.

In the past, I'd compared my job of being a kindergarten teacher to being held in a prison for eight hours a day. But now that I knew the reality of jail life, I realized my comparison was totally off-base. My kids with snotty noses, skinned knees, and the occasional confession of "Oops I didn't make it to the restroom" weren't all that bad. My classroom didn't smell of the sickeningly sweet odor of sweat, filth, urine, blood, and . . . was that feces? I was scared to accept the possibility. Whatever it was, it was all mixed up with the scent of bleach and a hint of bologna.

If the stench wasn't bad enough, the air conditioning in the jail was set to a permanent arctic blast that you'd think would clear out the odorous stank.

It didn't.

Because the room temperature was thirty degrees below my comfort zone, I'd been forced to beg for the blue paper pants and shirt I was currently wearing under and over my dress. I was a fashion nightmare freezing my backside off on the solid concrete bench that also served as my bed. Despite being new, my cell looked like it'd already been through hell and back. The light gray paint that covered the walls and my bunk was darker in the frequently used spots and had graffiti scratched into it.

As I read insult after insult carved into every inch of my cell, one thing became clear: most inmates knew diddly-squat about proper grammar. My five-year-old students could turn a phrase better than the previous occupants housed in this cell.

Unfortunately, my boredom led to an overactive imagination. For the life of me, I couldn't figure out what the previous occupants had used to write their vulgar comments on the paint. I needed answers to the wrong questions. Such as did they use the buttons on their shirts to write, "the po-pos on the take" without an apostrophe or a verb linking who was "on the take"? Or did they use the snaps on their jeans to say they should have sexual relations with a cop in a much more vulgar form? Surely they didn't use their teeth? I shivered at the images my mind created and decided to stick with the idea that they probably used long manicured fingernails.

Every woman in Texas had her nails done. It was a rite of passage.

Through it all, one fact rang true in my head: All of this was happening because I'd returned to my hometown to help my father out of a pickle. That alone burned my butt more than a rancher's red-hot branding iron. I fumed and paced for the first couple of hours until the deputy informed me I'd end up with blisters on my feet if I kept that up for my entire seventy-two-hour hold. That's how long it would be before the prosecutor decided whether to bring me up on charges.

Seventy-two hours?

Everything got real when she put a time frame to my incarceration, and fear replaced my anger. Fear that this situation wasn't just a short-term misunderstanding but rather a lifelong sentence. Fear that I could end up *staying* here—with three concrete walls and a fourth made out of solid glass that faced the booking desk. With a smell so bad, I wondered what the deputy behind that desk had done wrong to deserve such a lousy assignment.

It got even worse when the detective arrived and what I thought was an escort to his office turned into a short trip to a small interrogation room with two chairs and a small table. For the first time in my life I saw the Miranda warning in print. The bald-headed Detective Youngblood didn't read it to me but rather passed me the piece of paper and asked me to read it.

Out loud.

Then he asked if I understood my rights and, when I nodded, he told me he needed a verbal acknowledgment.

"Yes" came out of my mouth in vibrato form.

I signed my name and gazed down at the signature, which looked more like the chicken scratch of my five-year-old students than that of a teacher with a bachelor's degree. I looked up at the two-way mirror on the wall. Sheriff Mateo Espinosa was behind that glass; I just knew it. He was watching me suffer. I could tell from the detective's posture and the sweat on his head that he patted dry with a folded hankie. He was almost as nervous as I was.

Almost.

The interview started off friendly enough; at least his false smile showed some level of concern for my comfort. But then he started quizzing me about Marlene, my belt, and her scarf. It was at about that time that a light bulb turned on inside my brain. I was Hazel Rock's public enemy number one. If I didn't shut this down soon, I was going to end up *living* in this hellhole.

I requested a lawyer quicker than the high school quarterback would be saying "hut, hut hike" later that night. I glanced back at the sheriff hiding behind my reflection as we left the room and scowled. He didn't deserve a wave.

Once inside my cell, I tried to remember a name, any name, of a local attorney. My mind drew a blank—except for one.

Cade Calloway Senior. It's eye-opening to find that you're not quite desperate enough to dial your ex-boyfriend's father for help. I wondered what my limit would be before I buckled and dialed the number. Then again, the fear of him laughing and hanging up just might keep me from ever making that call.

There had only been one other time when I'd even considered risking the senior's ire: four years earlier, when Cade wasn't mayor but an up-and-coming NFL star. Not only had Cade gone on to play college ball but he'd ended up being chosen in the first round of the NFL draft. He would have been famous except for one hit. One sack he never saw coming. One play that ended his career and could have cost him his ability to walk.

I'd seen the story when it hit the national news. The vicious collision seemed to be on replay over and over again as they told about the injury—two broken vertebrae and a torn ligament in his neck, but no prognosis to go with it. At the time I'd been frantic. Searching every media outlet I could find for a report on his condition, I'd been close to ditching my life and coming home. It'd been my aunt who'd finally made the phone calls that calmed me down. Cade would make a full recovery, but the team and the league weren't up for taking the risk of keeping him on the roster despite his eagerness to get back on the field.

If I'd made it through that low point, surely I could make it through this . . . this temporary misunderstanding of the truth.

The phone rang on the opposite side of the glass and the deputy's voice broke through the mumblings of the drunk in the cell next to me. The deputy looked up at me, her deep-set eyes never giving a hint as to what she thought of me or the charges I faced. She nodded as if she understood some important fact that decided my fate and reached for something under the desk. My cell door clicked as she called out, "Ms. Warren."

I shot to my feet and approached the glass door framed with steel as it slid open, knowing that someone—probably my daddy—had straightened everything out and I'd be walking away from this miserable hole in a matter of moments.

The deputy nodded toward the black plastic phone on the wall that looked as if it came straight out of the 1970s. "I'm transferring a call for you. You can pick it up over there once it rings."

It wasn't what I wanted to hear, but I welcomed the chance to hear a friendly voice, despite having to use the nasty jail phone to hear it.

Even though I expected it, the din of the ring startled me, and I heard my neighbor in the cell next door snicker. Ignoring something that sounded like an antiquated catcall, I grabbed the gummy receiver and held it up: not too close to my ear, but close enough to hear the person on the other end.

"Hello?" My voice wobbled suddenly and my eyes were rimmed with unshed tears. My daddy was finally coming to my rescue.

"Charli, don't worry, honey; I'm going to get you out of there."

My tears stopped. Unless my father had received a sex change in the past ten years, the very feminine voice on the other end wasn't him. "Who is this?"

"It's Scarlet. I saw what Mateo did to you and I followed you to the station. He's gone and messed up everything. I've been waiting for the past two hours for that man to get off that fine butt of his and come talk to me in the lobby. You would think he didn't know what he was doing, the way he's handling this case." She sniffed, and I realized she was getting emotional for a completely different reason than I was. "The whole town is in an uproar over Marlene's death. Some people are talking about capital punishment, like they want to bring back the gallows or something."

The blood drained from my face. I felt it seep through my body, heading to my core to keep my heart pumping. If it didn't, I would have died on the spot.

"But everything's going to be okay. I pulled my video from the store and brought it to Mateo. He's viewing it now with the detective assigned to the case. He'll see exactly what I saw. You entered the Book Barn ready to conquer your demons from the past and three minutes later you ran out of that store like those evil spirits got the best of you and were trying to suck the blood out of your body or lop off your head."

I cringed at the thought of getting my head lopped off just as Scarlet paused long enough for me to ask, "Why?"

"Why . . . what?"

"Why are you helping me?" It didn't make any sense.

"Because we were friends in high school. We still are."

I wanted to say we weren't friends then or now. I hadn't even noticed her, except when her constant chatter had filled my brain beyond capacity back when I visited the principal's office almost as often as some people visit the beauty shop. But the voice on the other end of the phone believed I was innocent, and that was as friendly as it got in Hazel Rock.

Too afraid to believe my good fortune, I asked, "So you have a video?"

"Yup, from the minute you stepped out of the cab and got sprayed with dirt to the sheriff putting his hand on the back of your head and tucking you into his patrol car. Everything is there, plain as the pink armadillo that watched the entire scene from the doorway of the Book Barn."

I was beginning to hate that rodent. *She* was the real Book Barn Princess. Yet, at the same time, hope began to blossom in my chest. "Then you got the killer on tape too?"

"Well . . . I wouldn't go that far."

Her hesitation kept that good feeling from spreading. Scarlet wasn't telling the whole story. Which meant it was probably a story I didn't want to hear. I asked anyway. "Who else was on the video?"

"It doesn't mean anything, Charli. It's his store; I've got him on video coming out of The Barn for the past two years. It doesn't mean he committed murder."

Don't ask, don't tell wasn't an option for me. I'd quit hiding my head under rocks at the age of seventeen. My determination to get at the truth, however, didn't eliminate the warble in my voice. My question came out more like a whisper. "Who was on the video, Scarlet?"

Scarlet started backpedaling and I closed my eyes, waiting for that ax to fall. "I don't think he did it, mind you, but the sheriff's got it stuck in his head that your dad killed Marlene. And I'm pretty sure Mateo thinks you're covering for your dad while he hightails it out of town. I personally think our sheriff has lost his mind. You're not a killer; you're Princess Warren.

"Your dad is the town encyclopedia. If any of the kids needed a book for a report, your dad would find it. Without a library, your family's store was the only place the kids in Hazel Rock had before the internet took over. And you were our head cheerleader in your junior year, for Pete's sake. That's no easy task in the state of Texas."

I wanted to agree with her, but the part of me that grew up in Colorado laughed at the idea of cheerleading being that important to anyone.

Scarlet didn't notice the strangled noise from my end of the phone and continued on with a litany of superfluous reasons why I couldn't possibly be guilty of murder or aiding and abetting a killer. All of which made me sound more like a Barbie doll than a real life human being.

"You would have been a shoo-in for prom queen if you hadn't left town. Bless your heart, you were practically engaged to our mayor. What prom queen, first lady goes around killing her daddy's lover?"

I was starting to get the feeling that at some point during high school, Scarlet had put me on a pedestal on which I certainly didn't belong. I wasn't sure if she believed in my innocence or just believed someone with my popularity would never stoop so low as to commit a violent crime. Except Scarlet was forgetting one important fact that the rest of the town seemed to remember clear as day: I stopped being all of those things two weeks before I left town. Hazel Rock's darling daughter had turned into Hazel Rock's version of Belle Starr— a brazen woman known for scandalous love affairs and her ability to rob a man blind without batting an eye.

"Charli?"

I let go of the past that obviously still haunted me, and focused on who was going to get me out of jail. Not my dad, who'd apparently taken my place as the number-one suspect. Not Cade. Certainly not the sheriff. "I'm sorry; did you ask me something?"

"I'm sorry about your dad."

Unable to come up with anything else to say, I murmured a soft, "Thanks," and hoped she'd just let the subject drop. If I was going to be released and my dad was MIA, my means of escape was disappearing faster than it took Cade to turn his back on me. I needed to develop a plan to get home. Fast.

"It's not like the video shows anything," Scarlet continued. "Just him running out of the store and hopping into his truck. There could have been a hundred and one other reasons he was running like that."

I'm sure there were a thousand reasons why my dad had run out of the book store . . . but I wasn't going to think about the one reason that would make me stay. Because if I thought he was running out of the store to go to the airport to pick me up, the guilt would take over.

"You're sure the sheriff is going to release me?"

"Yes, ma'am. I'm sitting out in the lobby waiting to pick you up."

The woman I barely remembered from high school was waiting for me to get out of jail when there wasn't a soul back in Colorado, other than my aunt, who would dream of coming near me if they knew I'd been arrested on suspicion of murder. In fact, I'd probably lose my job just for being connected to this case. My principal was going to enjoy seeing me pack my bags and say good-bye to all the little five-year-olds who gave me my first gray hair. (I'd plucked it during my lunch hour after one of them had pointed it out to me in the reading circle.)

Would I miss my students? I bit my lip and pondered that question while Scarlet rattled on about my dad's innocence and Mateo's bullheaded stubbornness. I was surprised at her passion on both subjects and my desire not to think about either one.

I didn't want to be rude, yet I also didn't want to hold the phone any longer than I had to. And I certainly didn't want to return to that ten-by-ten cell that smelled like someone had defecated all over the walls and floor.

"Do you know when the sheriff is going to let me go?"

"Ms. Warren?"

I turned around as the deputy pushed the brown paper bag containing my purse, belt, and bootstrings across the Formica countertop.

"Yes?"

"Detective Youngblood just called and said you're free to go."

"Scarlet!" I said into the phone, "They're letting me go!"

"I just told you that."

She had, but I hadn't believed it was true until the deputy began opening the bag with *Warren* written on the outside in black Magic Marker.

"Don't leave. I'll be out ASAP." I hung up the phone without waiting for an answer. My faith in the truth had returned, along with my belief that it was time to get the heck out of Hazel Rock.

Chapter Five

"What is that?"

"It's my car."

I watched Scarlet open the driver's door that was literally the entire front end of her little white car. It was so teeny, it looked like a vintage toy from the 1950s, minus the windup knob on the back. Although neither of us were what I would consider large, it was going to be a tight squeeze. We were lucky I didn't have any luggage.

Scarlet slid across the seat and I climbed in after her.

"Did you make this car?" I asked.

Scarlet grinned like a pet raccoon. "It's a 1958 BMW Isetta. It's got one cylinder and thirteen horsepower."

"You're kidding."

She rotated the key in the ignition and the engine turned over. I swore, it sounded like there was a sewing machine mounted in the trunk. Not an adult sewing machine—one of those E-Z Stitch sewing machines for little girls.

"I think my dad's lawn mower has a bigger engine."

"Maybe, but this car is one of the original gas savers. It gets better gas mileage than most hybrids . . . and it's cute."

I looked around at the interior. It *was* cute, for a marshmallow on wheels. The exterior was solid white, with a small black circle on each side with a red letter *S* in the middle. The front windshield left me feeling exposed. The large rear window and the side windows that slid backward to open didn't help. I was pretty sure I'd ridden a few carnival rides that had cars like this attached to a wheel that rotated at slow speed. They called them Ferris wheels.

Scarlet pulled back the black cloth moon roof that covered the entire top to let in the evening breeze. I buckled my seat belt as she turned the radio on to a local country music station that made me feel even more claustrophobic as the tune bounced around the interior. "I don't think your car would look too cute under a semi," I said over the twang of a man singing to the woman who'd deserted him.

"It actually fits underneath no problem."

"You've tried it?"

"You only live once."

"I'd like to live longer than today." I gripped the handle on my side of the car as she zipped backward out of the parking spot and then drove down the road with more speed than I thought the car was capable of.

"I didn't realize you were so . . ." She stopped. I think it had just hit her that she really didn't know me at all.

"A stick in the mud?" I offered. It wouldn't be the first time I'd been called that.

She shook her head. "No, I was going to say afraid to try something new."

"What? I'm not afraid to try new things. I went skiing once." It was on the bunny slope, but I did it. "I've ridden a snowmobile." When that didn't impress her, I added, "And I've jumped off a cliff into a freezing cold lake for a polar plunge."

Her eyebrow rose skeptically.

"Okay, so it wasn't a cliff, but it was a rock at least six feet tall and the water was like ice!" I didn't tell her that I was the one who'd called it a polar plunge. Everyone else called it a summer swim in the month of July.

That big grin appeared on her face again and I got the impression she knew I was holding back.

I added the shocker I'd been saving for last as she pushed the pedal to the floor and passed a Crown Victoria I swore belonged to Sheriff Espinosa. "I'm the only teacher at Bobby V. Merrill Elementary who sits in the cutie pie booth at the school auction and takes countless whipped cream pies in the face every year."

Scarlet looked at my hair.

"I cover it with a shower cap."

"When's your school auction? I'd love to see that." She pulled in front of the cruiser and the headlights flashed bright for just a second. Scarlet waved in the rearview mirror.

"It's this weeken—" I started.

Scarlet began laughing so hard, I thought she was going to roll the car over.

"What's so funny?" I ask cautiously.

Cars honked as we buzzed by, doing at least ten over the speed limit. Nobody actually does the posted speed limit in Texas. It's an unwritten rule that you drive ten miles an hour over the number on the sign. The cops pull you over at twelve. Scarlet glanced at me as she tried to keep her eyes on the road.

"After what happened today, I needed a laugh like that."

"I could certainly use a laugh like that myself if you'd tell me what was so funny."

She was shaking her head again. "That's why you came to Hazel Rock."

"What?" My voice kind of squawked. It does that when I realize I've been caught in a lie.

"That's why you came back to Texas—to miss eating a bunch of whipped cream like a starving hog when he sees a troughful of slop for the first time."

I huffed my indignation. "I don't *eat* the whipped cream . . ." When her grin increased in size, I realized I'd denied the wrong part. "And I didn't come back to Texas to miss the school auction . . . it just happened to be on the same weekend that my daddy needed me to be here. If I hadn't missed my flight, I would have been back in time."

That wasn't what I'd told my principal, but what he didn't know wouldn't hurt him. And whether or not Scarlet learned the truth was irrelevant. I'd missed my plane; no whipped cream for me.

Scarlet persisted. "So you would have gone back this afternoon and done the pie-in-the-face routine?"

I skirted around the question. "It's for a good cause."

"Un-huh." Scarlet took the exit for Hazel Rock and stopped at the end of the ramp. "So you volunteer for this cutie pie booth every year?"

"Well, I . . . I . . ."

"Or you get chosen 'cause you're the only single teacher, right?"

I sighed. "Yes. A few years ago one of the coaches was in the booth and his wife brought her own pie . . . with a brick in it. He'd been having an affair with the music teacher. His marriage and his affair ended when the whipped cream got all bloody and the kids were traumatized. Now they pick the teacher with the least amount of drama every year—not the most popular one."

"And every year it's you because you have no life."

"I have a life!" I huffed.

"Really? 'Cause last time I checked, a person with a life has a smidgeon of drama that could stir things up."

"Trust me, when I get back . . ." I couldn't help but think I should be saying *if* I got back. "I'll be lucky to have a job. Being blackballed off that list for eternity would be too easy a punishment for spending the afternoon in jail."

"Would that be so bad?" Scarlet asked.

"Being blackballed? No, it wouldn't be bad . . . as long as I get to keep my job."

She shook her head. "I never pictured you becoming a teacher."

"I never expected to become one," I admitted.

"Do you like it?"

Once again she had somehow ruffled around in my feathers. "Of course—why else would I do it?"

"I don't know. It just doesn't seem like something you would do."

I understood what she was saying, The Charli Rae who Hazel Rock knew was a wild child. Not a bad child, just a free spirit who couldn't be held down. I wasn't that Charli Rae anymore. I was just Charli the kindergarten teacher—who'd been accused of murder. I still couldn't wrap my head around that.

Scarlet pulled off Highway 287 and hit the dirt-and-gravel road that went through the center of town. Main Street in Hazel Rock was everything I'd run away from.

Rustic. Quaint. Heartwarming.

Deceiving as all get out.

Chapter Six

We passed the quilt shop and the barber shop, which hadn't changed since I was ten years old. The brick facades were bleached from the relentless heat of the Texas sun and their original windows from the 1880s still rippled in the gleam of the moon. When I was a kid, my dad told me the windows were the same as a fun house mirror. I'd believed him until my sophomore year of high school. At the homecoming parade I'd stupidly called for everyone to make faces in the glass as we passed by the picture windows. It was then that I learned the waves weren't magic but due to the process by which glass was made before the twentieth century. Instead of being humiliated, I'd been proud that my dad had made me see magic in something so simple, and a little irritated with my peers for stealing away the mystic charm . . . almost like when Santa Claus had been stolen from me in my tween years.

Of course all of that was before Dad betrayed my trust and our relationship crumbled.

The diner, on the opposite side of the street, had once been a gas station in the 1950s but had been completely remodeled during my high school years. Along with its heritage from the Golden Era, it added a western flair with a neon cowboy. It was the only building in town that dated after the nineteenth century. The eatery attracted attention from the highway with its glowing "Hazel Rock Diner" sign lighting up the east end of town.

We passed a few darkened boutiques and antique stores, all with a western cow town flair, before my family's business came into view. Two pieces of yellow crime scene tape crossed over the front doors of The Book Barn Princess. I shuddered. *X* marked the spot of Marlene's life ending and my world turning upside down.

Scarlet parked in front of Beaus and Beauties and we got out of her toy car in one piece, a small miracle in and of itself. We turned and looked at The Barn in unison.

"What are you going to do now?" she asked.

"I don't know." I felt like a stray dog left in the middle of the road with no food, no money, and no roof over its head.

Her eyes softened. "Where are you staying?"

I hate being pitied. I let my gaze drift away before my eyes filled with tears. "I don't know." I sighed and tried to gain control of the emotions threatening to spill out of me.

"Do you have the keys to The Barn?" Her voice faltered, and I caught a glimpse of her swiping away a tear.

Geesh, if she kept this up we'd both look like my students had applied our makeup that morning. I cleared my throat. "No."

"I have a set of keys your dad gave me in case of an emergency."

"Really?" Dad had never felt safe giving the keys to anyone. The fact that he trusted Scarlet, of all people, made me wonder if she knew him better than I did. "I'm not sure he'd want me to have them." I confided.

"Don't be ridiculous. That's like saying Cade wasn't happy to see you."

I raised my eyebrow. She hadn't seen him walk out on me. She obviously still believed in my fairytale romance from high school, the one everyone thought would end in a happily ever after for the girl from the wrong side of the oil tracks.

Scarlet, however, was turning out to be the bright spot of my trip. She'd given me the warmest welcome of anyone, and I hadn't really given her the time of day when I first ran into her salon. I owed her more than I could repay, so I gave her the truth and let her in on my humiliation at the hands of her mayor. "Cade walked away without a word when the sheriff put handcuffs on me."

"He may have left you with Mateo, but trust me, he was working from behind the scenes. He's the one who started calling everyone to pull their video footage from our store cameras."

I shook my head, letting her know I didn't think that was for my benefit, but she continued. "When some people wanted to have a trial right on the front porch of The Book Barn Princess, Cade calmed the crowd down and told them you'd just arrived and had been unfortunate enough to find Marlene's body. He said that *before* I pulled the video. And he stood up, despite Mike Thompson accusing him of defending his piece of a—" She stopped before she confessed what the town really thought of Charli Rae Warren, but continued with her argument for Cade's affection. "He's looking for your dad right now."

That last part got my attention. He was looking for my dad? "Why?"

"I don't know. I suspect he still cares more than you think."

It took me about two seconds before I realized I was starting to get sucked in by the old Calloway charm—the same way the rest of the town had been and apparently still was. I rolled my eyes.

"I know you don't believe Cade still has feelings for you and I really don't blame you. So why don't you take the keys and sleep on it for a night?" Scarlet dug in her purse for my dad's keys, but the thought of staying in the apartment attached to the store made my stomach roll.

I shook my head, my desperation leading me to grovel. "Could I stay with you?" I asked the virtual stranger in front of me.

"I live in an eighteen-foot Airstream trailer behind the B&B. There's one bed and a teeny-tiny shower. I have to keep most of my stuff in the salon."

"Oh."

Scarlet pulled out the set of keys and held them out for me to take. Her outstretched hand lingered a little too long and she waggled the keys to get my attention. It was totally unnecessary, but it did pull me out of my trancelike state.

I took the keys and met her eyes. "Why would someone want to kill Marlene?"

Scarlet shook her head. "I honestly have no idea. I'll come by in the morning to see how you're doing," she offered.

I nodded and swallowed down my pride, clutching the keys until the ridges left an imprint on my palm. The apartment was half mine legally. It just didn't feel like mine. At least it hadn't before Marlene had called and asked me to sign the papers to sell it. Now I didn't know what to do. My dad was missing, the Realtor was dead, and I had no idea who the potential buyer was.

I hugged the only friend I had in Hazel Rock and crossed the street toward home.

Chapter Seven

A few accent lights dimly lit the aged stone courtyard in front of the hospital turned antique shop next to The Book Barn Princess. Stained by acid rain, the gray cut stone looked ominous despite the iron columns at the door painted bright white. The old "Hospital" sign was still displayed in the ironwork that trimmed the roofline of the porch.

In the middle of the courtyard, a gloomy rectangular fountain bubbled from a sunken hole the size of a coffin. At one end of the water feature there was a built-in bench said to have once been a step-down into the holy waters of the old baptismal font. It had been created for patients at the end of their lives who wanted to change their ways so they could enter the Pearly Gates and avoid those fiery pits of hell the old sheriff had always warned me about.

I never doubted that version of the truth . . . until Cade Calloway confided that it was actually a bathtub of ill repute. He told me *Hospital* was a code word the cowboys used when they wanted to get "nursed" back to health.

To this day, I pictured scantily clothed women hanging out the windows, waving at the cowboys who entered our stable, and now the fountain definitely looked more like a source of debauchery than soul saving.

I continued toward the alley that would lead me to the entrance to my family's apartment, in the back of the building where I'd grown up. A single bulb illuminated the spiked iron gate, but the alley itself was steeped in darkness. Up until finding Marlene's body, I'd never thought of the entrance as being spooky.

Now I wished the aluminum hood covering the bulb directed the light toward the alley and not the ornate iron bracket and sign that had more rust on them than white paint. Looking as old as the town, the oxidized sign brought back memories I didn't want to think about. We'd moved to Hazel Rock and hung the sign marking the entry to our home when I was eight. The words *Eve's Gate* were barely visible now; like everything else, they disappeared into the shadows, but my dad's housewarming gift to my mother still created a lump in my throat.

I used to secretly believe that sign was haunted by my mom's spirit. After her death, the motion of the sign swinging in the breeze reminded me of seeing her standing at the top of the steps to our second-floor apartment as she waved good-bye when I caught the school bus out front. Before my mom died, I'd never seen that sign move. I'd probably just been oblivious, but the fact that it moved as it was doing right now was enough to convince a young mind. So even if the noise was a little creaky instead of a singsong like Eve Warren's voice, I believed it was her.

Especially after it somehow fell and conked Cade on the top of the head the night he tried to get past second base. That sign made a screech and then an ungodly racket as it bounced off the back of Cade's head and hit the stone pavers. It was as if she wanted to bring my daddy outside to see what was going on. Which of course it did. I believed my mom was on a rampage that night. She gave Cade six stitches and put him out of the game the following week.

That of course was the way the old Charli looked at things. The here-and-now Charli heard the squeak of metal against metal and wished her childhood memories weren't so bittersweet. I also wished the dadgum sign would shut up because I couldn't see under the steps that led to our apartment.

I pushed open the surprisingly silent gate. That gate had given Mom a sense of security even though the back of the building was wide open down the hillside to the Brazos River. Right now it felt like I had no way to escape if someone came around the back corner of the barn . . . or, worse yet, if the killer came out of his hiding place in our apartment and made a run for it down the stairs.

"A flashlight would be really nice right about now," I complained aloud. Not that there was anyone to do anything about my predicament.

"Who needs a flashlight to meet an old lover in an alley?"

Despite my heart skipping several beats, I recognized the nasal voice behind me instantaneously. And he certainly wasn't any ex-lover of mine. It was Mike Thompson, the guy who'd called me Cade's piece of. . . property in front of the whole town.

I don't like someone insinuating a man controls any part of my body—including my behind. My backside didn't come close to the current trend of luscious lobes, so I wasn't quite sure why it'd been a topic of conversation at the impromptu town hall meeting in front of The Barn earlier that day.

Needless to say, my fear disappeared. Anger, and the fact that Mike was three inches shorter and weighed almost two hundred pounds more than me, squelched it down to zero. Mike might have a disgustingly dirty mind and repulse me completely, but he was more the sneak a peek, a grope, or even a kiss type of offender—not a cold-blooded killer. Violence wasn't in his repertoire. Besides, we had a gate between us, and I was pretty confident in my ability to get away.

Shadowed from the light above, I could still see the full beard he wore and that his hair had grown down past his shoulders. His brown, flowing locks were his one good feature. I'd always been jealous of the way he could tame those curls. Even now they glistened in the light from the lone light bulb.

The sign above him began to sway, as if a strong wind was racing through the alley. I squinted at it and wondered before turning my attention back to Mike. "I think we both know there was no love between us," I said with my arms crossed over my chest.

"Sixth grade, under the jungle gym," he reminded me.

I snorted. "I was swinging upside down and you came over and put your lips against mine. That's not a kiss." Technically, it was my first kiss. If I wanted to count it. Which I didn't. If any one-way kiss was going to count, then Justin Timberlake was my first kiss. I'd kissed his poster on my bedroom wall many times prior to Mike planting his slobbery wet lips on mine. (For the record, Justin's a better kisser.)

"It was a kiss in my book," he replied.

"Then you have a pretty pathetic book."

Mike ignored my insult and continued as if he hadn't slurred my name behind my back earlier that day, or just now.

"I dropped some books off at the store yesterday and your dad was supposed to pay me for them today." Mike held out his hand.

"You'll have to take that up with my dad." As if I would pay him a dime. I didn't even *have* a dime.

"Your dad isn't here." He waggled his fingers.

No kidding, Sherlock. If he was, I'd be long gone, I thought, but for Mike's sake I stuck to the path of least resistance. "The store isn't open," I said. My impatience was dying to spew out of me.

"You closed early."

"I didn't close anything; Sheriff Espinosa locked up." At least I thought he had.

"Either way, you owe me fifty-two dollars and seventeen cents," Mike persisted.

"I don't owe you a dime," I huffed. Seriously, where would I get fifty-two dollars and seventeen cents? The sign, battered by the wind, groaned above us.

Mike wasn't going to back down. "You own the bookstore."

"No, it's my dad's bookstore."

"From the way I hear it, you own half, so you're just as responsible for the debt as he is."

This was seriously getting old. "Come back when the store is open."

Mike shook his finger at me and smiled. "You're trying to skip town without paying me."

Of course I was. Obviously Mike had gotten a little smarter since high school. "I don't have any money on me. It was a business deal. Made in a place of business. During business hours. Come. Back. Tomorrow."

"Is there a problem?" A deep, rich voice broke up our ridiculous argument.

It was a voice that gave me goose bumps . . . and I hated to admit the visceral response it caused in my body. Especially because those vocal cords hadn't said a word to me after the cuffs clinked around my wrists.

"No," I said at the same time Mike answered, "Yes." We both looked at the man who now towered over Mike, his shadow making my view of my short opponent almost disappear.

The only thing that made this whole scene even remotely bearable was the gate still separating me from them. Plus the sign was making enough noise I could claim I couldn't hear what they were saying. I thought about turning and running up the stairs to the apartment, but unlike Mike, Cade Calloway still looked fit as a fiddle. He could probably catch me.

Drat the man.

My hands flew down to my sides. "If you want to help," I said and then paused. Cade cocked his head and waiting for me to continue. "Then you can tell this imbecile that if he sold books to my dad, he needs to talk to my dad about collecting the money, not me."

"Technically, you owe him as much as your dad does."

I think I may have growled at that point. Otherwise there was a rabid raccoon running around in the alley. "I don't have any money to pay him!"

"Maybe I should call the sheriff. She seems to be losing her temper and she's reneging on paying for goods her business received."

At that point the gate couldn't save Mike. I yanked it open and was about to grab a fistful of that luscious hair when he backpedaled away from me. Cade stepped in between us and my mom's sign crashed down upon us.

Well, technically it crashed on Cade's head and bounced off Mike's face. I caught it before it hit the ground.

"Son of a—"

"Don't you cuss in front of me, Cade Calloway." I pulled the sign close to my chest, afraid one of them would try to grab it. Five-year-olds cussed at me almost on a daily basis, but Cade wasn't going to break my mom's rule for a gentleman's behavior. Not that Cade was a gentleman, but I was beginning to believe once more that the sign really did hold my momma's spirit within it.

Mike was too busy whining about the scratch on his nose—even though he was lucky my mom had decided to slide down that long slope instead of gouging it off his face—and telling me he was going to sue me for everything I was worth to notice that I was keeping the sign out of his reach. I smirked at both of them. Served them right.

"Good luck with that, Mike."

Cade gave me a stern look as he held the back of his head and blocked my smirk from Mike's view. "The wind did it, Mike. You can't sue someone for an act of nature. How much does she owe you?"

"I don't—" I started.

Cade glared over his shoulder and I shut my mouth before I dug myself a hole six feet under.

"Seventy-two dollars."

"You said fifty-two dollars!" My voice sounded higher-pitched than a squealing pig.

"That was before you scarred me for life. Twenty dollars is getting off cheap!" Mike also had reached screeching level.

Cade grimaced, but the auditory pain didn't stop me. "I'm not giving you a dime. How do I know you're not lying about dropping off the books in the first place?"

It was Cade's turn to growl before interjecting, "How's an even hundred dollars sound?"

"A hundred dollars?" My voice squeaked worse than a rooster with strep throat. "That's robbery!"

Mike didn't miss a beat. "You're robbing me!"

Cade dug into his back pocket with one hand while holding his head with the other. Pulling out a hundred-dollar bill from a stack of God only knew how many, he extended it toward Mike.

Mike also got a look at the wad of cash. "I think it's going to take two hundred."

"I think you're pushing your luck," Cade said as he stepped toward him.

"I think he's plum out of luck!" I tried to step around Cade, but Mike snatched the hundred-dollar bill and ran as fast as his pudgy little legs would take him. I hoped he fell in the fountain.

No such luck. He scooted by it and disappeared around the corner.

"Well, sh . . . crap."

I looked to see what could possibly be worse than me owing my ex a hundred dollars and saw Cade's hand covered in blood.

"Oh my God, you're bleeding!"

"Ya think?"

"This is no time to get snippy with me. Let's get you upstairs and see how bad it is." I grabbed his arm and began leading him through the gate, noticing a large clay pot of purple pansies on the apartment side for the first time. My dad wasn't known for taking care of plants.

Cade's voice softened. "I'm fine."

"You're not fine," I insisted.

"You used to think I was fine."

I caught the question in his eyes and ignored the heat that rose between us. I wanted to walk away, just turn my back on him the way he'd turned his back on me. Then I remembered what my dad had done the last time my mom's sign split Cade's head open.

Despite being mad as all get out, Dad took Cade upstairs, got him cleaned up, and then drove him to the hospital. I didn't get to go with them on that trip. I was told to go to bed, but even then, I knew there was going to be a serious discussion between the boy who was my everything and the man I loved more than anyone. What I didn't know at the time was how much a few stitches could change my world.

Chapter Eight

"Ow!"

"Stop being such a baby."

"I don't think saying *ow* when someone is peeling back the skin on your scalp is unreasonable."

I paused, holding my medical 'instruments' in the air like the surgeon on my favorite television show as she let the audience know she was going to save her patient from certain death, and explained the procedure to Cade the best way I could. "It's a little alcohol and a Q-tip."

I gave him an alternative as our eyes met in the bathroom mirror. "You can let me do it or go to the hospital and get it cleaned out."

"I already told you I wasn't going to the ER."

Sitting on a kitchen barstool in the small bathroom that looked as if it belonged in an old western washhouse, the man took up all my breathing space. I swore his hazel eyes were going to be the death of me. I wanted to be distracted by memories of making the barn wood sign that said "Bath 5 Cents" above the claw-foot tub, but then I thought of how two people could fit in the tub.

That wasn't helping.

I looked back at the wound on his head, which probably needed a few stitches. "You should go get this sewed up."

"Are my brains hanging out?" he asked.

"No! Good gravy, what do you think I am, a monster?" Cade didn't have a chance to respond before I applied a liberal amount of alcohol to his injury. "If your brains were coming out of your head, I would have ignored what was coming out of your mouth and called for an ambulance."

I admit the wound was probably clean, but I didn't think it would hurt to be extra careful. Besides, I was enjoying his pain—just a bit.

"That's good enough." Cade started to stand up, but I pushed him back down. The last thing I wanted was for him to stand up in this room. Long and narrow, with the sink on one end and the tub and toilet on the other, we'd practically be on top of each other. That would be a little too tempting.

I wasn't an inexperienced teenager anymore, and this type of proximity could lead to a whole lot more than second base.

I opened the medicine cabinet behind the mirror. "I'm sure Dad's got some butterfly bandages; he always keeps a supply. Let me put a few on to help it heal."

Cade's shoulders relaxed, then stiffened as my chest accidentally brushed against him. Despite not looking at him in the mirror, I felt his scrutiny. He was checking me out, from my curls to my nonexistent behind, and wondering if that move was on purpose.

I wondered the same thing.

"Quit it," I said.

"Quit what?"

"Quit looking at my body like it's a fried turkey leg at the state fair."

"I wouldn't compare you to a turkey leg—too much meat, not enough spice, and definitely not something I'd want to lick—"

"Fine! Just stop." The air was definitely getting hot. I opened the package and began to apply one butterfly bandage after another. I felt the skin on his head pull as he grinned from ear to ear. Cade had a way of teasing me until I forgot everything but that smile. I refused to look at it and applied another butterfly.

"You're more like a long, lean strip of chocolate-covered bacon."

I scrunched my nose. That didn't sound appetizing at all.

"The key to its appeal is how you eat it. You don't jump in and take a bite; the flavors can't be appreciated that way. No, you savor the layers by slowly licking off all the dark, creamy chocolate that's so rich you're dying to sink your teeth into. Then, when you get to the bacon, you don't hold back. You devour it . . . let the spice nip at your taste buds as you wrap the lean curves around—"

"I get the picture. You like chocolate-covered bacon."

"It's an unforgettable experience."

This was an unforgettable experience. Drat the man. I changed the subject. "Four butterflies, but I'm not a doctor, so I doubt they'll stay on long enough for it to heal." I moved out of the bathroom before he could stand up and work his magic with his bacon talk.

Cade followed with the wooden barstool in hand. I turned my back to him lest we end up trapped in the hallway and scooted toward the long wood-planked bar in the kitchen. Then strategically placed myself behind it.

"What are you going to do?" he asked.

"Go to bed."

His eyes crinkled.

I leaned over the counter. "Alone."

His grin increased. "I meant, what are your plans? Are you going to stay until your dad gets back?"

"I don't know."

"He's going to need you."

"Like I needed him?" It was below the belt, but I didn't care. I was playing defense on several fields of play.

Cade's voice held sorrow. The emotion was distracting. "He loved her."

"Who?"

"Marlene. I'm worried about him." The heat was gone from Cade's expression. He was genuinely worried about my dad, which made my level of concern rise considerably.

I squelched it.

"Wasn't she a little . . . I don't know . . ." I hated to say it, but it begged to be said. "Wasn't she just a little too . . ."

"Refined?"

"Yes, refined. Dad lives in a barn. He's a fast-food kind of guy. The closest thing he knows to a restaurant is the Hazel Rock Diner. I can guarantee you, if I open this refrigerator there's a jar of jelly, a half-gallon of milk, butter, some unidentifiable leftovers from a meal he cooked that involved a can of hash, and a piece of chocolate cake or coconut cream pie. That's it. Well, besides the stash of bite-size Snickers in the fruit drawer."

That smile was beginning to form on Cade's mouth again. I told myself I hated it and looked out the kitchen window, still framed with the lace curtains my mom had hung twenty years before. They were clean but reflected the age of the building. "I can't see Marlene stepping foot into the Hazel Rock Diner, let alone eating two meals a day there like it was her own personal kitchen. Dad would be lost if they closed."

"They were opposites, I'll give you that. But the last six months was the happiest I'd seen Bobby Ray since you left."

If Cade was trying to make me feel guilty for staying away, I was done with the conversation. I'd left town for a good reason.

I turned on him. "You let those rumors run wild."

"Some of them were true." He tried to smile.

"Most of them were trash."

"It helped you move on."

"Seriously? Don't you mean move out of town?"

He sighed as if this conversation was old news. "The rumors made you hate me. With you hating me, I didn't have to worry about hurting you."

I wasn't letting him off the hook. "Your plan didn't work."

"You didn't look too hurt when I saw you at the diner with Hunter. Or Bryan White," he accused.

We were both acting childishly, but unfortunately I couldn't stop. "I was trying to make sure every boy in town knew I wasn't easy, and that I certainly wasn't pregnant."

He scoffed. "It backfired."

I think fire was starting to come out of my ears. "It would have worked if they'd had an honest bone in their bodies."

"They were teenage boys. They had to live up to my reputation."

"Your reputation was built on a lie!" Flames were definitely shooting from my eyes now.

Cade tried to add logic. Poor logic. "They didn't know that."

I rounded the bar and poked him in the chest with my finger. It was high time Cade Calloway owned his mistakes. "They would have if you'd told the truth."

"I never said a word about us and if I'd denied it, they wouldn't have believed it. Besides, the truth can be overrated in the locker room." He still had the logic of a teenager.

"Are you kidding me? Someone stuffed my locker with pregnancy tests!"

He had the grace to wince. "I saw that."

"Yet you did nothing." My hands went to my hips, demanding a reasonable explanation for his silence.

He gave a politician's answer. "It was twelve years ago. I was just as inexperienced with gossip as you were. I can't change it now."

"Gossip is your middle name. You're a Calloway. You could have tried. If not then, you could now," I insisted.

Cade wouldn't budge. "It wouldn't do any good. You heard Mike."

"Mike wouldn't have talked to me that way if you'd squelched the rumors when we were in high school."

Cade threw his hands in the air. "What does any of this have to do with your father?"

"He didn't stand up for me either! He plotted with your father—the two of them planned to break us up no matter what the price—and if my daddy hadn't made me put the stupid pregnancy book in The Book Barn's window, the rumors wouldn't have started! If it hadn't been for your lies, that photo in the paper of me putting up the display wouldn't have meant a thing!" My voice had returned to that shrill tone that hurt my own ears. It could probably kill a dog.

"How many times do I have to tell you—I didn't talk about you. Everyone could see you weren't pregnant. You were a beanpole."

"Our fathers plotted to break us up and you let them."

"They only wanted what was best for us."

"Your daddy wanted to save your football career. He wasn't worried about me."

"I wouldn't have made it to the pros if we'd had a baby," Cade reasoned.

"I wasn't pregnant! I'd like a little credit for the fact that I was smarter than that." Cade looked at the worn leather couch in the living room. It was the same brown leather couch where I'd almost given him my virginity. I would have if Cade's daddy hadn't knocked on the door and caught us in an extremely embarrassing position. I ignored the memory, and the feelings it stirred, and stayed on track. "If I had been pregnant, the baby would have been an act of divine intervention, not something that came from you."

"I would have claimed it." His act of selflessness was laughably too late and required way too much of my imagination.

"Oh, good grief. Are we really arguing about a baby that never was? A baby born by Immaculate Conception? I'm not Mary." I walked back to the kitchen, opened the fridge, and leaned on the door with one arm. Some sweet tea would hit the spot right about now—if I could lace it with whiskey.

"I don't think anyone could confuse the two of you."

I straightened up slowly and looked back at him, my voice low and dangerous. "What's that supposed to mean?"

"Just that she's ho . . . holy . . ." He stuttered, "And you're not."

"I think you'd better leave." If he didn't, I'd actually deserve to go to jail for murder.

"All I was trying to say was that your dad loves you. He did what he thought was best for *your* future. And mine acted in my best interest. Both of our fathers were wrong. I was wrong." Before his apology could sink in, he'd closed the distance between us.

I froze. I'd imagined this moment for years after I left Hazel Rock, and now that it no longer meant something to me, it was happening. "Are you apologizing, Cade Calloway?"

"I am." He nodded, the sorrow evident in his eyes. "I'm sorry I hurt you. I'm sorry I wasn't more mature. I'm sorry I listened to a ridiculous story about you possibly hurting my chances of getting picked up by the University of East Texas. And I'm really sorry I let my father's plan to break us up actually work at the expense of your reputation."

I forgot my anger and stared up at the mouth that had demanded too much of my attention.

Cade pulled me away from the fridge and wrapped his hands around my lower back. "We were great together. We never fought. Never bickered. But we made the mistake of never talking about the future."

A nervous lick of my lips drew his attention, but he continued. "We lived like tomorrow didn't matter, and it hurt us when others started talking about how we wouldn't be able to handle my career. Seeing you again has made me realize just how wrong they were . . . I was."

His mouth was closing the distance between us and I was powerless to stop him.

"We've never been able to stay away from each other." His voice had that deep, raspy quality it would always get right before he kissed me. Funny, how I remembered that so clearly.

"You've done a fine job of avoiding me all day long," I challenged, knowing that if I let him kiss me, I'd prove I'd done lost my mind.

His voice was barely above a whisper, but I heard every word before our lips met. "The day's not over."

Cade's kisses had the power to disarm, discombobulate, and define the meaning of desire. It never failed to amaze me how I could be completely sane one minute and rooster-in-an-empty-barn nuts the next, when I was in his arms.

'Cause what I was doing was C.R.A.Z.Y. But that old Charli Rae, the one who constantly got in trouble in her youth, was sticking her head into my business. Telling me I hadn't been kissed in months; a few moments down memory lane in Cade's arms wouldn't hurt anything. We were adults. Mature.

His hands slowly moved up . . .

And we were out of control. I pushed off his rock-solid chest, half-hating, half-loving the current Charli, who had some control.

"I think you'd better go," I said, my tone saying something completely different than my words. I cleared my throat and crossed my arms across my chest before I dared to look into his eyes.

They sparkled. Drat the man.

Cade turned and walked away. Opening the door, I thought he was going to leave without another word.

Then Princess walked in. Or rather waddled in, as if she owned the place.

"No," I said.

"She needs you."

"I don't need her; she's trouble." I thought about that scarf she'd planted near my purse. She was the reason I'd gone to jail.

Cade shrugged, as if all women were trouble. "She's pink. She's a freak of nature. They don't live long in the wild."

He knew that would get me. "I don't know the first thing about armadillos." All my frustration was starting to show. "She has to stay in The Barn."

"She's lived in the apartment and The Barn her entire life."

"But she stinks." And she did stink. Her odor was beyond rank.

"That's what those two tubs by the door are for. You fill them up at night and she'll bathe right when she comes in. She loves it."

I looked at the two plastic tubs. "It sounds to me like she'd be better off if you took her."

"No. They're territorial. She'd just try to come back and then you'd risk her getting hit by a car."

I paused, wondering if that would be such a bad thing.

Cade raised his eyebrows.

I threw my hands up. "Who would have taken care of her if I hadn't come back?"

The expression on his face said it all. Cade hadn't stopped by for me; he'd stopped by to take care of Princess.

"Oh."

"It's not like that—" Cade started to come back into the apartment, but I stopped him.

"It's fine. What does she eat?" I had no idea what I was going to feed her, or myself for that matter.

"Look in the pantry—it's full of cat food. Give her one can at night and one in the morning. In between she'll go outside and eat bugs, and your dad keeps some mealworms in The Barn for a treat."

"Uuuggg!" My capitulation was complete.

Cade smiled. "Thank you for cleaning up my injury. Get some sleep and we'll talk about finding your dad in the morning."

"Cade . . ."

He stopped and waited for me to finish. Probably waiting for me to ask him to stay. But I surprised myself and him by asking, "Do you think my dad could have killed Marlene?"

"No more than he'd be capable of killing his daughter."

My ex-boyfriend left the apartment and I finally realized I'd left the refrigerator door open. I looked inside and found blackberry jam, a stick of butter, a half-gallon of milk, two Tupperware containers of something that looked like stew, a piece of chocolate silk pie, and a carton of eggs. I'd forgotten his love of eggs. But behind the eggs I found what I was looking for. With the bag of Snickers in my hand, I turned toward the couch.

Princess was about to jump on the cushion.

"No!" I yelled.

She jumped straight in the air. Huh; so that's how they died on the road, I thought. Straddle one and they'll commit suicide by jumping into your undercarriage.

"I'll get your bath and your dinner. Just stay off the couch." I hurried over and filled both tubs and then her bowl that said "Princess" on the side. She took her time running back and forth between the tubs, making the water completely brown.

It was kind of gross. She stopped and licked her feet and then looked up at me expectantly.

"Are you kidding me?" I asked, then went and got a towel. I dried her off and she rolled and rubbed all over my hands. I had to admit, it was very cute.

Once I was done, I dumped the water off the porch and threw the towel in the hamper in my dad's room. I washed my hands and grabbed my bag of Snickers before plopping down on the same old leather couch Cade and I had made out on as teenagers.

I thought about the past and about the man who'd raised me. My dad was no more capable of murder than he was of standing up for a cause. He wasn't a chicken or weak; he just didn't get riled up over anything. When my reputation had been on the line, he'd told me to walk through town with my head held high and stop letting the gossip tear me apart. He just couldn't understand how one little slip of gossip could possibly matter. And he'd joined Cade's daddy in the plot to destroy my relationship with Cade, no matter what the cost.

Those couple weeks when I'd felt like I'd gone from Hazel Rock's homecoming princess to Hazel Rock's Jezebel didn't seem to bother anyone but me. At seventeen, I'd cried myself to sleep wishing my mom was there to bring the fire to Cade's backside and put the entire male population of Hazel Rock in their place—including my daddy. Because that couldn't happen, I did what I had to do instead.

Forgiveness was for a better person. I TPed the mayor's home, The Barn, and then moved on to Hunter's house and then Bryan's. After I was finished, I skipped town, taking my daddy's truck to the bus station in Abilene.

Now, a dozen years later, I sat looking at the photo on the wall of me dancing on my father's dress shoes while my mom laughed in the background. She'd been the only African-American woman in Hazel Rock, yet she never let the bias or whispers about her marriage to my daddy faze her. She gave me life. Backbone. And the ability to appreciate people for their character, not their skin color. If she'd lived, I have no doubt she would have taught me how to deal with gossip. But she hadn't, and that young girl in the picture with a spark in her eyes that wouldn't be denied had lost out on one of the most important life lessons she could have learned.

The picture captured a time when my life was simple. Both my parents were alive. Rumors didn't bother me, and the only complication in my life was my less-than-tame curls.

Today, however, I was once again faced with forgiving my dad. He'd stranded me in the middle of my own personal hell. Or I could repeat the past and run for the hills.

There was no argument; the mountains of Denver sounded awfully good.

I could even go for some whipped cream pie.

Chapter Nine

"Where are you?"
I dropped the bomb he wouldn't believe. "I'm in Hazel Rock."

"Get out!" My cousin Jamal said exactly what I wished I could do. Get Out.

"Does my mom know?" he asked.

"No. I didn't want her to make a bigger thing out of it than what it really is."

"What is it?"

"I came home." Uncomfortable with my choice of words, I rephrased my answer. "I came back to sign papers to sell The Book Barn."

"Get out!"

If Jamal said that again, I'd pull him through the phone connection and let him take my place. I closed my eyes and pursed my lips, trying to keep my temper and mouth in check.

"Why are you still there?" I could hear chips crunching in the background and pictured him sitting in front of the TV with a bag of Doritos on his lap, a beer in one hand, and a game control in the other.

"The Realtor was murdered." I explained. Poorly.

"Get out."

I sighed. Jamal was my Aunt Violet's only child and was more like an older brother to me than a cousin. He was also the exact opposite of me: never caused my aunt a day's trouble. He was smart. Studious. Self-sufficient. His social life consisted of people he met through the internet gaming system he had in his living room. He was socially awkward in person but an extrovert online.

Someday he'd make a horrible husband.

"Listen, I could really use a little—"

"Hey, Char, you know I love you—get him before he gets away!"

"What?" He couldn't possibly know about the kiss with Cade. Could he?

I heard the game in the background from his TV and breathed a sigh of relief.

"Sorry. I was talking to one of my teammates. I would love to be able to help, but if you're going to ask for money, I have to tell you I just invested in a new app that's gonna be killer." He grunted, and I knew he'd died during his game. He always grunted when his character died. "When are you coming home?"

"I–I don't know."

"Well, call me. I'll pick you up at the airport and we can take Mom out to dinner. She'd love to get together with the two of us." He hissed, and I pictured him narrowly escaping another death.

"Sure, tell Violet I'm fine," I said.

"Catch up with you later, Char." He disconnected and I wondered if I should just call my aunt myself.

But then she'd worry. Offer me money she didn't have. And I'd feel worse than I already did.

Stuck with nowhere else to go for now, I found a power cord in my dad's room and moved it to the kitchen counter to plug in my phone, happy he had the same type of cell I did. After stupidly eating a whole bag of Snickers for dinner, I found my energy levels were quickly dropping and a record-setting sugar crash was making the trip to my bedroom difficult.

Crossing the threshold was like walking back in time. Nothing had changed from the day I left. The white iron bed was covered with a hand-quilted bedspread in shades of lavender with matching pillows. My dad's military trunk sat at the foot of the bed, filled with more hand-stitched quilts made by my grandmother. The French doors leading out to the balcony were covered with the same light purple sheets that had faded in the summer sun. My antique oak dresser stood against one wall and the attached mirror still had darkened edges in the silver. It made me think of all the history, including my own, that had been reflected in that looking glass.

Toenails clicking across the wood floor alerted me to Princess following me into the bedroom, but I immediately shooed her back out and closed the door. I turned off the light, got undressed, and crawled into bed, letting the chocolate withdrawal do its magic. By morning the jumble of dreams I'd experienced about Marlene and my dad, her death, and the lost sale of the store made me develop a plan. I'd call Marlene's real estate company and request they contact the buyer to strike a deal for a reduced cost on The Barn. Then, with the sale of the store out of the way, I could focus on locating my dad, clearing his name, and getting back to my real life—the one that didn't involve murder.

One phone call later and my plans were shot to hell in a handbasket. In between her tears, the receptionist at Yellow Jacket Realty told me the real estate contract had expired at the end of business hours the previous day. Our buyer had already called and said the deal was off; he had another property that would work out much better—and it wasn't the scene of a homicide.

That brought up option number two: open the bookstore and make it profitable, which had always been a challenge. All I needed was short-term success; no career changes, just get the store out of the red and show that it was an investment purchase.

Decision made, I took a bath in the claw-foot tub that looked like Dad hadn't used it in ages, which he probably hadn't because my snooping revealed a newly added bathroom in the other bedroom that had a shower. My snooping also alerted me to the fact that Dad clearly hadn't been living in the apartment. His bedroom was clean, with the bed made and the closet mostly empty. He had a few shirts, a couple of ties, and his only suit—the same one he'd worn to my mom's funeral. A lone pair of black dress shoes collected dust on the floor.

Clean and wrapped in a towel, I padded to my bedroom and rooted through the few items of clothing that hadn't fit in my suitcase twelve years ago, which I was dang glad to have now. They smelled like cedar balls, but that was better than putting on the same dress I'd worn to jail. The bad part? There was a reason I'd left these clothes behind. Except for the cutoff jeans shorts that had seen better days, they were all associated with Cade. He'd bought me the matching panties and bras, which, unfortunately, still fit. And all the shirts had Cade's old football number on them in one way or the other.

Ugh.

I chose the shirt with the smallest number thirteen on the upper left-hand section. While identifying me as Cade's number-one groupie had been cute as a teenager, it was nauseating as an adult. Luckily, if anyone asked, the number and the color of the shirt also matched the current quarterback for the Denver Broncos.

At least one man would know differently, but I planned on avoiding him.

I put on my boots and assessed the look in the mirror. My curls were piled on top of my head in a messy ponytail and the entire outfit embraced working on the farm—something I'd never done, but that didn't matter. There was work to be done in The Barn.

I pushed Princess outside because she had no desire to leave the oversize doggy bed in the living room and locked the apartment. I swear, Princess was glaring at me.

"You can't stay in the apartment while I'm gone."

She blinked, then sat down. Who knew armadillos could sit down?

"Go play."

She shook her head and snuffled.

If she were human, I'd think she was saying, *No way.*

"I know you don't stay in the apartment all day. If you want in The Barn, just scratch on the door. I have work to do." I headed down the stairs, gave a final glance at my dad's pet, who hadn't moved an inch, and made my way past the silent iron bracket. It was freaky not having the sign swinging in the wind above my head as I went through the gate, but I wasn't in a rush to rehang "Eve's Gate." I was seriously thinking about taking it back to Colorado with me, so I left it on the coffee table in the apartment.

Pushing the key into the lock on the side door, I just about peed my pants when the door opened without me turning the handle. The girl screaming from the inside didn't help much either.

I jumped and then stared at the frozen young couple standing in the middle of The Barn. A few frightening beats of my heart later, we both demanded in unison, "Who are you?"

"I work here," said the girl with curly blond hair styled very similarly to my own. She had on a pair of low-rise shorts with a T-shirt and flip-flops.

"Nobody works here."

The boy—young, blond, and athletic-looking—stepped in front of her. "I don't know who you think you are, lady . . ." His chest was puffed out like a gorilla. Any minute he was going to start pounding on it and tell me not to mess with his woman.

"I get it," I said and waved his macho-protection attitude out of the way so I could talk to the girl. "I'm Charli Rae Warren. And you are ... ?"

She breathed a visible sigh of relief and held out her quivering hand. "Aubrey Buchanan. You met my mom yesterday at Beaus and Beauties."

I vaguely remembered Scarlet asking if Aubrey was supposed to work yesterday. Obviously this was the girl in question. "You do work here," I said.

"I did, before ..." She stopped, visibly upset by what had happened to Marlene.

"Aubrey ..." the boy started.

"How did you get in?" I asked, not giving him a chance to go all ape crazy on me.

"I've got a key."

That explained the unlocked door. I'd been about to give the sheriff a piece of my mind for leaving it unsecured.

"Were you scheduled to work today?"

"No, I ... I ..."

Her response irritated me. I didn't need nosy kids sneaking into The Barn when they shouldn't. "You came to see where Marlene was murdered," I said.

"No!"

I wasn't going to let her off that easily. Call me mean, but it felt like an invasion of my privacy and Marlene's. "Would you like me to show you where her body was? Where she lost her fight to live? Is that what—"

"I came to quit!" she yelled.

"Aubrey, you don't mean that," said her boyfriend. Then he turned to me. "She left ... her ... her term paper here, but we can't find it."

"Yes, I do mean it. I do, Darrin. I can't work here." On a sob, Aubrey burst into tears and Darrin pulled her into his arms. He looked as if he might join her any minute as he murmured in her ear.

Well, crap. I moved from one foot to the other. I'd done this to them.

Before I could apologize, Darrin beat me to it. "I'm sorry, Ms. Warren. We were trying to do the right thing."

"No, I'm sorry. Marlene's death has been hard for everyone. If I find the paper, I'll bring it by the beauty shop, okay?"

He nodded. Aubrey sniffed and murmured, "Thank you," before they walked out the door I'd just entered hand in hand.

Only then did I really see the interior of The Barn. The sight in front of me left my mouth hanging open.

"Fuzz buckets!" I wasn't talking to anyone in particular. Just myself. And the buzzing fluorescent light bulbs. And the rows upon rows of books. And the mess the sheriff had left me.

Black powder covered everything outside the tearoom. It was smeared over the cash counter and register. The pink princess merchandise was sprinkled with black polka dots. It spilled over onto the floor and left smears across the stained concrete. Even the glossy white doorframe leading to the back room hadn't been spared.

I slowly poked my head into the area where Marlene's body had lain. New fiction releases were strewn across the floor and I could almost see the fight she'd put up to stay alive. The covers on some of the mystery paperbacks were ruined. The same gritty powder dulled vibrant images and authors' names. Pages were bent and spines torn, as if the books themselves had fought, and lost, right alongside Marlene.

A shiver ran down my spine and I backed away. Then I realized I could follow the leads the police had observed and moved forward. Started at the point of discovery. They'd fingerprinted the books on the floor, a few of the shelves on either side. Boxes appeared to have been moved, but I couldn't be sure. The only thing I'd really focused on when I'd opened the curtain yesterday was Marlene's body.

They'd fingerprinted the doorway, the counter, the register. But when I opened it up, the drawer still contained money. I couldn't help but smile.

It was my first real clue. If there was money in the register, it couldn't possibly have been a robbery. I thought of Marlene's purse and stopped patting myself on the back. I didn't see it yesterday, but that didn't mean it hadn't been under the counter, in the tearoom, or in the back room. The police would have taken all personal property belonging to the victim.

I went upstairs, but beyond the railing it didn't look as if there was any fingerprint powder anywhere. Of course there wasn't anything to put powder on, unless you chose one messy stack over another to decide to dust for prints. Obviously the police had decided nothing of consequence had occurred upstairs.

I returned to the lower level and looked around. Fingerprints and photographs. That's all I could see coming out of the crime scene. I supposed they could have taken DNA, but where, I had no idea.

I returned to the tearoom and opened the refrigerator. I breathed a sigh of relief at the sight of a pitcher filled with tea and a bowl of lemons on the shelf next to it. I poured myself a tall glass of sweet tea and dropped in two tart lemon wedges. Then I got to work doing my least favorite thing—cleaning, starting with the front counter.

Almost two hours later, I'd thrown away a trash bag full of merchandise, photographing and cataloging each item to take a loss on inventory. It amazed me how quickly the business was coming back to me, yet at the same time I wasn't sure I cared for it sticking around in the recesses of my brain. I raided the petty cash fund, thinking my dad owed me for my time and everything else he'd put me through, and headed out the side door to get some real food at the diner down the street.

Scarlet met me in front of the fountain, her gaze straying to the number thirteen on my shirt.

"Quarterback for the Denver Broncos," I explained.

She didn't buy it, but didn't say, *OMW, girl, I wasn't born in The Barn yesterday* either. She nodded and asked, "Are you heading for the diner to get lunch?"

"Yeah; wanna join me?"

"That sounds like the best offer I've had today." She looked like her day had started out worse than mine. Granted, she was dressed a hundred times better than I was, in a red bottleneck dress that hugged every curve down to her knees, with five-inch heels to match. Her hair swooped down over her right eye in a glamorous wave like Jessica Rabbit and her makeup was perfect. But despite her glamourous appearance, there were circles under her eyes that told me she'd gotten less sleep than I had.

We headed down the street and I told her I'd met Aubrey and her boyfriend Darrin. She let me in on the gossip of Hazel Rock. Darrin was a senior, the star quarterback, and leading the town's dreams for a state championship. Aubrey was a girl from my side of town.

It really sounded like history was repeating itself and made me want to warn Aubrey to head for the hills.

We made it down to the diner, and I wondered how Scarlet had managed to wear heels in the dirt without breaking an ankle. Her skin was dry and smooth, while I was baking in the heat of the day and all too glad to step up onto the covered porch of the Hazel Rock Diner.

When we entered the restaurant, all the friendly chatter stopped. Dead silence surrounded us. I was very familiar with that particular sound.

Glasses and forks were suspended in midair and I wanted to say, *Seriously? Finish your bite.* Then turn to the table of high school students and say, *Drink your milk and grow up. Then we'll talk.*

I didn't, though. Instead, that hankering to run returned as everyone tilted, twisted, and leaned to take a look at me.

In the experience category, it ranked at about a two.

"Y'all need to learn some manners. That's not how y'all should be greeting a friend who's returned home after being gone for such a long stretch." Scarlet put her hands on her curvaceous hips as she waited for a response from the lunch crowd.

A few grumbled acknowledgments didn't appease her and she snorted her disapproval, ready to chew them up and spit them out any second. I grabbed her arm and headed for a booth in the back. I'd recognized most of the faces that were staring us down, from the barber to the baker. Thank God Hazel Rock didn't have a candlestick maker. The quilt maker, Betty Walker, however, was among them.

Along with a certain mayor and a football coach.

I avoided making any kind of eye contact.

"You can't let folks disrespect you like that," Scarlet insisted.

"I can't force them to respect me." I slunk into the booth the same way I had last time I'd graced this diner.

"Everyone deserves respect."

"Unless they seduced a football player or killed a Realtor."

"But you didn't. On either account."

"They think I did. On both accounts. I shouldn't have come." I started to get up.

Scarlet's blue eyes crystalized as she stared me down. "Don't you dare. You need to eat." She tapped the table with her index finger. "Sit."

I obeyed like one of my students, my body sunk down low into the faux leather bench seat with both shoulders hunched forward. I didn't do it because Scarlet browbeat me, I did it because I realized I was absolutely, positively starving and the bacon cheeseburger at the next table smelled like heaven. Yet the whispers circulating through the restaurant were weighing on me.

"I could have just ordered a pizza." My suggestion was half-hearted at best.

"Our pizza delivery stopped years ago."

"What?"

She nodded her head sadly.

"But that's impossible."

"Not when the size of the town's population drops the way it has in Hazel Rock. Everyone moved to Oak Grove when they built the new Country Mart there."

"Country Mart moved to Oak Grove? Why didn't Country Mart build the new store in Hazel Rock?"

"Cade's daddy wouldn't give them a tax break on the land. He lost his reelection over it."

"Cade ran against his daddy?"

That brought a smile to Scarlet's face. "He ran for mayor the following term and won by a landslide."

"Who was the mayor in between Cade and old man Calloway?" I asked, unable to fathom who could possibly beat a Calloway.

She shrugged. "You're going to find out sooner or later. It was Marlene."

I groaned and hid behind the grease-covered menu the waitress dropped with a slap against the wooden table. The town obviously held Marlene in high esteem—enough that she'd bested Cade Calloway Senior in an election.

"I heard you were back in town, Princess."

"Charli," I corrected the speaker before I realized it was Coach Purcell's form blocking my view of the rest of the diner's inhabitants. His girth had almost doubled, but his whistle still hung around his neck on a bright blue lanyard. His wardrobe hadn't changed a bit either. He still wore an oversize polo, but today it was covered by a long-sleeved Windbreaker with "Hazel Rock High School Football" embroidered on the front left pocket. Luckily, his long nylon shorts still covered his knees, but his skinny calves, which were in direct opposition to the size of the rest of him, were still exposed. The one thing that was different was the ball cap on his head. I didn't remember Coach wearing a cap, he'd had a full head of red hair that he had a tendency to grab and pull during the games.

I couldn't help but wonder if he had pulled it all out.

It was the smile on Coach Purcell's face that really caught me off-guard. The coach never smiled. He grunted and cussed at the football players. The rest of us didn't exist . . . unless we were football boosters.

"It's nice to see you, Coach." I wasn't sure whether my attempt at pleasantry would pass the Southern hospitality test, but Scarlet stepped in and took control.

"How's the team holding up in this heat, Coach? Are the new misters working for the boys?"

Coach's face lit up. "They've been a godsend, Scarlet. Thanks for getting behind that campaign. Those new haircuts are helping too."

I probably looked confused because the coach went on to explain. "We had a fund-raiser to raise enough money to buy water misters for the sidelines after one of the boys collapsed from the heat during our two-a-days. We auctioned off our hair to the highest bidder and let Scarlet shave any design the winner wanted on our heads."

My eyebrows shot up. I thought of all the dirty things people had shaved on their heads. Surely not.

"Within reason of course," Scarlet piped in, knowing exactly where my thoughts had headed.

"The Oak Grove coach won the bid on my head." Coach Purcell turned his head and pulled the school ball cap off, exposing hair that looked like he'd just entered military boot camp. The one difference? A bulldog with the letters OGHS was still visible despite his hair growing back enough to cover the skin.

"Oh." Oak Grove had been our rivals since before I was born. I knew it had to kill the coach to have that on his head, but he just laughed.

"It's for the team. We needed those misters and Coach Wiley helped us attain them with his five-hundred-dollar donation."

I nearly choked on the water the waitress had left for us. "Five hundred dollars?"

"He didn't think I'd wear a hat to cover it up. He misjudged our Hazel Rock pride." Coach Purcell smiled, his teeth surprisingly very white and straight, and put the hat back on his head. "We raised enough money to buy two misters and have plans to buy two more."

"I'm glad to hear it, Coach."

He nodded his head and gave Scarlet a half wink before turning in my direction. "That's not why I came over, though, Prin—Charli.

I'm sorry about what happened to you yesterday. It was an awful way to come home. I just wanted you to know that even though we are grieving over Marlene's senseless death, we know this has been hard on you too." He squeezed my shoulder in a gesture of support that was surprisingly comforting and not the least bit painful.

Stunned by his show of support, I just stared up at the man who had played a part in my breakup with Cade. He hadn't been directly responsible, but I knew Coach Purcell had told my boyfriend he didn't have time to be messing with me, he needed to focus on his football career.

That advice had gone a long way with Cade. So who was this new man in front of me?

"Once a member of the team, always a member of the team."

"But I wasn't part of the team," I said. Having a girl on the football team would tear this town apart—though I hoped to witness it one day.

"Our cheerleaders get the crowd into the game. I've come to realize they're an integral part of what makes us who we are. The Fighting Eagles of Hazel Rock wouldn't be who they are without our cheerleaders."

"Oh." I felt like I'd just received a pitch to rejoin the cheer squad. Or maybe the football team. I wasn't sure.

"If you need any help at the store, just ask. The team is here for you." Coach squeezed my shoulder once more and returned to his seat a few booths away. None other than the mayor himself was seated in the same booth. Cade winked at me from his seat.

"Coach Purcell married the cheerleading coach," Scarlet said. "I imagine she altered his opinions just a tad."

With the coach's blessing and the mayor's support, everyone else in the diner seemed to lose interest in me. Chatter resumed, and I was forced to admit some things had changed in Hazel Rock.

Chapter Ten

Coach Purcell's trip to our table broke the ice for the rest of the diners. During our lunch most of them stopped by to say welcome back and offer condolences for my loss. I kind of felt like it should be me offering the condolences. I didn't know Marlene all that well, but I accepted them graciously—after Scarlet kicked me in the shin.

She kicked me again when I started asking the mail carrier, who sat down at the table next to ours, if she'd seen anything suspicious at The Barn the previous day. She hadn't or I would have tolerated more bruises.

"That's Mateo's job," Scarlet hissed.

"Okay. I'm sorry. I can't help it, I just . . . I just need to know," I whispered.

Scarlet looked like she understood but let the topic drop without another word about it. Then she got me up-to-date on who'd left town for college and never returned, and who'd settled down with a spouse and kids. I couldn't see myself in that role anytime soon, so when she told me I was one of the few left unattached, I thought of Cade's kiss.

God, please let him still be among the single.

My prayers were answered a few minutes later when Scarlet announced that my ex was the most eligible bachelor in town. My eyes strayed to him eating lunch with Coach and I blushed when he caught me staring. Luckily, I was rescued by the waitress.

She plopped down a burger in front of me that was big enough for two and said, "Time to rock the house, girl."

My mouth watered. The diner's half pounder, known as The Rocker, was made up of two thick, juicy patties guaranteed to add plaque to my arteries, a sesame seed bun toasted with butter, two slices of locally made goat cheese, lettuce, tomato, and topped off with string-fried onion, and of course a side of ranch dressing. It was the *one* thing in Hazel Rock I admitted to missing . . . and craving on numerous occasions.

While I savored every bite, Scarlet talked about her salon and her plans for the future and nibbled on a Cobb salad. It looked good but didn't compare to the food in front of me. Content to listen, eat, and nod, I ignored the mayor and enjoyed myself for the first time since coming home. About halfway through the burger, however, I had to call it quits. I may have been able to squeeze into my high school cutoffs, but I was going to bust a seam if I ate one more bite.

I got the rest of my burger to go and Scarlet and I left the diner with a polite nod in Coach and Cade's direction. I was glad they'd chosen to sit toward the kitchen and not the front door. Walking past Cade would have meant we'd have to talk, and I wasn't quite ready to do that after our meeting of the lips.

Scarlet and I walked along the boardwalk, the sun beating down on us in between the roofs. Our steps clippitty-clopped on the wooden planks, my long stride offsetting her shorter, daintier progress.

"What are you going to do?" she asked.

I sighed and squinted into the sun. "I tried to see if the sale could still move forward, but the buyer is no longer interested. The real estate company said homicide scenes don't typically sell."

"I suppose not. And Marlene was a pillar of the community."

I nodded in agreement. The truth in that statement was beginning to hit home.

"I'm going to go by the office later this afternoon to see if I can talk to someone in person."

"Have you thought about staying and making a go of it?"

I did an about-face and was shaking my head before she even finished the sentence. Staying in Hazel Rock would be a big mistake. My dad needed me about as much as I needed a pie in my face every year. If lunch had taught me anything, it was that my daddy still had friends in town who would help him get back on his feet when he was ready. Besides, I had a life in Denver, with students waiting for me to return as soon as I could. "No. but I thought I'd open up the store long enough to make enough money to buy a ticket home."

"When were you planning on leaving?"

"Sometime next week. I priced an airline ticket and I think I can cover the cost with a few days of profit. It'll give Dad a start in the right direction, and if nothing else, I can always take a bus."

"I hate that this happened." Scarlet's voice cracked and she stopped so suddenly her arms and chest wobbled forward like a young filly standing for the first time. She was staring at The Book Barn Princess with the same open expression of pain she'd worn when she'd witnessed the removal of Marlene's body from the store on a gurney. I followed her gaze.

"OMW," she gasped. "I don't think you'll be making much money in the next week."

The front door to The Barn had turned into a memorial in shades of yellow and black. Balloons in the shape of bumblebees swayed in the dusty breeze. Decorative pots of yellow mums lined each side of the entrance with plush stuffed bees stacked behind them. Pictures of Marlene covered the doors; if I opened them, the images would swish right off into a crumpled mess and blow down the street like tumbleweeds.

The town would never forgive me for damaging the photos they'd taped to the glass of Marlene being sworn in as mayor, or of what looked like Marlene receiving the Chamber of Commerce award for businesswoman of the year.

The display was overwhelmingly huge. Texans believed in making sure everything is *bigger in Texas*—even if it meant your worst nightmare. The balloons and stuffed animals were all new ... and more abundant than the amount of toys I'd collected in my school's Christmas donation box last year. I couldn't just throw them away. Nor could I donate them to charity without looking callous. The plants I could at least bring to her gravesite or give to Yellow Jacket Realty or maybe a nursing home.

But the question remained: When could I do that without irritating everyone after they had only just started to warm up to me?

"Was that there when we left for lunch?" I asked.

"There was one balloon and one pot of yellow flowers when I crossed the street. I thought you put those out."

I shook my head, wishing I'd been that thoughtful. But I hadn't, and now the memorial was out of control. We watched as one of the big-haired blondes I'd seen leaving the beauty shop the day before parked her oversize SUV in front of the store. She removed a large floral cross with a stand out of the backseat, pushed the car door closed with her butt, which was barely covered by a hand-painted designer skirt, and walked up the steps to The Barn where she planted the floral cross directly in front of the doors. It wobbled for a moment as she bowed her head in prayer.

"Interesting. I thought Reba Sue and Marlene hated each other," Scarlet mumbled, more to herself than to me.

I felt like I should remain silent out of respect, but I couldn't. Besides, Scarlet had opened that door first. I leaned over and whispered, "Why did they hate each other? And what's the proper amount of time to leave a memorial in place?"

"Oh, just some silly argument about missing antique pieces from a house Reba Sue staged for Yellow Jacket Realty. She thought Marlene should pay for them and Marlene told Reba Sue she was the one who'd misplaced them, said they were never in the house to begin with."

That got my attention and put Reba Sue at the top of my list of potential suspects. Scarlet, however, saw the stupid light bulb light up in my brain and decided to turn it off immediately.

"Reba Sue didn't kill Marlene. She was getting a mani pedi when Marlene was killed."

I jumped on the obvious. "She needed a manicure? Were her nails broken? Did it look like she'd been in a fight?"

"OMW, Charli. Reba gets her nails done every Friday morning like clockwork, whether they need it or not."

When I started to ask again if her nails were damaged, Scarlet shushed me before I drew Reba Sue's attention in our direction. "No. Her nails were not damaged. She could have gone two more weeks with the manicure she had. Besides, Mateo already cleared her."

My shoulders drooped. A quick and easy answer to this whole situation was going to be harder to find than I thought. How could a murder in small-town Texas be difficult to solve? There were only so many possible suspects.

Scarlet then returned to the more important question I'd initially asked. "I would say you need to leave that memorial in place until after the funeral."

"After the funeral?" I said too loudly. Reba Sue's hand dropped in midwave as she frowned and got back in her vehicle, the black SUV spitting gravel in our direction as she left.

Her departure only encouraged the volume of my voice to rise. "I need to go home!" Desperate, I did the one thing my daddy had told me to never do—I begged. "Please, Scarlet, can I borrow two hundred dollars? I'm good for it, I swear I am. I've got to get back. I'll wire you the money first thing on payday."

Mateo strolled up behind us. "You can't leave town."

I turned on him. I couldn't help it. That appealing voice of his may as well have delivered a death sentence. "I have to get back," I insisted.

Sherriff Mateo Espinosa looked down on me with those dreamy eyes. I hate dreamy eyes. They make you melt when you shouldn't. Buckle when you know better. Dreamy eyes hadn't worked on me since I was seventeen. Even if the sheriff's eyes were the color of aged whiskey glistening in the bright Texas sun, I was immune.

Ignoring their drunken allure, I repeated my plea, "I *need* to go home."

Although he was shorter than Cade, Sheriff Espinosa still had more than a few inches on my five-foot, seven-inch frame. I could have sworn his eyes softened, but it could have been my tears of frustration blurring my vision.

"I need you to stay," he said.

I gulped. "Are you telling me I *can't* leave?"

"No, I'm telling you that it would be better for me and you, if you stayed until we had a suspect in custody."

"Why is that better for me?"

"Then your name will be cleared."

"I thought my name was cleared yesterday?" I gulped.

His eyebrow twitched, but he didn't say a word.

I turned back to Scarlet. "Can I borrow enough money for a bus ticket?" I'd checked out the price on my phone earlier that morning: $149, plus tax and fees. With meals, $200 should be enough to get me home and pay for my parking at the airport in Denver. Otherwise, every day I waited the amount of cash I needed to pay for parking increased.

Scarlet looked at the sheriff and I wanted to scream. He didn't know what was best for me, just what was best for his case.

"I'm . . . I'm really sorry . . ." she started, refusal written all over her crimson cheeks.

"I'm looking to buy a bookstore here in Hazel Rock." Another unwanted voice joined our conversation.

I looked up at Cade. Last night he'd wanted to lock lips and talk about finding my dad. Now he was talking about buying the bookstore so I could leave town. I looked back at the sheriff, who was now leaning up against the exterior of the Bluebonnet Quilt Shop. His arms crossed over his chest, the muscles in his forearms corded. He was either very tense or he had the most ripped forearms I'd ever seen. His face, however, remained emotionless.

Scarlet cleared her throat, and I couldn't help but wonder what was going on with this trio.

"Why do you want to buy The Book Barn?" I asked

"The Book Barn Princess," all three of them said in unison.

I rolled my eyes. "Why do you want to buy The Book Barn Princess?"

"Because your dad wanted to sell it and I don't want the town to lose the only bookstore within a twenty-five-mile radius."

It sounded heroic. At another time, I may have swooned. But now I wasn't buying it. If Cade was the heroic type, he would have defended my honor, and Scarlet and the sheriff wouldn't be acting as if life was about to get really weird.

Which it already had. I had no clue where my father was hiding out. Nor did I understand why he wasn't here to take care of Marlene. It made no sense.

"Has anyone seen my dad?" I asked, wondering if I should confess that he was no longer living in the apartment.

Cade looked across the street. "No."

The sheriff was more direct. "He's a person of interest in Marlene's death."

"That's ridiculous!" I exclaimed.

Sheriff Espinosa stood up straight. "Is it?"

Yes. Yes, it was. Yet I didn't say it, because even though my heart knew it was the stupidest thing I'd ever heard, my brain wasn't sure.

"The Book Barn Princess isn't for sale," I heard myself say. I'm not sure why I blurted it out. The last thing I wanted to do was stay and ruin my hopes and dreams, yet that's exactly what I'd just done. I'd doomed my future.

I turned away before my frustration spilled the tears down my cheeks. My dad was missing and he was a person of interest in the death of his girlfriend. I had no money other than the petty cash fund, which amounted to forty-three dollars after my lunch. And the one person I thought was a friend had turned down my plea for help.

I was officially stuck in Hazel Rock, Texas . . . indefinitely.

It seemed my daddy had raised a fool after all.

Chapter Eleven

Once I was in The Barn, the silence was unbearable. I felt trapped and alone, a feeling I hadn't experienced in years. I needed to take control of my future, not let anyone stand in my way. That included a dead Realtor and an absent father.

I looked out the front of the store to make sure Scarlet, Cade, and Mateo were gone, then went back outside and locked the door. I went around the back of the building, just in case Scarlet was looking out her window, and felt like a teenager sneaking out to meet her boyfriend. I headed for Yellow Jacket Realty two blocks down and one block over and looked for my father's truck along the way. Not that I expected to find it, I just hoped to see it.

The front of Yellow Jacket Realty hadn't changed since my childhood. A light yellow one-story house, it was accented with black shutters and a black door. Though the color scheme was the same, it had obviously been repainted over the years because the exterior looked clean and fresh. Including the yellow jacket wasp image on the sign out front.

Red-tip photinia shrubs lined the front of the house and the driveway leading to the parking lot in the rear of the business. I followed the well-maintained brick pavers to the front door and climbed the three steps to the covered porch where several black rocking chairs were placed neatly across the front of the structure. I was completely relieved to find the front door unlocked and that I'd at least get the opportunity to talk to someone. A cool blast of air-conditioning hit me in the face as I entered.

"May I help you?" With those four words I could tell the elderly woman sitting behind the reception desk was Southern born and raised.

She may not have been a Hazel Rock native, but she pronounced *help* without the *l*.

I smiled and poured on my own Southern charm. "Good morning, ma'am. I'm Charli Rae Warren," I started.

The smile dropped off her wrinkled face.

Dagnabbit. I should have gotten answers before I identified myself.

I changed tactics and pulled a tissue from my purse as I let my face crumple. "This whole thing has got me so upset, I'm not sure what to do with myself." I might have felt guilty except so far, I'd told the complete truth.

The woman behind the desk—Ruth, if the nameplate was correct—jumped up immediately. "Please, have a seat. Can I get you something to drink? Coffee?"

I sniffed. More allergies than tears, but that coupled with, "Do you have sweet tea, Ruth?" did the trick. Her wrinkles smoothed.

"Of course, dear. I'll be right back."

She disappeared into a back room and I took the time to blow my nose. Loudly. When Ruth returned with my glass of tea, I thanked her graciously and took a sip. It wasn't as good as my daddy's, but it was pretty close.

Ruth sat down next to me. "I want you to know that even though our dear Marlene is no longer with us . . ." She paused and closed her eyes. She inhaled through her nose and then exhaled through her mouth. Guilt blossomed in my chest. I squelched it. I was trying to find Marlene's killer, not hurt anyone. Ruth continued, "We here at Yellow Jacket Realty will do everything in our power to continue on with the sale of The Book Barn Princess."

I clasped her hand. "I appreciate that, I really do. I know this must be so much harder on you than it is me." I sincerely meant that. The death of a coworker in a small business could be devastating all the way around. I'd heard it in the voice of the receptionist when I'd called. "After all, Marlene was a literal stranger to me. But to you . . ."

Ruth stiffened. "Yes, I had to send our receptionist home this morning when I flew back early from my vacation. The loss has been . . . hard. I'm Ruth Busby, Marlene's partner."

Disappointment scattered my thoughts. In one sentence, Ruth had exonerated herself as a potential suspect. Marlene's partner had been on vacation when Marlene was killed. Unless she'd hired a killer, which I didn't think she was capable of, Ruth wasn't involved in Marlene's death.

"It's nice to meet you, Ruth," I commented. "I was hoping you could help me contact the previous buyer, I know your receptionist said the deal was no longer on the table, but if I could just talk to them . . ."

Ruth was shaking her head before I'd finished my sentence. "I'm sorry dear, but MCM is no longer interested in the property. Marlene's death . . ." Her voice faded.

I nodded. "Of course, I understand. Could you tell me what type of business MCM is?"

"MCM Incorporated was hoping to make The Barn into a mini mart."

I cleared my throat. Disappointed that I couldn't make the sale move forward. "I can see where that would appeal to the community of Hazel Rock."

"Yes, dear. That was always Marlene's goal. To serve the community." Ruth's voice became gruff, but it didn't sound as if sadness was the cause. More like irritation.

I tried for one more bit of information. "I have some of Marlene's belongings in the apartment at the store, where I'm staying . . . indefinitely." Again, that wasn't a lie. "I'm embarrassed to say I haven't spoken to my father, but I know he and Marlene recently bought a house together? We may not be on the best of terms, but I know her items would bring him comfort."

"Bless your heart, of course they would. And seeing your concern may mend the damage you caused in your relationship with your daddy."

I pulled another tissue from my purse and shoved it to my mouth before I blurted out that I hadn't caused a bit of damage in my relationship with my father. Obviously, she'd heard otherwise, and it had probably been from Marlene.

Ruth patted my leg in comfort and I swallowed down my pride, despite the kicking and bucking it was doing all the way down my throat that was worse than any horse pill a doctor could have given me. "Do you think you could give me the address?" I managed in a strangled voice.

Ruth grabbed a business card from the desk and hesitated. "I guess I'll have to remove these." She shook her head and wrote an address on the back before handing it to me.

"I wish you the best with your daddy. If the two of you could come in after Marlene's funeral, we'll work on a plan to move forward to sell The Barn."

I thanked her for her time and left before looking at the card. Marlene stared back at me—smiling like there was no tomorrow. And for her, there wasn't.

Chapter Twelve

The side door opened to The Barn and Scarlet walked in. "This is the last place you want to be, isn't it?"

"Not really."

She looked at me with disbelief.

"In the middle of a swamp filled with alligators would be a lot worse," I told her.

"Not if you had one of those alligator hunters with you."

"Really? Which one? From what I've seen, I'd be lucky if they didn't shoot me in the foot and bring a whole school of alligators to the scent of my blood in the water."

She laughed. "That's sharks, not alligators. Alligators are solitary animals who like dead chickens."

"They're reptiles," I corrected her.

Princess waddled into the room and sniffed my feet. Part of me wanted to punt her in the opposite direction. The other part was curious as to what she was up to.

Scarlet beamed that thousand-watt smile and pulled a chair up to the table I was sitting at in the tearoom. "Being stuck in a wrestling ring with a professional wrestler would be worse."

I couldn't help it; I smiled. Whether it was because of the rodent sitting up on her hind legs and twitching her ears and nose at me, or Scarlet cracking jokes, I wasn't sure. "How would that be worse?"

"You want to be slammed on a mat by a huge, sweaty guy with long, greasy hair who's got a female sidekick who will tear every curl out of your head because you've got better hair than she does?"

Princess squeaked. My smile grew. "I was picturing holding the mike and standing between a military hero and a mystery man in black—both of them with killer bodies."

I winced at my choice of adjective.

"We can't escape death, Charli. Even in Hazel Rock," Scarlet announced.

I stopped sorting through the books on the table, wondering what the heck I'd missed.

"Suzie Simpson died of lung cancer a month ago. I had to do her hair for the funeral," she said.

I flinched. I couldn't help it. The thought of touching the dead was too much.

"John Cavendar died in an accident last year on highway 152. He was going to pick up an engagement ring for his girlfriend. His casket was closed."

"That's a little different than what happened to Marlene." I looked over at the spot where she'd died. Even though I'd cleaned and there was no sign of a crime ever having occurred inside The Barn, I found my gaze constantly returning to the spot.

"Is that where she died?" Scarlet asked, following my gaze.

"What? No. No," I lied. The sheriff had asked me not to disclose the location and I'd agreed. I wanted her killer caught and thought it was better for business not to divulge the information to anyone, lest I get another memorial started inside the store. "I was just lost in thought. Sorry."

Scarlet nodded, but I could tell she didn't believe me. "What are you doing?"

"Going through some of the books that were damaged by the fingerprint powder." I placed a hardcover mystery novel off to my left.

"You could make stuff out of them," Scarlet suggested.

"What?"

"Book art." She said it like I was supposed to know what the heck she was talking about.

"What's book art?"

"It's when old books are repurposed into art or something useful."

I looked at her as if she'd grown a horn in the middle of her forehead. "Who would ruin a book?"

She looked at the stack of books on my left and right. The covers were blackened, pages torn, and several looked chewed up. I was hoping it was the work of my dad's rodent and not due to any other residents that may have made their home in The Barn. It wouldn't be the first time we'd fought off mice.

I bit my lip. "I suppose we could do something with these . . ." I put my hand on the stack of damaged hardcovers.

At the first sign of weakness, Scarlet pounced. She scooted closer. The sound of the chair screeching against the concrete floor made Princess perk up her ears and head in the opposite direction. That was fine with me.

Scarlet picked her Michael Kors bag off the floor and pulled out her phone. Next thing I knew, we were scrolling through photo after photo of the coolest things I'd ever seen—all made out of books. From ornaments to flowers to wreaths to beds and chairs and tables, counters, and even walls—entire rooms covered with book pages and book jackets.

"Wow. I never would have dreamed someone would destroy so many books to make a bed."

"People destroy beautiful living trees to make beds . . . and to make books."

She had a point. As much as I wanted to argue in the name of my love for books, the ugly truth was that trees died in the name of the written word.

Scarlet closed the app, then opened some personal photos. "I've made these out of books your dad gave me." She scrolled through picture after picture of beautiful decorations. Decorations I'd pay good money to own, like her trio of gourds of different heights and shapes. They had wooden stems, with twine to create the vines and leaves made out of colorful covers that kept the title and the author's names intact. The edges of the pages had been lightly painted different shades of orange.

"Two of the three gourds you can still read the book. The third was chewed up by Princess, so I was able to make its shape a little bit different," she explained.

"They're incredible."

"Thank you. I was thinking you could sell them in the store to help raise some money."

"But they're yours," I protested.

"Technically they belong to you. Your dad gave them to me."

"He gave the books to you . . . and you created something special and unique."

It turned out, Scarlet was equally stubborn. "And I'm giving them back so you can do something wonderful with them."

I could tell she wasn't going to budge, and I honestly didn't know what to say. I was touched by her generosity, but I didn't see how buying a plane ticket home was something wonderful for anyone but me. Plus, sometime in the middle of the day I'd resolved not to sell the store so I could stay and help clear my dad's name. "Thank you, but I can't—"

"Look, it's going to take you at least a week to make enough money to go home. In the mean time we can do some snooping and see what we can find out about Marlene's death and why your dad has disappeared."

How she knew what I was thinking was beyond me. If she'd wanted to help me buy the plane ticket or even just a bus ticket, she could have just loaned me the money. Instead, she was offering to help run the store. But since Marlene's funeral was scheduled for Thursday, I had to wait at least until Friday before I could even open the store. That was six days away.

"I appreciate your help, I really do. But I can't even open the store until Friday."

"You could have a backdoor sale."

"What?"

"A backdoor sale. As gruesome as it is, people want to see where Marlene died and they'll feel obligated to buy something. But you don't just want them to come in and buy a used book. You want them to buy more expensive items. With book art placed throughout the store, people—especially the women around here—won't be able to resist buying a piece of rustic-chic décor. Especially if it's got gossip attached."

I shook my head, wishing her description of The Barn was true. "This store is hardly 'rustic chic.'"

"You're right," Scarlet agreed. "It's more teen boutique, but the tearoom is dead-on."

I scrunched my nose and looked at it through the eyes of my teenage self. Everything in the store screamed of my youthful tastes. Everything except the tearoom, which I'd designed for my mom.

"I couldn't possibly take that many pieces of art from you. We'd need way too much."

"We'll make a stall just for young girls and put most, if not all of the tween stuff in there, along with chapter books and young adult theme books. That will make room for the new merchandise."

"Not all young girls like pink and delicate. A lot of girls like sports, vampires, and antiheroes."

"We'll add a little black for edginess and attract both."

I was starting to like her ideas. An overhaul of the store was desperately needed. "What about the boys?"

"We'll create a stall for them as well. Wrestling, horses, sports . . ."

I was pretty sure my male students back in Colorado didn't want horses or baseball bats, but I was starting to get excited. "And for all the geeks in between, we can make a gender neutral room."

I was beginning to see the big picture for The Barn's future. A future I wouldn't be a part of, but would help my dad once his name was cleared. "The rest of the store could look more adult."

Scarlet was catching the fever and I wondered if she should be designing spaces instead of hair. "The rest of the store just needs a little whitewash and stain to tone down the bright shades and it will be transformed in no time."

That's when reality kind of hit me in the face and my heart sank. I didn't have the funds to buy any supplies to redecorate. How could I possible get all of that done?

"Money is the game changer. You're talking about adult-priced renovations on a teenager's budget."

Scarlet wasn't swayed. "I've got leftover stain from my remodel, and I know your dad has some white paint stored in back."

"But it would take me forever to get it done," I insisted.

"The team is willing to help you. All you have to do is ask."

I blinked. Ask the football team for help? "I couldn't."

"You could. The town owes you."

The town *did* owe me. At least in my opinion. Although I wasn't sure they'd agree.

"Call Coach." Scarlet picked up the phone on the counter.

"I don't have his number."

She waggled the receiver in her hand. "It's programmed into the phone. Coach helped create this monstrosity with your dad."

I coughed, or gagged, I'm not sure which. "If he helped create it, why would I want him to do anything else? This is horrible." I indicated the pink wall behind me.

I think Scarlet was getting a little frustrated with my resistance.

Her shoulders lifted and then fell, and I'm pretty sure she was biting the inside of her cheek. "Because there's a woman in charge now. A woman who knows what's tasteful and what's tacky. With your guidance, Coach will get it done."

"But I can't pay him."

"You don't need to pay him."

"Of course I do."

"He owes your dad." Scarlet was worse than a rattlesnake in a bunny den.

"For what?" The only thing those two had in common was their age.

"Your dad is one of the major boosters for the team."

My mouth could have hit the counter, it dropped so far. "Wait . . . what? How could my dad possibly boost anything financially?"

"You'd be surprised."

"It's the middle of football season," I argued.

She punched in the number and I heard it ringing. "There's no practice or game on Sunday. They can help tomorrow."

The ringing stopped and a man's voice said, "Hello."

Scarlet's eyebrows raised and I snatched the phone from her hand just as Coach said, "Hello?" for the second time.

"Coach. It's Charli Rae Warren. I–I was wondering . . ." I rubbed my temple and scrunched my eyes closed. "Are you available to help do some remodeling at The Barn tomorrow? I know it's last minute, and I can't pay . . ."

"What time do you need us?"

"Us?" I squeaked.

"If you've got things to move, I'm bringing younger backs than mine to help out."

"Oh . . . say eleven o'clock?"

"Make it nine. I'll tell my players to go to the early service at church and be waiting outside the barn at nine a.m. . . . sharp."

Still dazed, I said, "The front door is kind of blocked."

"I understand. We'll meet you next to the fountain at nine. You can let us in the side door."

Somehow, despite the shock, I was able to end the conversation on a polite note. "Thank you, Coach."

"It's the least I can do."

I hung up the phone, wondering what had just happened. Maybe I had jumped the gun a little too quickly at seventeen . . . or maybe people could change their stripes. There was also the possibility that the universe had been altered.

My money was on the universe.

Chapter Thirteen

Scarlet changed and came back looking like Ann-Margaret: tight white capris with a blue-and-white-striped T-shirt with navy blue tennis shoes straight out of a movie from the sixties. I wasn't sure how she was going to keep her outfit clean but decided to let her worry about that. We spent the rest of the day and well into the night cleaning out three different stalls for our new tween sections. Despite my better judgment, I buckled to her idea of combining the self-help and relationship section with the religion section. She said if anyone asked, God was into people helping themselves and improving their relationships on Earth, as well as in heaven. It was a plan I thought I could sell.

Maybe.

The one new section I knew I could promote was the combination of diet, health, and fitness with cookbooks, food, and wine and the coveted sports section. For one, husbands and wives could shop together, and two, what better way to get into shape and eat right while preparing for the big game? Win-win. At least for the wives. I'd have to watch the guys' reaction to the changes.

The kids' stalls were awesome. Although all the shelves were white, my dad had painted the interior of every other stall bright pink, so we chose one of the pink rooms for the girls' section and brought every piece of pink froufrou gobbledygook we could find into the space—fuzzy tiaras and pens, along with journals and phone cases blinged out with crystals.

Scarlet grabbed a stack of book bags that we'd piled up on the floor near the girls' stall. "We need to make hooks out of old books to hang these bags on the outside of the stalls."

I stretched out my back. "Are you trying to write a Dr. Seuss story?"

Scarlet laughed with a little snort. "No, I've made a few for my trailer. They're hanging in my bedroom. You just attach a hook to a couple books that are stacked caddywhompus by screwing through them and into the wall of the stall."

I smiled. "Hooks on books on the walls of the stalls. I'm sure there's a kids' story in that somewhere."

Scarlet shook her head, her red hair glinting with strands of gold in the fluorescent light. "I saw a bunch of old doorknobs in a box in the tearoom. We could use those."

"Why don't we save that for tomorrow?" I suggested.

"It's a plan. It will be easier with the extra help." Scarlet nodded and wiped her hands on a dish towel she'd thrown over her shoulder. She was as clean as she'd been when she'd arrived.

I looked as if I'd taken a trip to the backyard with my dad's rodent and dug for grubs all night. And we weren't even close to being done.

We brought all the young girl magazines into the stall, leaving the display as is. It was the one thing my dad got right; every magazine was hung over a louver on a pair of old shutters. They were even separated by genre.

We finished up by adding the rest of the books. From Nancy Drew to a best-selling series about vampires and werewolves, monster princesses and utopian worlds. The stall was all about girl power—and it rocked.

Next, we moved on to the geek section. The white door turned into a stormtrooper thanks to Scarlet's artistic genius and a little bit of black paint. We left everything white on the inside of the stall and put a long bench down the middle of it with plans to have it painted black the next day. Once we poked holes into the paper shade on the black lamp sitting on a table, it would make the coolest Darth Vader.

My students would love it. I loved it. I was pretty sure Scarlet loved it by the way she kept eyeing it.

I marked three large rocks out back behind The Barn for the guys to move inside the geek stall the next day for additional seating. Then I moved on to the boys' stall—which was pink.

Scarlet disappeared for a short time and came back with a can of red paint.

"Where'd you get that?" I asked.

"Don't ask and I won't tell."

I took her advice and got busy painting the walls red, the whole time wondering if stolen red paint was better than pink. After the walls were done, I retreated to the apartment and got down my old baseball bat while Scarlet painted a baseball on the exterior of the stall door that had a cowboy hat tilted off to one side. We argued over putting half the sports magazines in with the boys' books, but in the end Scarlet won. The dads could spend time with their sons, and if girls wanted to look at them, they'd probably want to look at those books as well.

Scarlet donated a couple of black beanbag chairs she kept in the back of the salon. I secretly think she used them as her bed because there was no floor space in her trailer, but I appreciated it and vowed to make it all up to her someday.

By the time we'd finished the last kids' stall, we were exhausted. Scarlet's hair still looked perfect. Mine looked as if I'd painted the tips white. It was the story of my life.

We did have something in common—we were beyond starving.

"My mom sent Joellen to the beauty shop with a pan of lasagna this morning. Want to come over? I'll heat it up and put a couple of slices of bread in the toaster," Scarlet suggested.

My stomach growled. "That sounds awesome." We made our way out into the dark night. The town was quiet except for the low rumble of music and voices from the Tool Shed Tavern at the end of the block. Pickup trucks and muscle cars were parked out front and I had no doubt they filled the lot on the side of the building as well. Hazel Rock went from the family-friendly Hazel Rock Diner on one end of town to the Wild West bar at the other. Growing up in the middle of town, I could have embraced either side of the tracks. I'd ultimately chosen the diner side but had a few memories of the Tool Shed Tavern I wanted to forget.

"It's not as bad as our parents made it out to be," Scarlet said, glancing over at the bar.

I snorted. "Nothing ever is." It was actually worse than our parents had warned us against. "I take it you've been there a few times?"

"It's the only entertainment in town for the over–twenty-one crowd," she explained. "And every weekend they have a band. What's not to like?"

Smoke. Bad pickup lines. Spilled drinks. Lost souls . . .

The Tool Shed had been for the down and *way* out. It wasn't a place any parent would find acceptable—no matter what your age. "Do your parents know?"

"I suspect they've heard. You can't shake your hind end without the front end talking in Hazel Rock, but it's different now."

I raised a skeptical brow. "Is there dancing?" I hadn't seen any dancing during my time there, but maybe things *had* changed.

"You could call it that."

"What else would you call it?" I asked.

Scarlet grinned and did a hip swivel, followed up with a thrust. "Bump and grind."

I laughed as we walked to the other side of the street. "You lie!"

"My momma didn't raise me to lie."

My mom hadn't either, but that didn't mean I didn't embellish a tale or two along the way. "So everyone over twenty-one goes in there?" I couldn't help myself, I thought of *him*.

"If you're asking me if Cade bumps and grinds, the answer is no. Although I have seen him slow dance a time or two."

I knew how Cade slow danced. The man had moves that were as sinful as a preacher in a strip club. "I was actually wondering if the sheriff ever spent any time there." Which wasn't exactly true but was close enough.

Scarlet grinned. "He breaks up fights and acts like a cab driver to anyone who's dumb enough to walk out to their car after having a few too many."

"He doesn't wait to give them a DUI?" The old sheriff used to bring in a bunch of revenue for the town by arresting the Tool Shed's patrons driving under the influence.

"Nope. He says the bar is providing entertainment. The last thing he wants to do is hurt it."

"But people who drive drunk deserve a ticket."

"No argument there. Mateo just thinks a little intervention goes a long way."

I couldn't argue. Saving a life had to be a better outcome in anyone's book. "What about Oak Grove? With Country Mart moving there, the town must have developed a larger need for a police presence. Why is the sheriff hanging out in Hazel Rock?"

"There're four deputies and a sergeant who work through the

night in Oak Grove." Scarlet unlocked the door of her salon and turned off the alarm. We walked through the back room, where she grabbed the pan of lasagna from the fridge, and we headed to her trailer out back. I was immediately caught off guard. I'd been expecting a mobile home, but this was different—and cute. Scarlet's vintage silver Airstream trailer sparkled in the moonlight. A set of Adirondack chairs sat outside the door.

"That's adorable."

"Thank you. I think." I caught her smile in the dim light from a bulb on the outside of the trailer.

We made our way down the back steps and across a dried-up lawn with pavers that looked like flip-flops.

We entered her trailer and I was immediately thankful that she hadn't offered to let me stay with her. The two of us overwhelmed the space. I moved toward the end of the trailer, where a table stood surrounded by cushions fashioned after a 1970s Mexican fiesta. Decorated in bright oranges, yellows, and greens, the entire trailer was a blast from the past. The cabinetry was white with orange doors. The cushions on the couch and around the table were the same bright tangerine as the cabinets and had bright-colored paisley pillows neatly displayed across them. The windows were dressed in white curtains patterned with orange and yellow slices of fruit that made my mouth water.

"Wow."

"Yeah, it's pretty rad. Tight on living quarters, but I like it. There's wine, beer, or tea in the fridge. If you could get me a beer and help yourself, I'd appreciate it. I'll throw the lasagna in the microwave and have it done in no time."

I pulled out two beers and got napkins and silverware from the drawer she pointed to as she talked about how she'd acquired the trailer at an auction. She said it was her only hope of moving out of her parents' house after remodeling the salon. For six months she'd literally slept on the couch in the workroom of her shop.

That had to have been miserable, yet I could feel myself becoming claustrophobic in the tight space of her trailer. This was definitely not my preferred style of living.

"How did you get the trailer here?"

Scarlet set our plates on the table and sat down across from me. "Your dad."

"Really?" I took a big bite of the lasagna and instantly began fanning my mouth from the heat of the sauce.

"Yup. He heard I was looking for a trailer and took me to the auction. I bought it that day. He hauled it here, helped me level the ground, and put it in place. My parents were out of town, and when they came back, I moved into the salon to watch over the renovations."

"Who did the renovations?" I asked over another mouthful of delicious lasagna.

"Coach." Scarlet gauged my reaction over the top of her bottle of beer.

My fork stopped midway to my mouth and I set it back down. "Shut the barn door."

She laughed and took a drink of beer. "The man is a genius on and off the field. I told him what I wanted and he did the rest. Granted, I bought or made all the cushions and curtains, but the rest is all Coach Purcell."

"But he's responsible for The Book Barn Princess."

"He's color blind. He has no clue what it really looks like."

That explained it. My dad wasn't color blind, but he would wear a plaid shirt with plaid pants.

Scarlet and I talked for a while as we polished off the lasagna and finished our beer. I helped clean up the mess and then she walked me back through the salon. I hugged her good-bye and made my way across the street.

The noise from the Tool Shed Tavern was picking up, the bass was louder and the voices were more boisterous. A woman stumbled out of the bar and I realized it was Reba Sue. Dressed in a tight skirt with stilettos, she was having trouble maneuvering the wooden planks of the sidewalk.

A cowboy followed her out and immediately tried to put his arm around her, but she pushed him away. His voice was low, but there was a warning in it that pricked the hairs on the back of my neck. Reba Sue stumbled backward toward the door and almost made it back inside the bar when he yanked her toward him.

"Hey, leave her alone!" I yelled out without thinking.

The beyond-short cowboy wasn't about to take Reba Sue's rebuff or my intervention with a polite tip of his hat or say, *Sorry to bother you, ma'am.*

In fact, he did the opposite—without style. "Mind your own business—"

A car door slammed and the hollow thunk drowned out the less-than-ladylike name cowboy called me. All three of us turned toward the patrol car parked across the street from the bar. Mateo's eyes narrowed as he strode toward the fake cowboy, in real hero fashion.

It was kind of awesome.

One look at that uniform and the swagger it brought with it and the cowboy backed away from Reba Sue, hands raised.

In turn, Reba Sue took advantage of the distance and stepped into the light radiating from the neon liquor sign in the front window of the Tool Shed, hugging herself and the exterior wall of the bar, clearly shaken by the encounter.

I glanced back at Beaus and Beauties, but Scarlet was gone. A long-drawn-out sigh passed my lips, the kind that signifies capitulation, and I headed in Reba Sue's direction to see if there was anything I could do to help. My moment of nurturing, however, was interrupted before it began.

"I said, interlock your fingers and go down on your knees." Mateo's voice steeled with authority.

Anticipation of the inevitable violence hung in the air. Cowboy's hands were resting on his hat, Mateo's instructions to lace his fingers and get on his knees, however, were ignored. Spoken several times, heard several times, ignored several times. Cowboy's compliance was limited. And Mateo knew it.

Somehow, so did I.

An engine roared behind me. I jumped, my heart shocked into a full-out run by the roar. A dark truck raced down the street in front of me and I watched as the driver slammed on the brakes and came to a sliding stop. He blocked my view of Mateo, but I got an eyeful of Cade adding his own flavor of action hero. Whereas Mateo had swagger, Cade had the prowess of a quarterback avoiding a sack. Only now, as he hopped out of the driver's seat and ran around to the other side of the truck, I'd put my money on him making the tackle.

A crowd emptied out of the bar and I started to run in their direction, not sure what I could do but certainly not about to stand still and watch. Fear for Cade and Mateo made my feet move faster as the crowd surged forward. But the mass of spectators suddenly backed up. They moved like cattle being split between pens, and I was the post in between those pens as I rounded the truck.

Wondering what could possibly make them clear for me, clarity was delivered when a rock hit me in the arm.

"Ow!"

It wasn't my arrival that caused them to back away. It was the kicking and spitting handcuffed cowboy who was missing his hat as Cade and Mateo pulled him off the ground.

"Break it up, folks. There's nothing to see," Mateo instructed.

Except there was something to see: Cade and Mateo. The women were impressed by the show of masculinity, myself included. The men? Well, a little envy may have flowed through their veins. It was understandable.

I moved back near the bakery as a few people lingered, recording the cowboy being escorted across the street to Mateo's patrol car on their phones. Mateo patted the man down, removed a knife from inside his boot, and stuck it inside his own back pocket. The cowboy began to twist and yell at Mateo, who promptly loaded him in the backseat. The sight of his hand on the back of the man's head resonated through my body. I shivered with the memory.

The rest of the crowd finally returned to the bar, but Cade remained behind, distractedly running his hand through his hair.

Ever since I'd first arrived in Hazel Rock and opened the cab door, everything had felt foreign and wrong in my hometown. First Marlene's murder and now a man attacking a woman . . . and resisting arrest. It was like the Wild West had returned and I was the last to be notified.

I'd never seen anyone get arrested in Hazel Rock—other than myself. In the past, I'd experienced the bite of the old sheriff's handcuffs on my wrists a couple of times. What had just unfolded in front of me, however, was nothing like a teenager trespassing on a water tower. Or soaping windows. Or making out in the backseat of a car with the mayor's son.

The mayor's son . . . I looked back at Cade. He was taller and more handsome than ever. He was the prodigal son—returned—and better because of it.

I told myself I hadn't returned to The Barn yet because I was worried about him. Worried the butterfly Band-Aids on the back of his head had come off and needed to be redone. Yet that wasn't entirely true. Part of me was thinking about our kiss . . . I shook my head and wiped away the memory and started in his direction.

Until my feet froze. Reba Sue ran out of the shadows and put her arms around Cade's waist. It was an understandable thing to do. She was scared; he was a leader who'd come to her rescue. It didn't mean anything . . .

Then Cade wrapped his arms around her—tight. Familiar. Definitely not a stranger. He kissed the top of her head and my heart dropped to my boots. I looked at Mateo, who in turn was watching me.

Without a word, I turned around and headed home.

That dadgum skull of Cade's could bleed 'til the sun didn't shine. And I wasn't talking about sundown, I was thinking more like the end of time. It would serve him right. 'Cause I definitely had better things to do than waste a moment living a lie.

Obviously, Saturday nights in Hazel Rock hadn't changed much after all.

Chapter Fourteen

I let myself into the apartment and quickly locked the door. A brush across my ankle negated the sense of security the locked door provided. It scared the bejesus out of me and I jumped, swinging at nothing but air. Princess squealed at my feet, then scurried away.

I turned on the light and found the little rodent staring at me from behind the edge of the couch. "Holy crap, Princess. You scared me half to death. If you need in, don't rush past me without letting me know you're there."

I shook out the tension tightening the muscles in my shoulders feeling stupid for scolding an armadillo like she'd understand.

Still hiding, her ears shook like a momma's knees on my kindergarteners' first day of school. I sighed and bent down. "I'm sorry, girl, I'm not used to anyone greeting me when I come home."

Princess laid down her ears and I got the distinct impression she was ticked. Deciding not to test her temper, I turned and headed for the shower in my dad's bathroom.

Twenty minutes later, I felt more relaxed, dressed in Sweet Sixteen boxers and a tank top in lieu of my filthy clothing. I walked into the kitchen and stuck my face inside the fridge.

No pie. No Snickers.

Fuzz buckets.

Princess walked into the kitchen as well, looked at her empty bowl, and sat up like a half-starved little dog begging for food. Her front paws batted at me, and I could have sworn there was poodle mixed in her blood. It would explain the pink.

I opened a can of cat food and filled her ugly dish. Princess twitched her nose and dug in. Leave it to food to bring forgiveness.

Cade, on the other hand, was out of luck. Period. He'd be living in the outhouse. Forever.

I turned out the light and realized I'd left the bathroom light on in my dad's room. I went and flipped the switch off and was headed for my bedroom by the light from the moon coming in the front window when something caught my eye. It wasn't the built-in shelves that held all the photos from my childhood. It was the thin line of light along the floorboard below it. Princess walked in, stopped, and sniffed the floor.

She scratched at it and I backed away, my heart rate picking up pace.

I knew what was on the other side of that wall. More bookshelves inside The Barn's loft. To my knowledge there was no way to get from the store to the apartment without entering from the stairs outside. But by the light that was bleeding through the cracks, I was beginning to wonder.

I approached the shelves as if they held the secret of Al Capone's vault behind them. Because if I was right, there was at least a hidden compartment between the walls. If I was wrong, the floor had settled in the middle of the room, which could mean structural damage. Either way, I needed answers.

The worst part was that I didn't know who'd turned on the light on the other side. My dad could've snuck in and left it on, which would really irritate me if he didn't stop to check in on me. Or a killer could be waiting for me.

I shivered and grabbed my dad's bat from the other side of the room before I rubbed my hand along the inside of the shelf, catching some dust along the way. The wood was smooth, unlike the rest of the walls, having been milled and sanded to perfection before being painted a glossy white. On the first shelf I found something I didn't expect: a latch. But it wasn't just any latch. It was a dead bolt, painted white and set back from view, hidden by a picture of me dressed up as Tigger for Halloween.

I pulled the bolt, but nothing happened. Princess stepped back and waited patiently. What she was waiting for I had no idea because the shelves didn't push or pull open.

I searched the second shelf and then the third, where I found an identical lock. I pulled the second latch and took a deep breath. I looked down at Princess, who seemed to be telling me to grow a spine. Or a shell. Or something.

"I'm going. Don't rush me," I whispered.

I took a deep breath and yanked on the shelf. It gave way and opened, but not to what I expected. I was looking at another wall, with the beam of light still filtering out through a narrow track along the floorboard. Princess stepped forward and nudged it with her nose, pushing it open and letting the light spill into the bedroom from the cluttered loft of the store. In the middle of the floor sat a man, sifting through books by the beam of a flashlight that was pointed in my direction.

I almost screamed, but he beat me to it.

It may have had a throatier sound to it, but it was definitely right up there with scared half to death. I lowered the bat. He stopped, recognition dawning for both of us.

"Mr. Duncan?"

"Charli Rae Warren?"

It was Scott Duncan, Marlene's ex-husband. My math teacher, who'd pushed us to the brink of teenage insanity with daily home-work my senior year. He was young and nerdy, in a cute sort of way. A little on the skinny side, with a baby face and a soft mouth. He still looked the same—too young to be married to Marlene.

"What are you doing here?" we said at the same time.

"You first, Mr. Duncan," I said, arms crossed, bat still ready to whack some sense into him. After all, I did own the building, and he was breaking and entering.

"I . . . I . . ." He stammered and looked around at the books lying on the floor. "Marlene loved to read."

I remembered that about her from my teen years. The woman was our best regular customer. She came in every other day to buy a book. When I'd asked why she didn't just buy a couple of books at a time, I remembered her laughing and saying then she might miss the next best thing that someone brought into the store. It was a risk she couldn't take.

Mr. Duncan continued to look around at the books, as if they would give him all the answers. "Go on," I ordered in that teacher voice of mine I used to address the bully in my class.

"I just wanted to be in the last place where Marlene was alive." He moved a brown leather satchel behind him and out of my view.

Something in my chest melted and guilt filled my heart. It was my turn to stammer. "I'm . . . I'm sorry, I didn't . . . I didn't mean . . ."

He waved me off and brushed the back of his hand across his eyes. "It's okay. I should have asked if I could spend time here. Your dad never minded me coming into the store when he was out."

Seriously? Another person Dad let come and go as he pleased? "How did you get in?" I asked skeptically.

"The key under the flowerpot."

"What flowerpot? There're thirty out there."

A sad smile crossed his face. "It was nice of everyone to remember Marlene that way."

It *was* nice. A pain in my backside, but nice. I waited for his answer.

"The one inside the gate. Everyone knows your dad keeps a key there."

Everyone but me. Was there a key to the apartment out there as well?

"I heard you were a teacher now," Mr. Duncan continued. "Do you teach math?"

I laughed. "You could say that. I teach kindergarten."

"Oh." His disappointment was palpable. The bond he was hoping for wasn't going to happen. We were both teachers, but he worked at the high school and I dealt with snotty noses. I guess you could put them in the same category, but I didn't think he thought so.

"I didn't know there was a way between the barn and your apartment. That's . . . that's pretty cool," he said as he dusted off his hands and stood up.

I had to admit it was cool, but it didn't make me feel any better that I'd exposed the secret passageway to Mr. Duncan. Granted, he was shorter than me, with a short-sleeved, yellow, button-down shirt hiding his skinny frame. His jeans were cinched tight with a dark leather belt sporting a big buckle in front. He wore boots that made quite a bit of noise as they scraped across the floor. I wondered how I didn't hear his bootsteps earlier.

Not that I thought he was the killer, but then again . . . why not him? He could be a jealous ex-husband who couldn't let her go.

I thought about the wife who'd delivered a brick pie back in Denver. The woman hadn't even been five-foot tall and couldn't have weighed a hundred pounds. Yet she'd sent that man to the hospital for surgery.

My grip on the bat tightened.

"Mr. Duncan, I can appreciate you wanting to reminisce. I know this has got to be very difficult for you—"

"Don't."

"Excuse me?"

"Please don't kick me out. I won't bother you. You won't even hear me."

He looked at me with eyes filled to the brim with unshed tears.

Princess nudged me and looked at Mr. Duncan. Her nose was twitching, as if she didn't want to see a grown man cry. It was the last thing either one of us wanted to see.

My shoulders sagged. "All right, but I want you out by midnight, Mr. Duncan."

"Thank you, Charli. I really appreciate it." He stuck out his hand for me to shake. "And please call me Scott."

Hesitant, I reached for it, surprised by the strength he displayed in his grip. His eyes, however, were friendly, not mean or made of the stuff ax murderers came from. "Good night, Scott."

I turned and went back to the apartment with Princess on my heels. I held the shelf open for her and she scurried past.

Never in my wildest Hazel Rock dreams did I think I'd hold a door for an armadillo.

Chapter Fifteen

The alarm went off at eight-thirty, and for a minute I was lost in a strange familiar room. It came back to me when I saw the prom photo on the dresser. Hazel Rock. Murder. My dad missing. I was stuck and I had to find out as much as I could to help clear his name.

Then I wanted to get out of this town faster than a roadrunner being chased by a coyote—except I didn't feel as if the roadrunner was gaining any ground.

The sheriff's display of business as usual the previous night didn't allow me to sleep peacefully. Not that he'd done anything wrong. On the contrary, he'd done everything right. But I'd had dreams of my father and the sheriff in a similar showdown at sunset with the sun cresting the horizon at the end of town. It'd been a mixture of the O. K. Corral and a squirt gun fight. My dad and I used to have squirt gun battles in the stalls of The Book Barn. Nothing dangerous, just fun-filled laughter. My nightmares through the night, however, were nothing to laugh at.

The last thing I wanted was my father facing off with the sheriff. The violence the night before had made the case against Bobby Ray seem real.

And that scared me.

I dragged myself out from under the quilt, made the bed, and got dressed. I'd absconded with a few book-themed T-shirts from the bookstore the previous day and pulled on a turquoise T-shirt with *Get Cozy and Read On* printed across the front. It was either that, or wear Cade's jersey.

That wasn't happening. Anything was better than the number thirteen in orange or blue.

I was also wearing a pair of low-rise khaki cargo shorts that really didn't go with my boots, but such was life. I put my hair in a pony-tail, knowing that soon the curls were going to be completely out of control. One of these days I'd get to the store and buy some hair products to calm it down.

I microwaved an egg and ate it in about three bites before brushing my teeth and heading down to meet the team. All twenty of them were already gathered around Coach in the courtyard, waiting for me.

I cringed. "I'm sorry—did I get the time mixed up? I didn't mean to be late."

"You're not late. You're right on time," Coach said.

I looked at my watch. Eight-fifty. I was ten minutes early, wasn't I?

"On time is late," several voices said at once.

I looked around at the young, fresh faces, wondering what exactly they were talking about.

Coach Purcell laughed. "Fifteen minutes early is on time. On time is late. That's what I expect from my boys."

I returned Coach's smile, remembering Cade saying something like that back in the day. "How could I forget?"

I unlocked the side door and the boys piled in, taking up most of the space.

Gathering the boys around me in a huddle, Coach asked, "What do you need us to do, Princess?"

Some of the boys snickered.

"Charli. Call me Charli." I smiled, feeling that sick drop in my gut as all of them assessed me. I cleared my throat, refusing to be in-timidated by all the testosterone in the room.

"Sorry, Charli. Old habits die hard." The coach winced, stum-bling over the word *die.* The boys immediately lost interest in me as they started looking around for signs of the crime. As if blood and guts would be scattered across the floor and the shelves in The Book Barn . . . *Princess.*

The real diva, whom Dad had named the store after, had impecca-ble timing. Princess the armadillo showed up in the doorway and scared a boy well over six-foot tall half to death.

He yelled some weird boy scream and would've punted her across the barn as I stood there sucking in wind, if it hadn't been for one of his teammates pushing him back.

"That's Princess, you moron!"

The boy looked at me, confusion clouding his eyes. "I thought *she* was Princess."

I smiled weakly. "I'm Princess One." I pointed at my dad's pet, "She's Princess Two."

Princess made a noise like she thought we were all crazy—she might be right—and waddled away.

"Please be careful you don't hurt her while you're here today. She's my dad's pet," I said.

"Don't those things carry like the plague or something?" The boy peeked around the stall, watching Princess's departure.

I stared at him blankly, not sure how to respond because I didn't know the first thing about armadillos. Yet, as far as I knew, the plague no longer existed.

"She's been tested. She's disease free," Cade answered from the doorway. His tall physique still looked too good to be true in a pair of basketball shorts and a T-shirt with the sleeves cut off. The sheriff was right behind him, dressed in cargo shorts and a T-shirt tight across the chest. His sleeves were intact.

Some of the boys acted like they didn't quite believe Cade's statement, while others didn't care what he said—the mayor and the sheriff were more intimidating than a diseased armadillo. I was just ticked off the man had the guts to show his face in my barn. Especially with Reba Sue right behind him, dressed in designer capris and a tight T-shirt that probably cost more than my meals for the week.

"Scarlet said you needed some help cleaning out The Barn?" Cade asked.

The sheriff raised his eyebrow. There was a hidden question under that brow. He wanted to know if I'd tolerate Cade's presence. The guy in question, however, seemed clueless. Smiling, he winked in my direction.

Unbelievable. I rolled my eyes at both of them. The sheriff laughed and the mayor looked between the two of us as if he'd missed something.

What he'd missed was the opportunity to get in my bed. That bird had flown the coop when he'd kissed the top of Reba Sue's head last night.

Reba Sue chose that moment to step forward. "I got some of your mail." She shrugged. "It happens all the time."

I looked down at the stack of bills and held back a groan. Her helpfulness was rather questionable, but I put on a smile and said what was expected of me. "Thank you. I appreciate it."

I turned away from the three of them and immediately put several boys to work in the loft, which was so messy my dad had been forced to hang a rope across the stairway to keep customers from going upstairs. I instructed them to divide the books into three sections: one to sell, one to donate and one to trash or make something out of. Then I told Coach I wanted the tiara light fixture moved to the girls' section and told him I'd have the old fixture that was in the back room painted and ready to hang in the main entry.

I put Reba Sue in charge of the tearoom. I figured playing hostess would suit her best, especially since she'd brought several cases of vitamin water for everyone to drink, saying it was a healthier choice than well water. I moved on to Cade and the sheriff, neither of whom were exactly on my good side. I gave them the worst job of all: the boulders in the backyard, which I wanted moved into the geek section.

"You've got to be kidding me," Cade said.

"I suppose if you're not up to it, I could ask Scarlet and Joellen to help me."

Mateo almost rolled his eyes but refrained and elbowed Cade when he started to argue. "I've got just what we need in the back of my truck." Cade followed him through the barn, looking back at me and clearly wondering why I was mad at him.

The man had no conscience. Which ticked me off even further, but once they were gone from view, I breathed a sigh of relief. Moving those boulders was a challenge I didn't even want to try to tackle. And if one of them got bit by a snake or stung by a scorpion while doing it, that was his own fault.

I checked in on the boys in the loft and snatched up the box of girlie magazines from the 1950s they'd found before Coach or any of the other adults noticed. They were totally embarrassed for the most part, but a few tried to act like they were as old as their size made them look. One went so far as to ask if I was free for dinner.

It was a new low. I hadn't had a date in eight months, and now high school students saw me as desperate date material. As if I would let a teenager take me to dinner on his allowance money. I immediately set some boundaries.

"The magazines will be our secret, and if you find anything else like it, you will immediately put it in this trash bag." The one who'd asked me out gave a sly smile. "Unless you'd prefer that I have a word with your mommas about what you've been up to."

His smile disappeared and the group got back to work, grumbling about a term paper that was due in a few days and how far behind they all were.

I made my way down the steps with my boxful of magazines, then stopped and looked up at the plain white steps. One of the pictures of book art Scarlet had shown me the previous night came to mind. The kick plates of the steps needed to be painted like book bindings and the walls in the stairwell needed to be lined with shelves—full of books. It would make a statement.

I balanced my box on the railing and grabbed my cell phone from my cargo pocket, typing a reminder note to myself. Once that was done, I headed for the storeroom to put away the unmentionables. Princess stood at the entrance to the storeroom, right in the spot where I'd stood when I'd found Marlene. I turned away, determined not to dwell on the memory.

"Have you seen Coach?" I asked Darrin, the current quarterback for Hazel Rock and Aubrey's boyfriend.

"He went into the back room to wash his arm. He cut it while he was taking down the tiara."

Fuzz buckets. That was all I needed. I turned back toward Princess and the curtain. "Were you trying to tell me that Coach needed me?" Princess just turned and walked away. I could have sworn by her expression that she was calling me an idiot for not understanding her message sooner.

Sue me for not speaking armadillo.

I pulled back the curtain and found Coach standing where Marlene had died. His long sleeves rolled up around his forearm as he casually patted several cuts on his wrist with a paper towel.

It was worse than someone failing to walk around the gravesites in a cemetery.

Coach walked right onto Marlene's resting spot. His feet were planted in the middle of Marlene's chest—at least in my mind they were. He didn't realize his mistake. There were no signs that a horrible crime had occurred under his tennis shoes. The permanent chalk outline of her body was only in my head—where it glowed in bright neon yellow.

Coach looked up from inspecting a particularly nasty cut on his arm. "Prin—Charli, are you okay? You're as pale as a ghost."

My breath hitched before I was able to answer. "I–I'm fine. I just don't like the sight of blood," I lied. Blood didn't bother me in the least—unless of course you were talking about it leaving someone's body in mass quantities. I was pretty sure that would leave me speechless.

"Here, let me take that box from you. One of the boys should have volunteered to carry it for you."

"No!"

Coach jumped and I realized I'd overreacted.

"I mean, I've got it, don't worry. Are you okay?" I asked as I shoved the box under the sink and washed my hands.

"It's just a scratch. Nothing to worry about." He dabbed at his arm with the paper towel one last time before wadding it up and throwing it away.

Just then, the sound of books falling across the concrete echoed through The Barn. Aubrey's voice, filled with panic, followed. "Scarlet!"

Coach and I went through the curtain at the same time, his sweaty body rubbing against my arm. Boys were gathered in the front of the store near the register and it sounded like a herd of cattle was making its way down the steps. But I saw Scarlet first. Her red hair piled high on her head in a Grace Kelly–style bun, she raced from the tearoom to Aubrey's side, knocking football player after football player out of her way.

I followed with Coach right behind me. Aubrey stood at the register, her hand covering her mouth with a look of pure terror on her face. Books were scattered across the floor in front of her like my five-year-olds at nap time. Some faceup, some facedown. Some with their covers curled around their bodies, others with their arms and legs spread wide like the books that were splitting their spines.

"What's wrong?" Scarlet asked as she reached for Aubrey and turned her around to look for any injuries.

Aubrey's eyes focused on me, her look of terror turning to horror. I'd never believed there was a difference between those two expressions, but I saw the change in Aubrey's face—felt it, even. Looking at me was worse than whatever had frightened her to begin with, which was more than a little unsettling.

She pointed at the counter.

At first I couldn't read it. Not because it wasn't legible but because it was unfathomable that someone would write a message on the smooth white surface in of all things . . . blood.

But that's exactly what it was, and once I got past the gore, the letters and the message became clear:

Leave

I couldn't help it. I looked at Coach, meeting his hazel eyes dead-on, ready to take the fight to another level. I looked at his arm and his gaze followed mine. He had the decency to blush.

"That wasn't me."

"Then who was it?" I accused, looking around at everyone assembled, ready to fight back for every wrong I'd ever experienced—which they had nothing to do with, though that didn't stop my ire.

"It's paint." I turned to find Scarlet holding up the can of red paint we'd used the day before.

"Paint?" I heard my voice squeak.

She nodded. "It's dry and the paint brush is hard." Aubrey moved to Darrin's side as Scarlet held up the can we'd used the previous day along with the paint brush.

All eyes were on me, waiting for me to say something.

"What's going on?" Mateo made his way through the crowd of football players.

"Someone wrote *LEAVE* on the front counter. We thought it was written in blood, but it turned out to be paint," said Darrin, who now had his arm around Aubrey.

Mateo slipped past Cade and Reba Sue, who just happened to be clinging to the mayor's arm, then gingerly took the paintbrush from Scarlet's hand. He held it by the bristles, along with the handle on the can of paint, and set them at the end of the counter. As on the day I'd met him, a scowl drew the sheriff's brows together. "Has anyone else touched any of this?" His eyes scanned the crowd, each person getting that piercing look I'd received just a couple of days ago as they shook their heads in denial.

He turned to me. "When was the last time you used the paint?"

"Yesterday, around nine o'clock." I knew exactly when it was, because at the time, I'd been counting the minutes before I could quit and get dinner.

"When did you lock up for the night?" He pulled a pad of paper and a pen from the back pocket of his jeans and started taking notes.

"About that time," I answered, wondering why he would question me in front of a room full of potential suspects.

"No, you didn't," Cade interjected.

"Excuse me?"

My irritation didn't daunt him in the least. "I came by at eleven and the door was wide open. I checked the store, didn't find anything, and locked up. Then I knocked on your apartment door, but you didn't answer. I called Scarlet, and she told me you guys had worked late and that you were ready to drop when you left her place around ten-thirty. Your door was secure, so I left."

Scarlet nodded her head in agreement. "That's when I asked him to help today."

"I locked the store—" I insisted, but I was still stuck on Cade saying he'd stopped by. He had some nerve—comforting Reba Sue and then dropping by The Barn like nothing had happened. It made me wonder if the mayor's job title now included warming the bed of every single woman in town.

Scarlet corrected me. "I don't think so. We walked out of the store with one thing on our mind—lasagna."

She was right. The thought of homemade pasta had consumed us when she and I had finished for the night. "How did none of us notice this until now?"

"Those books were stacked at the front of the counter. No one could see it until I picked them up," Aubrey explained.

"How did you lock the store last night?" I asked Cade accusingly.

"With my keys. Your dad gave them to me."

"He what?" My dad guarded his keys with his life, yet in the last couple of days two different people had said he'd given them a set. None of this made any sense.

"He'd gotten in the habit of leaving the store unlocked. When I started hounding him about it, he gave me a set of keys and said to quit waking him up in the middle of the night to lock the doors."

"Why is the mayor checking doors late at night?" It was more a question to myself, but because I'd voiced it aloud, Cade felt obligated to respond.

"I check to make sure all my tenants are locked up. We don't want any temptation for a crime spree."

"Tenants?" My curiosity got the best of me. "How many tenants do you have?" I didn't ask if Reba Sue was a tenant.

It was the first time Cade had looked sheepish since my return. "All of the stores, except The Book Barn Princess, Beaus and Beauties, the diner, and the Tool Shed."

"You're kidding." Everyone looked at me as if what he'd said was old news or wasn't any big deal. But what Cade was talking about was one man—the mayor—owning 80 percent of the town. "You own the quilt shop and the pottery shop?" I asked.

He nodded.

"The barber shop and all the antique stores?"

Again he nodded.

"And none of you have a problem with that?" I looked around the room.

The kids shrugged. Coach stepped forward. "It beats the alternative."

"What's that?"

"The stores ending up empty with no businesses to fill them."

"But . . ."

"Hazel Rock was turning into a ghost town after Country Mart left. The mayor rescued it from that," said Mateo. His voice was soft, yet it captured everyone's attention, and most of the kids nodded in agreement. Cade was their hero. Not only had he graduated from Hazel Rock High but he'd gone to college and played in the NFL.

Cade had the entire town and a sheriff in his back pocket . . . and keys to every bedroom. What more could a man ask for?

Chapter Sixteen

Mateo stayed to work on crime scene number two at The Book Barn Princess while the rest of us headed to the diner for a bite to eat—on Cade's dime.

The money he was throwing around was beginning to make me think thoughts I had no right to think. But I couldn't help it. My ex-boyfriend had the means and the motive to kill Marlene. Especially if he wanted to own the town. The standing joke during our childhood was that it should be called Calloway, Texas, not Hazel Rock.

Cade's daddy, however, had remained steadfast in maintaining history, which I'd always thought a little out of character. He was powerful, egotistical, and critical of his only son. Yet he'd knocked down the talk of creating a Calloway, Texas, with a swift and stern speech during halftime of the opening football game my freshman year of high school.

The town had loved him even more after his speech. He'd spoken eloquently of how the blue-green–colored rocks reflected in the river and were so beautiful they could compete with the bluebonnets of Texas. Nobody bought into it, except the entire population of Hazel Rock. Our ancestors settled down and created our small town because of it, and apparently the voters weren't about to give that up.

My guess? The river itself was the main reason they chose this area. Water could be hard to come by in mid-July. Plus, the land around Enchanted Rock was already settled. But the mayor's moment of humility was met with cheers almost as loud as the win his son delivered later that night.

Had Cade ever agreed the town deserved to have its own name, or was he caught up with making his *legacy*, a term my generation seemed to obsess about? Cade's smile appeared as real as it had when he was eighteen, but his confidence may have taken a hit when his professional career died. Plus, he'd put his coveted career before our relationship. Would he put his need to succeed before the town? Did he want to own every business and finally have a Calloway, Texas? Would his ego drive him to commit murder? So many people had committed murder for less, and I wondered if I ever *really* knew the boy I'd loved.

"Are you going to tell me what's bothering you?"

"What?" I shook my head loose from the haze of the past and focused on Scarlet sitting across from me in the booth.

"You're off in the clouds, staring at Cade like he's up to something when all he's done since you came back is stand by you."

I leaned forward and whispered the question I shouldn't ask. "Don't you find it odd that he's doing all this?"

She folded her arms and I knew I'd made a mistake. "No. I find it odd you're questioning him."

But I couldn't let it go. I leaned in farther across the wooden table. "I haven't seen him since we were kids."

Scarlet gave in and leaned over, our faces inches apart. "He's probably the best friend your dad has in the whole state."

I couldn't have been any more caught off guard. "What?"

Scarlet rolled her eyes and held the menu up in front of us, as if we were discussing the food instead of my conspiracy theories. "Have you not been paying attention?"

"Of course I've been paying attention." I pointed at the chili cheese fries with bacon and sour cream.

She shook her head and turned the page to the salads. Rabbit food didn't appeal to my empty stomach.

"I don't think you have," she lectured and pointed to a strawberry and chicken salad with spinach, black beans, corn, and avocado, all topped with a Margarita-style dressing. "Your dad disappeared after you left town. From what I heard, he was so depressed he couldn't function. And if I remember right, the store didn't open for about a month. It was Cade who brought him back and got him to reopen The Barn."

"I . . ." Something like shame crawled up my back and had the nerve to sit on my shoulder. I brushed it off. "I didn't know my dad felt anything, except maybe relief that he didn't have to deal with my drama."

"I wouldn't expect you to know. You weren't here. But Cade was. Wherever your dad went off to, Cade found him and somehow compelled him to come back. Made him promise to go to the games or he wouldn't play. Made the team go up to the store and ask your dad for books. He didn't care if they asked for vintage girlie magazines or car manuals, so long as they made him work at finding it.

"He had the athletic boosters giving out coupons—buy two books, get one free—to everyone who bought something at the concession stands during the game. He talked the yearbook staff into creating a calendar with pictures of all the athletes in the bookstore reading books. The calendar sold like hotcakes and has become an annual tradition."

"Who paid for that?"

"Cade."

I looked over at the boy I'd known, who'd grown up into a man I didn't. He was talking to Darrin and the coach. From the bits and pieces I could hear, they were strategizing next week's game.

Aubrey interrupted the conversation and all three men looked at her. "This is why you should go to the University of East Texas," she explained. "They use the Don Coryell style of offense." She pushed aside her silverware and napkin and began drawing circles, Xs, and lines on the paper place mat, becoming animated about what she had to say. The men listened intently. Darrin's eyes lit up before he pulled her into his arms and squeezed a giggle right out of her. Then he kissed her temple, and Aubrey had more than one lone star of Texas shining in her eyes. Coach and Cade seemed equally impressed, nodding their heads in appreciation.

It was another aspect of the young couple's relationship that was different than mine had been with Cade. I never would have felt comfortable enough to put my two cents into a football conversation with Cade and Coach. In fact, I had often walked away when Cade started talking about the game. Not because I wasn't interested but because I'd always felt like I was intruding. Now, I wondered if I'd contributed to our breakup.

Maybe Cade wasn't all about himself. Maybe he did care about other people the way I once thought he had. Yet, if I didn't believe Cade killed Marlene, I'd have to look in my father's direction, and that wasn't sitting well with me at all.

I turned my attention back to Scarlet. "Where did Cade find my dad?"

She gave me a look that dared me to take a risk. "I don't know." She nodded in his direction. "That's something you'd have to ask him."

For a moment I couldn't move. Then the disappointment in my lack of spine flashed in her eyes before she shook her head in resignation. It seemed Princess wasn't the only one who disapproved of me backing down. Scarlet became interested in the ice in her glass as she stirred it around with her straw. With each clink, I heard her disillusionment.

"That's exactly what I'm going to do." I stood up and walked over to Cade before I lost the nerve. I was ready to listen, give him a chance at being a friend, and a friend only, if it meant finding my father.

His eyes met mine the moment I stood up. As if he'd been waiting for me to make a move the entire time. With the grace of an athlete, he unfolded himself from the booth and met me halfway, concern written across his face.

His hand reached out and touched my arm as he searched my face for answers. "Are you okay?"

I took a step back, not wanting him to think I was just another woman in a long line of women who wanted that kind of comfort from him. His hand dropped.

"Yeah. I'm good. I just need to know something," I said.

Our conversation was starting to draw attention. Not because it was particularly interesting but because he was the mayor and I was the girl who'd left town in a cloud of rumors.

"Why don't we sit at the counter?" Cade put his hand at the small of my back and led me to a barstool made out of an old saddle. Anywhere else it would have felt weird, but in Hazel Rock it was right at home. I straddled the worn leather and turned toward Cade as he took a seat to my left.

"Where did you find my dad after I left town?" I watched his face, looking for a denial or a lie.

But his only reaction was a defeated shake of his head. "I already looked. He wasn't there."

"Where was it?" I asked.

The waitress came by, and Cade ordered a sweet tea for me and a glass of water for himself. I wanted to say I already had one at the table, but I needed answers and the faster she left, the better off I was.

As soon as she departed, he said, "At my family's cabin near Enchanted Rock."

I drew back in surprise. Our families had never been close. "How did he get inside your family's cabin?"

Then Cade dropped a bomb. "J. C. told him he could stay there as long as he wanted to."

"Your dad?" I couldn't believe it.

Cade nodded. "He recognized his part in your dad's misery."

"Oh." There wasn't much else to say. We sat there in silence, thinking about our dads; both had made huge errors and both seemed to make an effort to fix the damage they'd done. Could I ask for more?

"Did J. C. allow dad to use it again?" Someone had to know where my dad was.

He shook his head slowly. "No. I even drove up to make sure he wasn't lying to me. Your dad wasn't there."

I hadn't realized how much hope I'd held that Cade knew where my father was. He could very well be dead somewhere out in the middle of nowhere, his body left for the coyotes to ravage. "Where would he go?"

"I don't know."

Cade didn't sound defeated. Stumped, maybe, but not doomsday-ish, the way I was feeling. "Where did Marlene live?" I asked, hoping it was in another county and the police just hadn't made it there yet.

Cade's response tore that dream in half. "In town. She and your dad bought a house together."

"So it's true?" Dad's almost-empty closet made a lot more sense now.

"What?"

"I suspected my dad hadn't been living in the apartment, but I wasn't sure."

Cade nodded and took a drink of the water the waitress had just delivered with a flirty smile. I ignored it, telling myself it didn't matter. Just like Reba Sue and Cade embracing didn't mean anything. A couple weeks from now these people would be in my past once again.

It wasn't quite working. I caught myself glaring.

"Your dad moved out about a month ago. But he still used the apartment. He couldn't quite let it go."

"How do you know so much about my dad?" I wondered if what Scarlet had said was true. Had Cade been his friend or just a mayor wanting the approval of a voter?

Cade shrugged and almost looked embarrassed. "We're friends. Friends talk."

It was time to find out if Cade really was the same person I knew growing up. "How did you become friends?"

"Through football. After you left, your dad didn't have much to do, so he kept busy supporting the team. He came to games and talked to me about how I did afterward. It started one Saturday after I had a bad game. He sat me down right over there and told me I was projecting too much. The defenders knew where I was going to throw the ball before I did. From that point on we met every Saturday to discuss how I'd played."

"And when you went to college? Surely it didn't continue." It just sounded too weird, my dad and my ex-boyfriend hanging out together.

Cade shrugged. "I came home on Sunday and we had brunch. It was like having my own personal quarterback coach. Your dad took a deeper interest in my skills than my dad ever did."

"But your dad lived for your career," I insisted.

Cade shook his head, the sadness in his eyes dulled through years of acceptance. "My dad wasn't interested in teaching me anything. He was interested in bragging about my success. There's a difference."

We sat in silence, the smell of the grill making my stomach growl. Cade didn't say a word about how he'd helped my dad come out of his shell or the dark place he'd disappeared into. Just that my dad had helped him during his time of need.

That's the way I knew my dad—the guy to turn to in your time of need, not the other way around. Unless of course you were a teenage girl with a broken heart.

Chapter Seventeen

Mateo showed up at the diner shortly after my conversation with Cade and announced the all clear to return to the bookstore. Not everyone was enthusiastic about the prospect of more work in my bookstore. The store where I was getting creepy messages delivered in graphic style and a woman had been murdered. I felt the need to give them all a pass.

"I understand if y'all don't want to go back to The Barn..." I started to say.

Coach Purcell interrupted. "Don't be ridiculous. My boys aren't afraid of a few words scribbled in paint. But you'll need to buy some more water. My boys won't drink the well water."

I was about to get offended by his comment about our well water, but then I saw the boys stand up taller, jutting out young chests that wanted to belong on men. Cade and Mateo shared a knowing look, like they were reliving their own teenage drive to manhood.

Then Aubrey did the same thing, only she was ready to take the lead. "Let's go whip that Princess into shape!" she yelled.

I was pretty sure she'd recognized how bad the words sounded as soon as they left her mouth. If it'd been me, I would have crawled under a rock, but Aubrey stood tall at five-foot-two and allowed the shade of red to cover her face and neck as more than a few guys snickered in response.

Darrin stepped up, "You heard her, it's time to get to work." His support did the trick. He and Aubrey led the pack back to The Barn together.

I turned to see if Cade saw us reflected in them, both the similarities and the differences. The mistakes and missteps we'd made were being handled so much better by the next generation to graduate from Hazel Rock High.

He was watching me, pain visible in his expression. "I should have done that," he confessed.

"Done what?" My question was barely audible, but he heard it. Both of us recognizing my need to hear his response.

"When the guys talked, I should have shut it down immediately. I'm sorry. I was immature and hurting and I just thought . . ." Cade shook his head and looked away for a moment. "I'm not that guy anymore."

He wasn't. I knew he wasn't, and I needed to let go of the pain that had built walls between us. I didn't want a relationship with him, because it was obvious he hadn't grown in that department. But we both needed to heal. From what Scarlet had told me, Cade had been paying his debt to me since the day I left town, and he'd more than paid in full. I touched his arm.

"I'm not that girl anymore either. I may not be as carefree as I once was, but I'm a heck of a lot stronger." It was true. My teen self wouldn't go back year after year to the cutie pie booth and take the heckling and the abuse. Sure I'd avoided it this year, but it wasn't because of embarrassment or humiliation. I actually enjoyed the camaraderie and fun of the whole event. No, I'd avoided it this year simply because of my hair. Vanity to the extreme.

I smiled and took the arm Cade offered as we walked out of the diner together. Scarlet, Mateo, and Coach were standing together, staring at the exterior of The Barn.

"That pink seriously has to go," I said.

Cade and Mateo were holding their breath. Neither one daring to agree or disagree.

"What's wrong with it?" Coach asked. He was definitely color blind.

"I think you could get by with a whitewash. It'd be cheaper and it'd take on the boutique look I think your dad was trying to accomplish . . . plus you could leave the name across the loft door. If you destroy the name . . ." Scarlet bit her lip and shook her head.

She was right of course. If I tried to repaint the whole barn, it would cost me a fortune I didn't have. And my dad had changed the name for a reason. Granted there was an armadillo sleeping under the counter who had her likeness on the front of the store, but both were a tribute to a daughter who'd left and hadn't returned. The sooner I accepted that, the better off I'd be.

"Yeah, but I'm not going to be around that long and I really can't afford to pay someone to do it." That was the understatement of the year. If I ever got out of the debt I was carrying, I was going to cut my credit cards in half, then shred the pieces so I wouldn't be tempted to put them back together.

"I've got some extra whitewash we didn't use on one of my construction sites. You could use it," Cade volunteered.

"I can't—"

"It's helping the town's overall appearance. And hopefully keeping anyone else from thinking about painting their salon purple." Cade winked at Scarlet, who punched him in the arm.

"That was a joke, Mayor Calloway. I was never going to paint Beaus and Beauties purple. Now go get a few cases of water like the Coach said." She linked her arm in mine and pulled me off the porch to cross the street.

"But I can't afford to pay anyone to paint it," I whispered to Scarlet.

She promptly turned her head back and ground my pride into the dirt. "Mayor, I'm sure you'll make arrangements with Coach to have The Barn painted?"

"Scarlet!" I hissed and would have stopped in the middle of the road if she hadn't ignored me completely and dragged me with her toward the store. She looked over her shoulder, obviously expecting a response from Cade.

He laughed and nodded his head as he and his old mentor followed us. "Yes, ma'am. Coach and I will get on that right away. Mateo will make a run for the water." Cade winked in my direction right before Scarlet pulled me inside The Barn.

I didn't see Cade or Coach for the rest of the afternoon, we were too busy moving stacks of books from one end of the store to the other to notice they'd disappeared. Scarlet grabbed Aubrey, Darrin, and Brad to help her carry over some of her artwork. To be honest, I hadn't thought much about selling it until I saw it.

It was one of those lightbulb moments. Electricity crackling through my brain like lightning in a dark cloudy sky. Where there had been signs of the darkness winning the night, light broke through.

Scarlet's art was brilliant.

She had gourds of all sizes and shapes—all made out of books. The covers had been removed and the pages fanned by the front one being glued to the back. The rectangular shapes now shorn into the various profiles of fruit and vegetables. The edges of the pages painted various shades of orange, off white, brown, and even some apple red, while others had been left natural. The stems ranged from sticks to book spines twisted into curves above the plump fruit forms. Some had leaves made out of lace or burlap, and others utilized the covers as cute cutouts of foliage. The ones I liked best had no adornments beyond the stem and a little Spanish moss.

Then Scarlet brought out a beautiful tea set I seriously wanted to keep for myself. The teapot, made in the same fashion as the gourds, didn't have a lot of shape to it. Tall and cylindrical, it had a circular top that had been cut out of a book page and then adorned with gold silk flowers to make a knob handle on top. There were gold emblems attached to the front with ribbon and lace, which made it look like a family crest. The spout and handle were created from more pages, curving and spiraling with the grace of real silver. There was a shorter creamer decorated in similar fashion with the bottom edge cut to give it an inward curve. A spoon, which I suspected was découpaged silver, lay next to it. The two teacups reminded me of *Alice in Wonderland*, but the saucers were the coup de grâce. Aged yet beautiful, the original covers for Agatha Christie's *The Body in the Library* and *The Moving Finger* were now cut into the appropriate-size circle with an inner rim that hugged the teacups in the middle of the plate and completed the set. Miss Marple would have been proud of the attention to detail.

The set was absolutely stunning. To say they were pieces of art was an understatement. Scarlet didn't just have mad skills as a hairdresser, she was an artist.

"OMG, Scarlet, are you sure you want to sell these?" I asked.

A little part of that bookworm I'd seen in the principal's office during high school returned. "You don't like them."

It wasn't a question. It was more of an I-knew-it type of statement laced with self-doubt.

"Are you kidding me? I love them!" I practically yelled.

Scarlet didn't hear a word. She began rattling on about destroying the written word and art shouldn't destroy art. I grabbed her arm before she could put the tea set back in the plastic tub.

"Scarlet, I absolutely, positively *love* them."

"Really?" She wore two shades of red I'd never seen on her face before: embarrassment and something I couldn't fathom. Humiliation.

She doubted my *absolutely, positively*. It always worked with five-year-olds.

I smiled. "Really. They're so beautiful, I can't imagine selling them."

"You don't think they're an insult to the author who wrote them?"

I frowned, thinking about what she'd said. I suppose some people might take it that way, but I didn't. I'm not sure why I didn't perceive it as a slight on the author's talent. I just saw it for what it was: creating a treasure out of something I cherished.

Scarlet turned away. "I knew it. Marlene was right. Readers will be completely offended by what I've done to the soul of our humanity."

I didn't know what Scarlet was talking about, and for a moment I stood in stunned silence. With downcast eyes and shoulders slumped, Scarlet grabbed for the tub to pack her art away. It was only then that I began to realize the gravity of the moment.

"I'll get them packaged up and—"

I couldn't let her finish. "Scarlet, I love them one hundred percent."

Hope appeared in her eyes as she looked up.

I continued. "'Cross my heart and hope to die.'" I raised my hand across my chest and made an *X*. "'Stick a needle in my eye,' throw my body to the crows, and let my spirit doze." It was the wrong thing to say in The Barn, but I didn't care. It was the right thing to say to Scarlet.

The upturned corners of her mouth turned into a laugh and I smiled. The two of us standing feet apart and looking into each other's eyes was a moment of genuine friendship I hadn't experienced in years.

"I would be honored to sell your book art," I told her.

"It's my donation to the store."

I shook my head in disbelief. "I can't let you do that."

"It's for your dad, Charli. He's done more for me than I could possibly repay. Besides, I made these for him out of books Princess destroyed."

We both looked down at the armadillo, who had chosen that moment to wander out of the back room, a piece of paper hanging from her mouth.

"She has a habit of tearing apart some of the books," Scarlet said.

I remembered the sound of pages being torn up in the loft the first day I'd returned to Hazel Rock. At the time I'd thought it had been a killer lurking in the shadows. Now I suspected it was a rodent with a hard shell.

"Did my dad see your work?"

"No. When I showed them to Marlene, she told me absolutely not. So I never even attempted to talk to Bobby Ray about them."

"When he gets back, that will be the first thing he notices. Not the paint or the redesign of the interior but the art we have on display."

"That's what I thought, but Marlene—"

"Didn't know my daddy as well as you."

Scarlet beamed with pride. She hugged me hard with a hint of a tear in her eye but quickly pulled back and picked up the tea set to return to work.

"What would you think about having classes in the loft and teaching people how to create different items? We supply the books, the tools, and all the decorations," I said.

"OMW! That's exactly what I proposed to Marlene. She wanted no part of it." Scarlet was bouncing in places that wouldn't even jiggle on my body.

"I love it! You can teach the classes if you have time?" I cringed, hoping I wasn't asking too much.

"Time?" She laughed. "It's not as if the men of Hazel Rock are beating down my door. My nights are totally free. We can teach them together, but we'll need a big table."

I frowned. I didn't have a table.

"You're talking to the right man." For a big guy, Coach could be scary quiet. Neither one of us heard him walk up to us.

"You have a table we could use?" I asked.

"No, but I've got milled logs that I've been meaning to use."

"That sounds expensive."

"Not to me it doesn't. It sounds perfect." Cade winked at Coach, who nodded, as if a deal had been struck.

No, no, no. I couldn't be indebted to Cade any more than I already was. I squared my shoulders. "I'm sorry, I can't accept it," I told Coach.

Coach frowned and Cade overrode my decision. "It's not for you. It's for Scarlet and Bobby Ray."

His comment stung, but no one seemed to notice except me.

Scarlet squealed. "We'll have the store looking better than ever in no time flat." She began giving orders once more. "Aubrey! Darrin! Let's get these tubs moved toward the front of the store."

Princess didn't seem to care for the amount of activity that was going on and disappeared somewhere on the second floor. I hoped she wasn't going to tear up any more books. I'd like to be the one to choose which books were repurposed and which ones remained intact.

The paint on the counter was cleaned off before we'd returned. Mateo apparently took the service part of his job very seriously. I didn't care what his reasoning was as long as I didn't have to look at the eerie message any longer.

By the time the sun went down, I thought everyone would be ready to leave. On the contrary, some of the player's mothers arrived with fried chicken, potato salad, ranch corn, and herb biscuits. The entire group sat on the ground out by the fountain and ate the hearty dinner on the plates and silverware from the tearoom. All that was missing was a bonfire and red plaid tablecloths to make this the end-of-the-season football feast.

"Why aren't you eating?"

The sheriff stood above me holding a plate of food, his snug white T-shirt hugged every muscle across his chest and abdomen. I couldn't help but admire the results of years of working out. The splatter of white paint on his arms told me he'd been helping Cade transform the face of The Book Barn Princess. The difference was astounding—on two sides. But they were the sides that mattered most, the front and the courtyard sides where I was going to have to direct customers until after Marlene's funeral.

I smiled and invited him to join me by sweeping my hand across the vacant pavers next to me. "I–I was just thinking."

He nodded and sat down with his legs crossed in front of him, his ball cap hiding his dark eyes in shadow. I had no doubt he was watching me. That's what the man did.

"What's got you tied up in knots?" he asked.

"I'm not . . ." There was no use denying it. I was uptight and pretty much everybody knew it. "I was just thinking about my dad."

I waited for him to say something, but he just nodded his head and took a bite of his chicken leg.

"Have you had any luck finding him?" I sipped my tea, acting as casual as could be.

"Nope." He took another bite.

I waited for him to say something more, but his bite was followed by another and then another. I forged on with a theory I'd been too afraid to think, let alone voice. "You don't think . . . you don't think that maybe . . . maybe he's hurt and can't return home, do you?"

The sheriff finished chewing the bite in his mouth, took a sip of tea, and then wiped his mouth carefully, making sure not a speck was left on his face before he answered the question.

"No, I don't think he's hurt."

I expected him to say something more. Give me his opinion as to why my dad hadn't returned home. Instead, Mateo took another bite of chicken.

"Then why hasn't he come home?"

He wiped his mouth once more, then tipped his hat back so I could look into those deep chocolate eyes of his and said, "You tell me."

I scoffed at such a ridiculous statement. "If I could, I wouldn't be asking."

He searched my face. For what I don't know, but I was beginning to get a bad feeling about the sheriff sitting down with me.

"My detectives sent your belt off for DNA testing." He took another bite, his eyes never leaving my face.

The image of my pink leather belt with rhinestones and studs wrapped around Marlene's neck made my throat clog. I didn't want to think about it, but there it was, thanks to the sheriff. Her face darkened, yet lacking color, a deep, purplish-gray hue that took away all the highlights of her makeup. Her mouth open, her tongue swollen. I wanted to gag, but I shook my head to rid the image instead.

"That's good. It will lead you to her killer." My voice sounded strangled.

"That's the plan." He continued to scrutinize my expression. "If you remember, I've got your DNA sample from when you gave it to the detective the other day."

"I thought I was in the clear."

"You are, but if we find the DNA of a relative of yours on the belt . . ."

Suddenly, I understood. "You think my daddy did this?" That welcoming tone I'd had when he first approached me vanished from my voice.

He tilted his head, his hat falling back down over his eyes as he put a forkful of potato salad in his mouth. He was watching my reaction, his eyes trying to read my very soul.

"Well, you're dead wrong," I growled.

The sheriff paused and I realized what my words sounded like, but the last thing I had on my mind was to threaten the man. "What I meant to say was that my daddy isn't capable of murder. It's not in his blood to fight—for anything."

"You said yourself that you hadn't seen your father in a decade." He took one last bite, then folded his napkin and dropped it on the empty plate in front of him. All he needed to do now was pat his belly, lay back, and take a nap.

I pictured him with a cowboy hat tipped over his face, a piece of straw hanging out of his mouth and his boots crossed at the ankles. I could even see the silver star on his chest and a gun on his hip.

"What would you do if my dad walked up right now?" I asked.

The sheriff didn't mince his words. "Take him into custody and question him in regard to Marlene's death and his whereabouts for the past forty-eight hours."

Whereas he'd taken me into custody because I was at the scene of Marlene's death and a total stranger, Mateo would take my dad into custody because he knew him. Knew that my dad not being here was all kinds of wrong. The irony was eye-opening.

"How well do you know my dad?" I asked, my blood starting to get as hot as the midday sun.

"Well enough."

"What's that supposed to mean?" I demanded.

Mateo sighed. One of those male noises that said, *God help me deal with this emotional female.*

I don't like that type of sigh. I was on my feet before he could start shaking his head in a I-knew-that-was-coming manner.

"If you've got something to say, Sheriff, I think you'd better say it." We were starting to attract attention.

Actually, *I* was attracting attention. I was good at it. Mateo was just sitting there.

"All I was going to say was that everyone is capable of murder." His tone was much quieter than mine.

"Not my daddy," I growled again, because no matter what our differences and the number of years that had passed since I'd last seen him, I knew my father. He wasn't capable of the act of murder, let alone killing the woman he loved.

Mateo stood up and towered over me. I could see his eyes as he peered down, searching my face for what I had no idea. "No offense intended, Ms. Warren." He tipped his hat and said, "I best be moving on."

With that he was gone and I stood in the middle of the courtyard looking at all my neighbors, new and old. All of them watching me. All of them with the same expression on their face.

Approval. By standing up for my father, I'd won their approval. It was surreal. After twelve years of wanting it, I finally got it.

I was home to stay—until I cleared my daddy's name.

Chapter Eighteen

I rolled over and smacked the crap out of the annoying alarm on the nightstand. A nightful of bizarre dreams had made for a few fitful hours that I'd like to do over. Instead, I was dreading another day of wiping snotty noses on a bunch of five year-olds. I yanked the sheet up over my head and groaned, stretching for the corners of my king-size bed—that wasn't king size. In fact, it was only full size.

I suddenly remembered where I was and peeked out from under the sheet, lifting one corner high enough to see the swaying piece of wood hanging from the ceiling by three pieces of rope at the side of the bed. Waking up in Hazel Rock still seemed unreal—as if it couldn't possibly be happening.

But it was.

My dad had made the hanging-wood nightstand for my bedroom in Texas when I was a little girl. We didn't have enough money to buy one, so when a tree by the river toppled over and needed to be cut, he turned it into a nightstand, two end tables, and a bench in the backyard. I was looking at the smoothly sanded finish of a five-inch piece of that tree. Braided rope suspended it from the ceiling in a rustic design my mom had come up with, way before all those home improvement shows. I caressed its surface, thankful to see it once more.

Then I remembered the conversation I'd had with the principal of my school the previous night. I had one week before I would be on unpaid leave. If I missed more than three days of work after that week, he would consider it my resignation. I gulped down the fear that wanted to rise in my throat and swung my legs out of bed. I had twenty minutes before Scarlet was going to meet me at the diner for breakfast.

I made it in eighteen, thanks to taking a bubble bath the night before. The diner was busier than I'd dreamed it could be at seven o'clock on a Monday morning.

Hadn't these people ever heard of a drive-through or a breakfast bar on the run?

What about a Pop-Tart?

I found it hard to accept that so many people would take the time to have breakfast at a full-service, sit-down restaurant during the week, but apparently small-town Texas still liked its biscuits and gravy every day, not just on Saturday and Sunday.

Scarlet was sitting in a booth toward the back and I walked past all the smiling patrons feeling as if I'd been transported to another dimension.

"Morning, Princess. Welcome home," Mr. Draper said over his cup of black coffee. His dark, weathered skin and windblown, curly white hair gave credit to every year he'd spent on his cattle ranch.

I paused for a moment and smiled. "Mr. Draper, it's nice to see you."

"Your daddy would be right proud of you, little lady." He smiled, showing off teeth that weren't anywhere near as white as his bushy eyebrows.

"Thank you, sir." I nodded and headed toward Scarlet.

"That girl has a loyal heart in her chest," Mr. Draper said to the young man sitting across the table from him.

I didn't know him, but I was betting he worked for the old guy from his response. "If you say so, Mr. Draper."

"Charli! I heard you were back in town watching out for your daddy." Joe Buck stood up from the booth he'd occupied and hugged me tight. He was like a big teddy bear, soft and mushy all over, with a spirit as genuine as the smile that was a constant on his face. His cheeks glowed—literally. I used to tease him about putting on makeup that made him glisten like the actors on the red carpets, when in actuality he had a natural complexion every girl envied. As Cade's offensive center during high school, we'd spent a lot of time together, and from the way Cade told it, that smile was a killer after he crunched the defensive tackle on the other side of a football.

"Joe . . ." I managed to squeak out.

He laughed, and I felt his belly tighten before he released me and rubbed my ponytail like he was flopping the ears of a dog.

It used to make me mad when he did it in high school. Not because it was mean but because my vanity got the best of me. But Joe flopping it around wasn't going to hurt it a bit.

"Some things never change." I smiled up at the big man I hadn't realized I'd missed until that very moment.

"Some things changed for the better." He eyed me up and down, giving me an appreciative once-over.

"Careful now. I might have to knock you on your backside." I poked him in the chest and his smile got bigger.

"Sounds like a good time to me."

I laughed at my old friend who was now married with his first little one on the way. According to Scarlet, Joe wasn't just married, he was deeply in love with his wife, Leila, and had inherited the Tool Shed Tavern when his parents retired to Houston.

It was only then that I noticed his companion. Mike Thompson, the man who'd made my debt to Cade even larger. He was watching me with unveiled animosity and I couldn't help but think I should be the one who was thoroughly disliking him right then.

But Mike was sitting with Joe, so I decided he must have some likable qualities I didn't know about.

"How's your nose, Mike?" I smiled, trying to be polite. I think I succeeded in looking like I'd seen a dead rat in the middle of the table.

He rubbed his snout gingerly. "I'm still considering my option to sue."

Joe laughed, and I remembered how he could turn a fight into a party. His humor was infectious and irresistible. Mike actually started to smile until Joe punched him in the arm and laughed even harder. If he'd hit me like that, I would have been on my butt nursing a broken arm. As it was, Mike was holding his biceps while trying not to cry.

"You're such a riot, Mike." Joe wiped tears of pure joy from his eyes. "Look, you made me cry."

Mike's lip quivered. "You're not crying because of me. You're crying because of the damage to the bar last night."

Joe stopped laughing and his eyes narrowed. "If you didn't have the kind of voice that drove the women wild on Friday nights . . ."

"I took that as my cue to leave and patted Joe on the arm. "We'll catch up later."

A few other patrons said hello: Franz the baker and the quilt shop owner, Betty Walker, who still looked like they had a thing going on between them, and of course, Coach and Cade sat together with a notepad between them, discussing plays. Both nodded but were in a deep discussion that I wouldn't dream of interrupting.

That was never my role.

One of the antique dealers, Mr. Diaz, told me to bring over any old books I came across and he'd give me a fair price. I made some noncommittal comment, knowing the chances of me doing that were slim. My mom and dad had always been against that strategy. It went against their desire to be *the* source of books, new or old, in the community.

I finally made it to where Scarlet was sitting in a booth with her head down as she texted someone on her phone. "I didn't think you'd make it back here," she said without looking up.

"I didn't think anyone in this town would treat me like they just did ever again." It was reminiscent of the days when I was the darling of Hazel Rock and could do no wrong. Well, I did wrong, people just made excuses for my wild ways back then. Things like driving my daddy's truck at fourteen when the forecast said we had a 10 percent chance of rain and I didn't want to get my hair messed up for picture day. (I used to have issues about my hair. I probably still do to some extent.)

The old sheriff wasn't too happy with me when he pulled me over. I thought he was going to lock me up and throw away the key. But Mr. Draper had come by and talked him out of writing me a ticket. Said I was a good girl and we needed to teach our young'uns to respect the law, not fear it. The sheriff had muttered under his breath about them being one and the same and then parked the truck and let Mr. Draper take me to school.

My dad had picked me up that afternoon in that same truck. Told me I'd have to make him some oatmeal butterscotch cookies if I wanted to stay on his good side. It had cost me two batches of cookies and one pumpkin pie for Mr. Draper. Well worth staying out of that stinky jail.

That time.

Scarlet brought me out of my reminiscence. "Why would they treat you badly?" She looked up, her face a mark of perfection in porcelain white.

"Um, hello? Do you remember how they were treating me before I left?" I asked.

She looked puzzled for a moment. Then finally accepted that she wouldn't remember whatever I remembered and shook her head. "Nope. I remember you being the center of the world in Hazel Rock."

"That was before Cade broke up with me."

"Because you cheated on him with that boy from Denver."

My mouth dropped. "That boy from Denver was my *cousin*." I may have fumed a little bit at that point.

"Your cousin?" She said it as if I couldn't possibly have any relatives outside Texas.

"My Aunt Violet's son? Jamal is my cousin." Those bad feelings were starting to come back.

She blinked. "Huh. I never heard that one."

I tried to keep my voice down. "Of course you didn't. At that point I could have shouted it from the water tower and nobody would have heard me."

Scarlet looked down at her phone and began texting again. "I seem to remember you shouting quite a bit from the water tower and everyone heard you."

I sighed. "That was different."

Never looking up from her phone, she asked. "How so?"

"I was trying to get everyone to rally around the team." Hadn't I told this story a zillion times?

She looked up long enough to blow air out of her nose at the absurdity of my youth and then returned her gaze to the text she was receiving. "By yelling from the water tower in the middle of the night?"

"It seemed as good a time and place as any," I muttered, trying to defend myself with no real conviction behind it. She was, of course, right. I'd gone up on the water tower on a dare from Joe. That infectious smile of his could also be used to goad people into doing stupid stuff.

That night I'd learned how stinky the jail was. The sheriff had been woken up out of bed and wasn't about to respond to a call about obnoxious teens without someone paying the price. His determination to lock up the troublemakers started and ended with me.

Out of thirteen kids, I was the one who went to jail. Most of our friends had scattered like the wind, but because I was on the walkway at the top of the tower admiring the stars on the back side, I hadn't seen the sheriff coming. He'd used his siren to get my attention, and when I saw him, I seriously thought about pretending to faint. Except everyone knew I was an adrenaline junkie. The chances of me fainting were slim to none.

As I climbed down with his spotlight on me the entire time, I noticed one person had stayed behind. Cade. He'd tried to talk me out of climbing the ladder in the first place. I wouldn't listen. I was my own woman. Yet he'd stood by, despite being out after curfew, and tried to reason with the sheriff.

When the lawman wouldn't listen to the illogical arguments of a boy in love, Cade had had the decency to argue with him and kept him from putting handcuffs on me. Then my boyfriend went to wake up my dad, who came to get me before the sheriff could lock me up in his two-cell jailhouse.

And that marked the beginning of my downfall. The mayor didn't want his son hanging around a common criminal.

"Did you know Marlene was married?" Scarlet asked.

Holy schnikies, the look on her face made me squirm. "Yeah, to Mr. Duncan, our math teacher. Please tell me they were divorced."

"Yeah, they've been divorced for years. But apparently Mr. Duncan has been getting drunk at the Tool Shed every night since Marlene died. Last night he ended up in jail."

I thought about what Mike had said about the bar being damaged the previous night and wondered if Marlene's ex was responsible for the damage. "I can't see Mr. Duncan getting *that* drunk, can you?"

She shrugged. "Stranger things have happened. Including who posted his bond."

I knew I was supposed to ask who did it, but I also knew I wouldn't like the answer. I asked anyway. "Who posted his bond?"

"My sister Joellen just texted me. She overheard Mrs. Calloway talking to Mary while she was getting her hair done. Mrs. Calloway said your daddy posted his bond."

I scoffed. "Why would my dad post Scott Duncan's bond? My dad was engaged to his ex, and if you haven't noticed, the sheriff is digging pretty deep to locate him. Besides, my daddy would have come to see me if he'd stepped foot in town."

Wouldn't he? Scarlet looked at me. Waiting for me to accept my dad's neglect.

"How was he able to post Mr. Duncan's bond without Mateo pulling him in for questioning?" I asked.

"Apparently he went to a bondsman in Oak Grove and paid the fees. Mateo wasn't real happy about missing him."

I had no doubt the sheriff was fuming. Even if he had a tendency not to show it, Mateo didn't like to be bested. By anyone.

The second tidbit finally sunk in. "What Mrs. Calloway?" If the man had a wife, I might hit him with a brick cream pie for kissing me the way he had.

"Cade's momma," Scarlet replied.

I'm pretty sure she saw the momentary guilt that crossed my face as I thought about making out with a potentially married man. It was bad enough that he was seeing Reba Sue . . . okay, I wasn't going to go down that road again.

Changing the subject, I leaned forward so no one else could hear. "Did you hear about the bar getting damaged last night?"

"I heard Cade and Coach talking about it taking two deputies to take Mr. Duncan to jail."

"No way!" My voice got a little loud and Cade looked in my direction. Our eyes met across the room and a shiver ran up my spine. He still affected me more than I cared to admit. Drat the man.

Scarlet turned to see who had drawn my attention, a knowing smile crossing her face.

I ignored it. "Did he get into a fight or did he just go off and tear the place apart?"

"Someone apparently started disparaging Marlene's character, saying she didn't have a loyal bone in her body." Scarlet took a sip of her coffee.

"Wow, that's kind of harsh to say about a woman who was murdered." I eyed her coffee, wishing I had one with cream. "Who said it?"

Scarlet nodded her head toward Mike Thompson.

I was practically lying across the table as I whispered, "You're kidding me."

She shook her head. "Nope. I'm as serious as your daddy was when he said The Book Barn would never be the same without his princess."

My eyes fluttered as I processed what she'd said and slowly sat back in the booth. "He said that?"

She smiled sadly. "That was right before his armadillo showed up."

I couldn't help but smile. "Not exactly the cutest creature I'd like named after me."

"Maybe it has something to do with her coloring," Scarlet suggested.

"Or your tough-as-nails attitude." My hair moved as he spoke close to my ear. Somehow that man had snuck up behind me and leaned over my shoulder to send sparks through my body.

Scarlet grinned.

"Abuse tends to tear or toughen your skin," I said with as much conviction as I could without sounding breathless. Judging from the increase in the size of Scarlet's grin, I'd failed.

"I just came over to let you know that my offer stands to buy The Barn."

"Why? Are you planning to call in the debt I owe you for painting it? 'Cause if you are, there are still two sides that need to be painted." I was irritated. Not with him but with my reaction to his proximity. Cade and Scarlet, however, didn't know that.

Scarlet's smile turned upside down, and without even looking at him, I could feel Cade stiffen. He cleared his throat and straightened before answering. "After seeing how good The Barn looks this morning, I can see even more value in the investment . . . and I thought you'd like to return to Denver."

"I'm not going anywhere 'til my daddy's name is cleared," I said with more conviction than I thought I had.

"Sometimes these cases take a while. How long are you going to wait?"

If I were paranoid, I'd think he might be trying to run me out of town. "Then The Barn will stay open until it's done." Period.

Cade wouldn't let it go. He pushed. "What about your job?"

I shrugged as if it meant nothing. "It's a job." I couldn't believe I said it, yet I suddenly realized it was true. The job I had viewed as my career was just a job. I loved my students, even the ones with potty mouths, but in the bookstore I felt *alive*. After working 'til the late hours of the night, I had been wired, ready to keep going if I hadn't noticed the looks on the others' faces. While I'd been energized, they'd looked exhausted, so I'd called it quits. After they all left, I'd stayed a little longer just savoring what was mine. Because despite all the bad things that had happened there, The Book Barn Princess was a part of me.

I could sit down with a book and disappear to another land, another world, or even another time. I could explore the Amazon, fall in love with a Civil War soldier, or fight next to the Jedi and save the galaxy. I could learn to carve. Learn to cook. Or even learn to cuss in another language. Not that I would—but I could.

And certainly all of that was available to me on the internet, but I'd come to realize just how much I missed being physically immersed in it all. Being able to share that potential with others was a dream come true—literally. And that scared the bejesus out of me.

Chapter Nineteen

After breakfast I left the diner and headed for my daddy's house. I had a little time to snoop before I had to be back at The Barn and now seemed as good a time as any. I really wanted to see where he'd lived with Marlene.

And if I happened to find him at home, more the better.

It didn't take long to find the address. It was an old Victorian two blocks over behind the beauty salon on Sunset Drive. The house was green with white gingerbread surrounding the porch and the gables. The windows were dark but still welcoming, with lace curtains adding to the home's charm. I could see why my daddy had moved, even though it hurt just a little bit.

I walked up onto the porch and saw a pot of pansies identical to the one outside the apartment sitting next to the front door. Instantaneously my old ways perked up my heart rate. I looked around the neighborhood, but the streets were quiet and barren, all except for the steady, bored bark of a dog behind the fence of his yard. I bent over and tilted the pot and there it was: a key.

I grabbed the small silver key and looked around one more time before sticking it into the lock and turning the handle. A click and a squeak later, I was standing in the middle of the entry, wondering how stupid I could get.

"Hello?" I called.

My greeting met silence.

"Hel-looo," I called out again, louder this time. "Daddy, it's me—Princess."

Like he wouldn't know who *me* was.

I crept into the living room on my tiptoes. There was no doubt about this. I was breaking and entering . . . into my father's house.

Surely I could talk my way out of that?

The living room didn't have a lot of furniture: an antique couch and matching chairs with an old mahogany desk that had papers scattered across the top.

I flipped through them, looking for anything that might stand out. An electric bill in my dad's name, a credit card bill in Marlene's. One glance at it told me the woman liked her shopping, but nothing looked out of place. There were a few junk mail items and something from the city about the upcoming mayoral race next year.

I looked around the room and found a few photos of Marlene with my daddy. It was strange to see. He looked older but happy. I didn't look too long because I was scared I'd see the same kind of happiness in his eyes he'd had with me and my mom, and I wasn't ready for that. Especially knowing he'd lost his second love too soon as well.

I walked into the kitchen, which was decorated more in a seventies décor than one that fit the house, but by the construction plans sitting on the counter it looked as if they were ready to remodel. I made my way to the second floor and found two vacant bedrooms. The third had a queen bed that didn't look like anyone had slept in it. I moved to the closet and found my dad's clothes along with Marlene's when something tugged at my chest.

It felt a lot like guilt. Guilt for snooping. For spying. For interfering in his life when I had no right to do so. Yet I continued to the dresser. Because despite my guilt, I was determined to push forward and find something in Marlene's stuff that would lead me to her killer. It was the only way to clear my daddy's name.

I went through Marlene's closet, her drawers, her nightstand, but found nothing. Nothing. Nothing.

Defeated, I turned and looked around the room before heading downstairs. I peeked out the front door before exiting and locking the door. I hesitated, scared to put the key to my daddy's house in such an obvious place, but then decided he might need to get it and put the key back under the pot.

It was nine-fifteen when I made it back to The Book Barn Princess and stood looking around the store all alone. Technically, I wasn't *alone* alone. I had Princess staring up at me with her beady little eyes wondering what I was going to do next.

This was insane.

My cell phone rang and I pulled it out of my pocket. My cousin Jamal's name flashed on the screen. He was exactly who I needed.

"Jamal!" I answered on the third ring.

"Char, are you coming home anytime soon or have we lost you to Texas?"

I laughed and looked down at Princess. "I was going to call you tonight after the grand reopening of The Barn."

"The what?"

"I'm reopening The Book Barn Princess for business in thirty minutes." I smiled and let those words sink in. They felt crazy but good.

"Get out! Princess? You put Princess on the end?"

I laughed again. God, it felt so good to laugh. "Nooo, Daddy had already put Princess on the end of the name and painted The Barn pink."

"Get. Out!" He was laughing, and I knew someday my Aunt Violet and Jamal would come through the front door and *love* the new store. *I* loved the new store.

"Pink." I grinned. "Big and pink."

"You're not coming back, are you?" he accused.

For a moment I hesitated, and then I laughed again. Only this time it wasn't filled with joy but rather more like I'm-so-stupid-crashing-down-to-reality-I-think-I-might-cry laughing.

I knew from experience that The Book Barn barely made it in the black each month. It'd always been enough to put food on the table and keep the lights on, but that was it. I suspected Dad had given The Barn an expensive facelift hoping it would do the trick, and when it didn't, he'd put it up for sale. And here I sat thinking the exact same thing—my remodel would do the trick. Not that the changes in the store this time around had been expensive per se, but it had been labor intensive and I owed a lot of people favors—including an entire football team.

"What if I fail? What if I don't raise enough money to get home, let alone set up a legal fund for my dad?"

"Wait, what? A legal fund? You didn't say anything about a legal fund. Is your dad in trouble?"

I cringed and realized my mistake. I was relying on the entire town of Hazel Rock. I couldn't possibly involve my cousin or my aunt in this mess. I laughed again, but I know it sounded fake.

"Don't be silly. Listen, I gotta go, but I'll call later on in the week, okay?"

"Sure, Char. But—"

I didn't give him a chance to continue. "Bye, Jamal." I clicked my phone off.

Princess rubbed against me like a loving cat. Being rubbed by a shell, however, wasn't exactly the same thing. It hurt and kind of creeped me out. I stepped back and she gazed at me like I'd just delivered the worst insult possible.

I couldn't even take care of an armadillo. What made me think I could take care of the store?

"Sorry. I gotta get used to you rubbing against me."

Princess sneezed and waddled away.

I shook off the feelings of doom and started brewing some tea, then put out a dozen cookies I'd purchased at the bakery. My emergency fund was precariously low, so I was hoping I'd earn enough money to put food in my mouth this week. I needed to quit eating at the diner and start going to the grocery store. Problem was, I didn't have a car and I'd have to ask someone for yet another favor. How many favors would my new old friends allot a charity case who shouldn't be asking for funds from anyone?

I went out and watered the memorial to Marlene that I'd decided to maintain and keep as neat as possible until Friday. Actually, Thursday night after dark was sounding better and better. If I didn't take care of it, I'd have a bunch of pots with dead flowers blocking the entrance by the end of the day. That was the last thing the store needed. Especially when the memorial wasn't just growing by the day, it was growing by the hour. More plants, balloons, and signs that said, "We love you, Marlene" and "RIP Marlene" had been added since I last looked. There was one new sign that caught my eye and made me wonder.

It simply said: "Forgiveness."

It was posted right next to a five-foot column cactus. Who puts a cactus at a memorial?

I picked up some of the stuffed bumblebees and placed them in as neat a display as I could manage, then moved the A-frame chalkboard that read *The Book Barn Princess Is Open!* to the courtyard, where the arrow could point to the side door. With one last look, I went back in the store and got ready for the crowd of customers that would hopefully be pouring through my door at ten o'clock.

A wistful smile crept across my face. I'd always liked to dream big.

I put the fifty dollars of start-up cash in the antique register my mom had picked up at an estate sale when I was seven years old. She said it was worth a week of us eating fried bologna. At the time I didn't think so. I ate the bread and dropped the meat in my napkin. Now I loved the ornate scrolls of the machine and the sound of the ding when I opened the drawer of the register.

I still avoided bologna at all possible costs.

I swept the floor since we hadn't gotten to it the previous night, and returned the dustpan to the back room, refusing to think about walking over the spot where Marlene lost her life. I didn't have to worry about it too long, though, because I soon found Princess tearing out pages on a first edition of the Nancy Drew mystery *The Secret of the Old Clock.*

The noise I made sounded like a ghost dying, which in and of itself was a little spooky. Princess jumped straight up in the air—the only way to describe it would be a hunched-over cat on a hot tin roof, the Texas sun included in that image.

She even made a noise that competed with mine on the spooky scale.

"Princess, no!" I waved my finger at her as if she was a five-year-old. She pouted, turned around, and waddled out the curtain.

I picked up the pages and wondered if it could be rebound, which would cost me an arm and a leg I didn't have to spare. I thought about Scarlet's tea set crafted out of Agatha Christie's Miss Marple mysteries. Could she make something out of this too? The woman was a creative genius—Scarlet, that is. Ms. Christie was beyond genius.

I hung up the dustpan and broom and returned to the register with the book and ten torn pages in hand. They were all legible except for the very last page. It had a hole in the middle the size of my fist. Apparently, Princess liked the taste of Nancy Drew. Then I noticed that one page was completely missing. It was no doubt in the digestive tract of a hard-shelled rodent.

Glancing at my watch, I was shocked to see that it was five minutes to ten. I quickly stashed the pages inside the book and stuck it under the counter. I looked around to make sure everything was in order and made my way to the door. With any luck I'd get a handful of customers who would pay for dinner. It wasn't exactly the best way to do business, but I had to pay myself somehow.

I took a deep breath to get myself in the right frame of mind. I pulled down my skirt and unlatched the top half of the door from the bottom. The door originally had been designed for a horse to hang its head outside, but since The Barn didn't have any equestrian inhabitants, a human head would have to do.

The first thing I noticed as I started to push open the door was the noise. Voices carried and bounced off the stone buildings and I couldn't fathom what could create such a stir. When I got the door halfway open, someone grabbed it from the outside and pushed it open the rest of the way.

"Excuse me," Mr. Draper said as he pushed the door against the exterior wall and a crowd of people stepped out of his way.

The entire courtyard was full. Not that it was a large courtyard; it could only hold about fifty people, but there were more people there than I had ever seen in town. Most of them were familiar, and if not readily recognizable, I knew by the people they were standing with where they belonged. Scarlet was in the middle of the crowd, flanked by Joellen and Aubrey, who I was pretty sure should have been in school.

Tracy and LouLou from the bakery were talking about a new cinnamon roll recipe and still had on their aprons. Franz, the baker himself, was helping Mrs. Walker with a shopping cart. I was pretty sure it said Country Mart on the seat, but it'd been spray painted blue.

Coach stood next to them with his assistant coach and Mrs. Phelps, my high school English teacher, who had to be approaching eighty.

Joe Buck stood behind Cade. Joe's smile was bright and he had his arm around Mike Thompson's shoulder like he'd dragged him there and wasn't about to let him sneak off. Mateo was there, although I'm not sure why. Maybe he and the blond female deputy with him were there to keep the peace. Or they expected my father to show up.

I highly doubted it.

Several of the servers from the diner stood together off to one side, taking turns glancing at their watches and cell phones since it was getting close to lunch and that meant their time to earn the most tips.

I looked at Scarlet, who nodded in Cade's direction. and my eyes returned to my high school sweetheart.

"On behalf of the citizens of Hazel Rock, we'd like to give you a formal welcome home and wish you the best with The Book Barn Princess," Cade said and handed me a key.

"Wh-what's this?" I asked, unsure of what he was giving me the key to. His heart? The store?

"It's a key to Hazel Rock. We know you've run into hard times since coming home, but we wanted you to know that we appreciate everything you've done to the store to make it fit in with the rest of the town."

"I . . . I . . . thank you," I finally spat out. It was about as far from eloquent as it got.

Coach wasn't about to be outdone. "And for the art classes these two lovely ladies are going to start, I've made something special." Coach and Joe Buck moved to the side and exposed an eight-foot table sitting in the courtyard.

"Isn't it beautiful?" Scarlet asked.

It was beyond beautiful. I wasn't sure what type of wood it was, but the planks were rounded on the bottom like uncut logs bound together, with a flat, smooth satin finish on the top surface.

Scarlet beamed. "And this here," she said as she scooted past Mateo with what looked like an elbow to the ribs, "this is for donations to your dad's legal fund." She handed me an old safety deposit box converted into a bank. On the front, scrolled on the clear glass in gold it read BOBBY RAY'S LEGAL FUND. Bills of every denomination—including hundreds—filled the interior.

I didn't know what to say. The town was stepping up and supporting my dad—and me. My eyes filled with tears. I tried to blink them away, but two spilled down each cheek.

Scarlet wiped her own eyes and handed me a tissue. "OMW. I think you'd better open up that store before the floodgates open up around here."

I laughed, and there was a loud whoop from the crowd.

"The Book Barn Princess is open for business," I proclaimed. "Step on in and enjoy your trip to a whole 'nother world!"

Chapter Twenty

It took every able-bodied man and woman to get the new table to the second floor. When Scarlet mentioned we needed a second one, a collective groan filled The Barn. At that point, Coach looked at me and told me the next one would be built in place. I heartily agreed.

The day turned out to be a huge success. Every piece of book art sold except for one pumpkin. But it wasn't just any gourd; this one was special. Made out of a *Cinderella* book, it was above and beyond what fairy tales are made of.

The pumpkin was shaped into Cinderella's carriage, with the tips of the pages embossed in gold leaf and lit from the carved-out interior, which held a battery-operated candle. The wheels were made of heavy gold jewelry wire that scrolled around so smoothly I had a hard time imagining anyone could bend it without putting in at least one kink. Scarlet had papier-mâchéd two toy horses with several book pages and curled thin strands of more gold-leaf paper edges for the manes and tails. It made the hair look ablaze with fire. The horses' bridles were made of gold ribbon and draped delicately over the carriage seat. The hooves were also in gold leaf, and I had no doubt the entire project had to have cost her a chunk of change and time.

Scarlet had snuck it over on her lunch hour and it now sat on the shelf above the register. I was glad she had proclaimed it property of The Book Barn Princess and not for sale to several of the big-haired customers who just happened to follow her to the store. While she was there, Scarlet told me the gossip about Marlene had hit an all-time high at the beauty shop that morning, but she wouldn't go into detail.

"I think it's time you were reintroduced to the Tool Shed Tavern," she said. "I'll come by to pick you up at seven. *Monday Night Football* will mean an early crowd."

No one ate the cookies I'd set out—except me. I would have eaten more, but Mateo had shown up with grilled chicken and a side of broccoli salad for me at lunchtime. He didn't want to get a call for service about a young woman passed out behind the counter.

Scarlet, who'd stuck around until after he left, said Mateo was smitten.

Seriously? I laughed it off, not ready to think of the man in that way.

After ringing up my last customer a few minutes after six, I locked up the store and balanced my register. The big news of the day: there was $257 inside the cash drawer and $1,500 in the box for my dad's defense fund. Not too shabby for my first day's work.

I paid myself fifty dollars and hoped that would be enough to get me through the week. It was definitely below minimum wage, but a girl's gotta do what a girl's gotta do to bail her daddy out of trouble. I put fifty dollars back in the register and locked it up. The rest of the money went in a bank bag we left under the register and then I headed for the tearoom to lock up the funds in the safe.

Except the safe wasn't there.

All I found was a stack of dusty, damaged books hidden in its place under the counter. It looked like the safe hadn't been kept there for years. I made a mental note to locate the safe tomorrow and said good night to Princess, who crawled out of her bed and yawned in my direction. I never would have thought an armadillo could yawn until I saw her do it. I let her outside to roam around the dry riverbed in back before heading upstairs to grab a quick bite to eat.

Scrambled eggs never tasted so good.

I brushed my hair and my teeth and was swiping on a fresh coat of mascara when I heard a scratch at the door. I looked out the glass-paned door and found Princess sitting on the porch, waiting patiently to get in. At least I assumed she wasn't irritated. It was kind of hard to tell when I didn't know what an impatient armadillo looked like.

"That was awfully fast." I opened the door wide enough for her to enter.

Princess cocked her head and waddled past me to the kitchen. Before I had the door locked, I heard a bowl scooting across the floor.

"I take it that means you're hungry."

Princess pushed her bowl with her snout in response.

About that time, I got a whiff of her special scent and ran for the sink with her tubs. "First, you bathe."

Ten minutes later she was clean and pushing her bowl around the floor again.

"What flavor do you want tonight? Tuna? Chicken? Liver and other gut innards?" I asked as I opened the cupboard that contained stack upon stack of canned cat food.

I held out two cans of food for Princess to choose from, one red can and one blue. She stood on her hind legs and rested her front paws on my wrists. The feel of her claws digging into my skin was worse than that of a cat, but I held my comments to myself. Her ears twitched as she sniffed both cans, looked at me, and blinked before nudging my right hand, which held the blue can of tuna.

"Tuna it is." I pulled away, trying not to topple her over, and opened the can. She started eating before the bowl touched the floor and I had to admit her skinny little tongue was kind of dainty and cute in a weird sort of way as it slid out and gathered one small bite at a time. But it was the food dish that held my attention as with each lick it squeaked across the floor.

I couldn't help but wonder if Marlene had made it. The jewels were haphazardly attached to the aluminum dish, some in clumps and others spread too far apart to form a pattern. The whole thing appeared to be done in the style of a five-year-old's art project. Not that I was judging it—just noticing whoever'd made it didn't have my momma's eye for design.

I hate to admit that the idea of another woman living in the apartment ate at my craw. This was my family home. A home that belonged to the original three amigos. No one else.

Even if two of the amigos were gone.

My phone rang and I grabbed it off the counter, expecting Scarlet to tell me to get my butt in gear. "Hello?"

"Princess?"

If Scarlet were here she'd say, *OMW*. My response wasn't quite so polite.

"What the . . . Daddy?"

"It's me, darlin'. I can't tell you how good it is to hear your voice." He sounded the same as he had the day I left.

"Where are you?" I asked. I wasn't sure yet if I was happy he was calling or mad that he still hadn't shown up in person.

"I think you're better off not knowing."

"But—"

"I know Mateo is looking for me. I don't want you to be accused of harboring a fugitive."

"Then come home. We can get this straightened out."

"I can't."

"Why can't you?" I asked, my voice tight with a growing sense of irritation.

"There's something I need to do first."

"What could possibly be more important than Marlene's murder?" I demanded. The silence on the other end immediately made me regret my angry outburst. "I'm sorry."

He sighed, as he always did before a particularly tough explanation. "It's okay. I deserved it."

"Not this time."

"No, but in the past I have."

I couldn't argue with that, but I'd come home in order to move forward with my life. I needed to move forward. Funny how you make those sudden realizations when you least expect it. "We can talk about that later. Right now we need to go talk to the sheriff."

"Mateo's a good man; I'm not worried about him."

"I am!"

"Don't be. What I want you to know . . . no, that's not right. I *need* you to know that I didn't mean to hurt you, but I was wrong. I screwed up. I should have known J. C. was behind that unexpected shipment of pregnancy guide books. A gift horse is never a gift. I should have sent those books back," he confessed.

"Yet when the rumors started you didn't say a word. You kept those books out in the store window and told me to just ignore them. To walk through town with my head held high!" I sounded like an angry teenager.

My dad's voice was low, he sounded almost ashamed. "I couldn't beat J. C. I owed him."

"Owed him for what? What could you possibly owe Cade's daddy? What was more important than my reputation, Daddy?"

There was a long pause, and I didn't think he was going to answer. When he finally did, his voice was just a whisper. "The roof over our heads."

"Wh-what?" I knew I'd misunderstood him. We owned our roof—didn't we?

He finally broke the silence. "When your mother died, her medical bills broke us. That's why I wanted to sell The Barn after she was gone."

I closed my eyes, unable to face what I'd done to my dad, my family. "But I wouldn't let you."

"It was all you had left of her. You were only ten."

My anger was gone, replaced by a sense of foreboding. "So you turned to J. C.? Why not the bank?"

"The bank wouldn't refinance The Barn. We didn't have any equity in it. I got a loan from J. C."

Even though I knew why he'd done it, I had to ask. "Why?"

I could hear his voice cracking as the tears poured down my cheeks. "Because I'd do anything for my little princess."

"Oh, Dad. Why didn't you tell me? If we'd only talked it through . . ."

"It was my burden to carry, not my baby girl's."

"But all these years I thought you conspired—"

"I wasn't innocent."

"You weren't guilty then, just like you aren't guilty now. Come home. We'll work it out." My voice cracked on old emotion I'd wrongly thought was gone. I missed my daddy.

"I can't." I could almost see him shaking his head.

"Why?"

"Just promise me you'll be careful. I think I know why Marlene was killed—"

"Then go to the sheriff and tell him everything."

My father wasn't swayed. "I have to take care of something first."

"What?" I'd tear my curls out if he didn't answer. "What could possibly be more important than this?"

"Your future."

Fuzz buckets. I closed my eyes, wishing all this would just go away. I was just as responsible for all of it as anyone. "Daddy . . ."

"I'll call you before I come home—just to make sure you won't swing a bat at me by accident when I show up."

"Daddy—" I started, but he was gone.

"I love you." The dial tone didn't respond. I shoved my phone into my purse and threw it over my shoulder. Then I blew my nose and looked in the mirror. No one at the bar would notice I'd been crying. The lights would be too dim.

I walked back into my bedroom, grabbed a scarf and wrapped it around my neck. Then I grabbed the keys off the counter before telling Princess, "Don't wait up. I may be late."

Chapter Twenty-one

Scarlet was in the courtyard waiting for me when I went through the gate. Her red hair pulled up off her neck in a messy updo that turned spiky at the top. Her long bangs were no longer smooth, silken curls but appeared brash and edgy, just like the rest of her. Jessica Rabbit was gone. I was now looking at a younger, shapelier version of Scarlett Johansson as the Black Widow in a black leather miniskirt and five-inch stilettos that still didn't bring her up to my height. Her breasts were threatening to spill out of a royal blue peplum blouse that hugged every curve. I'm not sure she wouldn't have fallen out if it hadn't been for the sheer black lining that looked like a long-sleeved blouse underneath and gave the illusion of respectability.

I looked down at my own outfit. I would disappear next to a vixen like Scarlet.

"OMW. Next to you, I look like a fat ogre," she said.

"You're kidding, right? Because I'm feeling about as shapely as a piece of barn wood."

Scarlet laughed and linked her arm with mine. "Then I suggest this ogre take her best piece of barn wood to the hottest bar in town to see how much trouble they can stir up."

"The Tool Shed Tavern is the *only* bar in town."

"Exactly." She looked at me—hard. She scrutinized the redness of my eyes and the puffiness around my nose. "Have you been crying?"

So much for nobody noticing. "Allergies," I lied. "This isn't like a biker bar or anything, is it? I'm not exactly looking for trouble."

"No, it's not, but trouble is brewing in Hazel Rock. I can feel it in the air."

A pickup truck with darkened windows slowed down as it came

up behind us. Its shiny black paint and extralarge tires made it clear the driver loved his vehicle. The truck rumbled as it passed, the vibration traveling through the town and my body. I was pretty sure if I'd still been in the apartment, I would have felt it.

"Who's that?" I asked as we continued toward the bar.

"Don't pay him no mind. That's Scott Duncan. He's going through a midlife crisis."

"Aren't you supposed to buy a sports car when you go through that?" I thought of Mr. Duncan in the loft, sneaking around the store. The same Mr. Duncan who'd called my daddy away from the bookstore when I was seventeen and a newspaper photographer just happened to take a picture of me placing those infamous maternity books in the display window.

I should have asked Daddy about him. It seemed especially important now that I realized there was no way I would have missed the rumble of his truck outside The Barn when I'd caught him in the loft. Mr. Duncan didn't want to be seen that night, which was understandable . . . to a point. Now it was kind of making me think twice about allowing him access to the store whenever he wanted, even if it was to reminisce about Marlene.

My dad may have shown him where to find the key, but my comfort level was deteriorating fast.

"What red-blooded man in Texas would want a dinky little sports car when he can put that same money into the monster truck of his dreams?" Scarlet said.

I shrugged. I'd obviously been gone too long to understand. "So what did you hear that made you think we had to check out the gossip at the bar?"

Scarlet leaned in close. "Marlene was stepping out on your daddy."

"What?!"

"You heard me. Apparently, that's why Mateo thinks your daddy killed her. It was a crime of passion, in his mind."

"But that also means there's at least one other suspect," I argued.

"You're right and you're wrong. It means there are at least *three* other suspects."

"Three?" My voice growled with anger at the woman who had duped my daddy.

"Mind you, it's just the rumor mill. But supposedly, Marlene was seeing her ex-husband, Dean MacAlister, and—you'll love this one—Mike Thompson."

"He's half her age! And . . . and . . ."

"A slimeball with beautiful hair."

"Exactly!" I thought of the man who'd tricked Cade out of a hundred bucks and put me in debt to my high school sweetheart for a few books I wasn't even sure existed. "How does a woman who catches a sweet man like my father end up cheating on him with a boring math teacher she discarded in the wind, a mechanic, and an immature computer geek who has the natural gift of even turning off a woman of God as soon as he opens his mouth?"

"Shhh." Scarlet waved as Scott Duncan crawled out of his truck. "That's what we're going to the bar to find out." She turned up the volume as she greeted our old math teacher, who didn't look nearly as lost as he had when I'd found him snooping in The Barn.

He waited for us but didn't seem happy about it. On the contrary, Mr. Duncan appeared more irritated by the second. He ran his fingers around the collar of his short-sleeved button-down shirt as he waited for us to catch up.

"Remember Charli Rae Warren?" Scarlet asked. "She was a year between the mayor and me." Scarlet pushed me forward and I awkwardly held out my hand, unsure whether I should pretend he had been caught red-handed prowling in my store or not.

"Of, course," he said smoothly. "How could I forget? I'm sorry for your loss, Charli."

Again, I wasn't sure how to respond. I certainly wasn't the one who'd lost my old flame. Marlene was a distant acquaintance to me, not my ex-wife I supposedly still loved. "You too, Mr. Duncan. It's got to be pretty hard on you."

He nodded. "It is on everyone, I suppose." His eyes traveled between Scarlet and me. I gave a slight shake of my head to let him know I hadn't breathed a word about his afterhours visit to the store. His relief was visible. I, on the other hand, wasn't sure I should keep his secret.

"How's your father holding up?" he asked.

Yet again he left me tongue-tied. As far as he knew, I had no idea how my dad was doing. Yet I had to admit his question had a sense of desperation to it, as if he was at a loss as to what to say and had blurted out what he thought would be expected of him. He was as bad a liar as I was, and by the look on Scarlet's face, she knew she was missing something.

"I haven't seen him yet, but I'm sure I will when he's ready to talk about it."

Mr. Duncan nodded. "I'm sure he's glad you're home." He didn't leave any room for a response as he nodded at both of us and added, "Have a good night, ladies," and slipped past us into the bar.

"That was weird." Scarlet looked after him, completely puzzled by the exchange. I chose to shrug it off, as if I didn't know what to think of it—because I didn't.

We went into the bar and I was surprised by the interior. The last time I'd been in the Tool Shed was when I was ten years old. Not long after my mom died, I'd come home from school one day and The Barn was locked up tight. A short time later I'd found my daddy's pickup parked in front of the bar for the first time in my life. Not sure what to think or that there could be anything wrong with a ten-year-old walking inside a liquor establishment, I pushed open the door and strutted right in. The place was dark and dingy and full of smoke that made me cough.

The bartender had looked up and yelled immediately, "Get your butt out of this bar, young lady!"

My dad looked up from the drink perched between his elbows with a look of horror on his face. That was the first time I'd recognized the Tool Shed as a place not fit for kids or mourning husbands.

Daddy grabbed the bartender by his shirtfront, growled something in his face, and shoved him away before stumbling off his stool in my direction. I wasn't sure what shocked me more, the fact that he'd gotten angry at someone or the way he'd swayed as he walked—unable to pass the two rough-hewn timber columns that separated the bar from the dance floor without grabbing hold of them for support.

By the time he'd made it to me, I knew he needed to lean on me. I wasn't sure why, but when we got outside to the truck, he told me we could leave it there for the night. The walk home would do him good.

That was the first and last time I'd stepped foot in the bar, so when we walked in and my eyes didn't immediately start burning from cigarette smoke, I took that as a good sign. Joe Buck had done an incredible job transforming the Tool Shed from a depressing, down-on-your-luck hole in the wall to an upbeat bar and grill. And from the look of it, the crowd was well into a celebration for the football game of the week. The fact that it was the Big D's team playing the City of Brotherly Love didn't hurt. The rivalry brought all the fans to cheer and jeer together.

Scarlet grabbed my hand and we squeezed our way through the standing-room-only crowd that currently wasn't happy about a touchdown being called back on a holding call. There were loud complaints being yelled at several large TV screens in various locations in the bar. I couldn't help wondering if Cade was among the unhappy fans.

We passed several people I'd known in high school. Sarah and Debbie? Kathy and Gwen . . . or was that Vicki and Gwen? I honestly couldn't remember. I smiled politely as Scarlet hugged and air kissed the two I thought were Vicki and Gwen before we moved on to two seats that were magically vacated at the bar. After being on my feet all day, I was happy to take a load off.

"You don't remember them, do you?" There was a hint of amusement in Scarlet's eyes as she tugged down her skirt.

I leaned in and confided with a yell, "I'm honestly having a hard time separating them from my students."

She giggled, but our conversation ended as Joe approached us.

"Well, well, well. Look who's here. Thank you for bringing her in, Red. You'll have to introduce Princess to my Leila when she comes around."

"Will do, Joe. In the meantime, I'd like a Sex on the Beach."

"You and me both, Red. Maybe you could tell Leila I deserve it."

"Maybe you should sweep your wife off for a romantic weekend to the Gulf."

"I'm afraid there won't be any romance for this bartender until after the Super Bowl." He swept his arm out, indicating the crowd in the bar. "We live for football."

That was a given in Hazel Rock, Texas. Even the sign welcoming you to town was in the shape of a football. It was either that or a star—the town had voted for the football well before I was born.

"What can I get you, Princess?" Joe asked.

"It's Charli now," I yelled over the sudden outburst of cheering for a touchdown by the home team. Joe squinted, trying to make out what I'd said, as he pointed to his ear. I gave up on trying to get him to call me Charli and told him I'd like a frozen Amaretto Sour if he had one.

"Anything for the Princess of Hazel Rock." He turned and walked down to the other end of the bar as I rolled my eyes.

"You may as well let it slide. That's how people remember you." Scarlet pulled out her larger-than-life smartphone from the fifties-style clutch purse she'd set on the bar. "Lean in for a selfie."

Not wanting to offend her, I leaned in for the photo and found out she had an ulterior motive. Behind us, to my left, another gentleman had just joined the group of football enthusiasts standing around a café-style table. Dean McAlister was the best mechanic in town, but with four kids by four different women, he wasn't exactly the catch of small-town USA. Sure he looked good for a man in his early forties, with brown hair curling around his neckline and a strong jaw with happy eyes. He worked hard and was an honest businessman. But when it came to his love life, the man didn't know the meaning of the word *loyalty*.

Scarlet nudged me and we smiled for the photo, which actually turned out pretty good. "He's somebody we need to talk to."

"How am I going to approach him without him thinking I'm looking for something I'm not?"

"Ask him about a rental car."

"A rental car?"

"Yeah. Dean's got a couple of vehicles he lets people use while he's working on their cars. I'm sure he'll give you a deal." Scarlet winked.

I couldn't keep the sarcasm from seeping into my voice. "At what price?"

Scarlet laughed. "Grow some backbone, girl. You're from Texas— and we don't back down in Texas."

She was right. Except I'd learned how to keep to myself and avoid adversity in Colorado. Approaching Dean was going to mean all kinds of trouble—I could feel it in my bones.

Chapter Twenty-two

"Go! Before he moves on and it becomes awkward." Scarlet reached over and turned me toward Dean, both hands on my shoulders.

"Why don't you come with me?" I sounded like I was back in high school, but I didn't care.

"Because I'm waiting for our drinks. Now go. Unless you really don't want to help your daddy?" Scarlet challenged.

"I didn't say that."

She raised her brow and I sighed with resignation.

"Hold my seat."

Scarlet beamed, but I ignored it and slid off the stool. Five steps later, I was tapping Dean on the shoulder, ready to get more information about his affair with Marlene and who else had a motive to kill her. Dean turned around, expecting someone much shorter than me, and when his eyes finally reached mine I felt like I'd been thoroughly undressed. I couldn't help the shiver that traveled down my spine. Dean, however, reached out to shake my hand.

I returned the gesture even though I knew he wouldn't let go, which of course he didn't. I pulled my hand back with a gentle tug.

"Princess. I heard you were back." His drawl elongated every word.

I debated on getting right down to business but let my Southern up-bringing dictate my greeting instead. "Hello, Dean. How are you?"

"My day just got brighter." He sidled up next to me and put his arm around my shoulder.

I would put money on Dean running out of women who would fall for that line in Hazel Rock. Looks could only get you so far. Yes, the man was total arm candy—if you wanted an older man to warm your bed and leave as soon as he found pleasure somewhere else. He did own MacAlister's Auto Shop, which was the best in the area, but along with his success he also had four kids and four child-support payments.

I slid out from under his arm, blurting out my excuse for approaching him before I got the information I needed. "I came over to see if you had a car for rent."

Talking business did the trick. Dean's expression changed and he gave me his undivided attention. "You should have told me you needed the truck worked on." He'd been known to work on some vehicles for free when families ran across hard times. It was *that* version of Dean that I liked.

"It's not the truck." I blushed because I knew I couldn't afford to pay him to rent a car but suddenly realized how much I could use a vehicle. "My dad's taken off with the truck and, well . . ."

"You're kind of stranded in Hazel Rock until he gets back," Dean prompted.

"Yeah."

"I heard you're having trouble with the water from the well at The Barn. How much can you afford?"

I didn't know what he was talking about with the well; as far as I knew, it was fine. But then again, maybe that was why dad had moved out. I decided to ask Scarlet about it later and then focused on one of Dean's good qualities. He didn't believe people would try to get something for nothing, yet I had no doubt some people had taken advantage of his generosity over the years.

I stretched my wallet as far as it would go. "Ten bucks a day?"

"Twenty-five for the week, and if you need it longer, we'll talk."

"I'm not sure when my dad will be back. He could show up tomorrow . . . or Thursday." Thursday was the day of Marlene's funeral. I waited to see if my mentioning it would have an effect on him.

It did. Immediately.

His face softened, and for the first time since I'd known the man, I saw real emotion cross his face. Not the generosity he'd shown toward others but pain for a personal loss mixed with what might be guilt. "I can't imagine Bobby Ray missing Marlene's funeral. The whole town will be there."

"Will you?"

"Of course. Back when we were just kids in our early twenties, Marlene helped me buy the auto shop. She was just starting out at Yellow Jacket and I was ready to start making a name for myself."

"There isn't any other reason?" I asked.

Dean's eyes narrowed as he searched mine.

"I know." My voice was soft, but Dean heard every word and his shoulders slumped.

"I'm a weak man. Marlene and I went way back. She's the one woman who never wanted anything in return from me."

I was happy I'd obtained a little bit of information to help my daddy's case, yet sad that his fiancée, Marlene, hadn't been worthy of his love. I hid my disappointment and asked, "So she was a friend . . . with benefits."

The smile he gave me was kind of sad. "She was a *good* friend . . . with benefits."

I pushed further. "Even after she was engaged to my father?"

Dean looked away, refusing to meet my gaze. "Even then," he confessed.

Suddenly I felt my eyes filling with tears. I blinked them away before asking, "Didn't she love my dad?"

"In her own way, yes."

I couldn't let Marlene off the hook that easily. "What does that mean?"

"Marlene was . . ." Dean cleared his throat, as if what he was about to say would be hard to swallow. "She was the female version of me. Being tied to one person forever seems like a mighty long time to keep someone happy."

It suddenly dawned on me that Dean was afraid. Not physically but emotionally. Taking a risk with his heart was the last thing he wanted to do—would ever do. "So never committing is better than losing someone you care about?" I asked.

He tapped the side of his nose and smiled. I'd identified his fears without him admitting a thing.

"When was the last time you and Marlene . . . ahhh, danced?"

There was a flash of shame in his eyes, but he squared his shoulders and confessed his sins as if he was sitting in the confessional on

Saturday morning. "Two weeks ago Marlene and I danced the night away. It was the last time I saw her."

Two weeks ago.

It was shocking to hear that the woman my daddy loved had cheated on him so recently. Especially because he was prepared to give up his past and sell The Barn to make her his future. For a moment I wondered if my dad really had killed Marlene in a fit of jealousy. But couldn't Dean be just as jealous of the man who was stepping in on his dance?

Before I had time to ask another question, a waitress came up and put a clingy hand on Dean's arm. Her big blond hair was full of hair spray. She wore a plaid denim short-sleeved shirt with the pearl buttons open all the way down to the knotted shirttails, showing off plenty of her perky, man-made breasts. Her denim shorts exposed long legs born from hours at the gym. The look on her face was exactly what Dean liked: a sultry pout.

"Sugar, I am so glad you found me." He leaned over and whispered something in her ear that caused her to lick her lips. Dean finished off his beer and put his empty bottle on the waitress's tray. "While I use the men's room, could you get me another beer and Princess here . . ." He pointed to my empty hands.

I shook my head. "I'm fine. I've got a drink waiting for me at the bar."

Dean nodded. "Then I'll see you at the shop first thing in the morning." He winked at the waitress and disappeared into the crowd.

The waitress started to leave, but before she could, I asked, "Excuse me; could you tell me how often Dean hooked up with Marlene Duncan at the bar?"

Her face grew wary. "Are you a cop?"

"I'm about as far from a cop as you can get."

"Why would you ask if Dean was hooking up with Marlene?" She seemed genuinely stumped.

"Because Dean isn't exactly the discriminating type?" I suggested.

The waitress leaned toward me, her tray balanced steadily behind her as she displayed a tattoo between her breasts. If I wasn't mistaken, it was the stem to a piece of fruit. She sneered as she looked me up and down. "He's taken."

I leaned back. "Excuse me?"

"Dean's taken."

"I know he and Marlene—"

A look of shock crossed her face and I realized my mistake instantaneously. Just because I knew one secret didn't mean I knew them all. "What I meant to say was that he and Marlene were friends, and I was asking him if he knew of any other men she'd dated."

"Wasn't she engaged to that old guy who owns the bookstore infested with rats?"

"Rats? The Book Barn doesn't have rats!" I realized my next mistake a little too late. Defending the store was the last thing I should be doing while trying to get information.

I tried to smooth over my mistake. "I mean, I hadn't heard that one." I pushed her for more. I needed to know if Dean could be a suspect. "I heard Marlene had a thing for good-looking guys."

"Marlene liked to dance," she replied.

That's what Dean had said, only he'd meant much more than a bump and grind on the dance floor. "Really? Do you think she could have been cheating on her fiancé with other men?"

"I saw her in here a few times with her ex, and when she couldn't find someone else, Dean took pity on her." The light bulb went on and darkened her blue eyes with anger. "Are you telling me my boyfriend chose *her* over me?" Her hand went down her body as if the thought of a man choosing another bed partner with fewer attributes than she had was an impossibility.

I hesitated, not sure how to deal with the wild card I'd dealt myself. "I wouldn't go that far . . ."

But obviously she thought I did. Her free hand went on her hip. Her lips pursed and her eyes sparkled with a jealous flame.

"You got some nerve, coming in here, accusing Dean." She looked me up and down from head to toe, dismissing my skinny frame like a stray tumbleweed blowing across the street. She grabbed the mug of beer on her tray.

As she reared back to shower me with my least-favorite drink, I ducked and the ale struck the only Philly fan in the whole bar. If that wasn't bad enough, the guy was two sheets to the wind and grumbling about the upside-down score that left his team heading for a loss. He turned around and punched a Dallas fan before I could utter the words, *Sorry, that was meant for me.*

His one punch was followed by a second. The new victim stumbled back into another guy who had at least one sheet swaying in the breeze as well. I cringed and tried to stop the third guy from getting involved, but it was like trying to stop a bull on its way to a heifer in season. My feet flew out from beneath me as I slipped in the beer and ended up on the floor with the crowd around me throwing punches and insults faster than a WWE wrestling match.

I crawled toward the bar where Scarlet sat back watching the action with a smile on her face. "You'd think it was Friday night," she yelled over the din and held out my drink.

I grabbed a napkin and wiped the beer off my knees. "This happens a lot?"

Scarlet squinted, trying to read my lips, and then nodded. "Usually when our football team loses."

I took a sip of my drink and watched a woman break a pitcher over some guy's head. More beer sloshed on the floor and dripped down his chin.

Dazed, I downed the rest of the best frozen Amaretto Sour I'd ever had. Then I set my glass on the bar and watched Joe Buck start tossing patrons out the front door of the bar.

My jaw tightened from the sour bite of my drink. "We should help."

Scarlet laughed and shook her head. "Joe's got it down to a science."

At that moment I saw Mateo enter the bar flanked by two deputies, Joe Buck pulling up the rear. Mateo grabbed the first two guys he encountered who were throwing punches and handed one back to each deputy. The deputies immediately got the brawlers' attention by getting in their faces. At first the football revelers bristled and chest-bumped. Then sanity clicked, and with their heads bowed in submission to the deputies' authority they followed instructions to have a seat on the floor. Those who didn't obey, got put on the floor with their wrists zip-tied behind their backs.

A break in the crowd formed, leading right to where I sat next to Scarlet.

The sheriff, with his arms crossed and feet shoulder width apart, still had a don't-mess-with-me look on his face. It was the same expression he'd worn as he made his entire way through the bar. His words, however, were just for me. "I should have known the trail would lead me straight to you."

I raised my hand and waved, trying to look as innocent as possible. Mateo wasn't fooled. He grabbed my upper arm and marched me outside.

So much for changing my ways.

Chapter Twenty-three

"What in the blue blazes did you think you were doing in there?" Mateo asked before muttering something under his breath in Spanish. He practically dragged me to his patrol car and opened the passenger-side door.

"Am I under arrest?" I squeaked as he opened the door and shoved me inside with his palm on the top of my head. Déjà vu was definitely setting in.

"Should you be?"

I looked at him, afraid to utter a word lest I incriminate myself.

"*Dios mio.*" He slammed the door closed and I watched him stalk around to the driver's side. I jumped when he got in and slammed his door as well.

"What did you get yourself into now?" His voice held the accusation of a prosecutor facing down the man responsible for the Texas Chainsaw Massacre.

"Nothing!"

"I haven't seen a brawl like that since . . . since I don't know when." Mateo flexed his fingers over the steering wheel.

I think he wanted to put them around my neck.

"Scarlet said it happens on Friday nights when the team loses." My tone may have come off a little condescending. It wasn't my intention; it just happened.

"Our team is winning, in case you failed to notice."

A knock on his side window startled us both. Scarlet was standing on the other side with her arms crossed.

He turned the key in the ignition and rolled down the window. "What can I do for you, Ms. Jenkins?" Mateo's voice scraped out the polite words as if they were the last thing he wanted to say.

Scarlet didn't waste any time on good manners. "You've got no right to detain Charli."

"*Princess,*" he said, making it sound like he thought I was anything but royalty, "started a brawl in the bar."

"I didn't see her throw any punches," said Scarlet.

"You were talking to Joe with your back to the action," he countered.

He had no way of knowing that, but he was a dadgum good guesser. Mateo rolled up his window, dismissing Scarlet before she could argue. His forehead was beginning to sweat and his jaw made a grinding noise when Scarlet knocked on the glass even harder.

I made the gesture for her to quit by slicing my finger across my neck. Scarlet crinkled up her nose but decided to wait and folded her arms. It wasn't a second later that a large drop of rain hit the windshield. Then another.

They started coming down faster and Scarlet looked up at the dark night sky. A big grin crossed Mateo's face for the first time since I'd met him. Scarlet threw her hands in the air and returned to the covered porch of the Tool Shed.

"How much have you had to drink?" Mateo asked, turning to me and resuming his normal blank look.

I refrained from rolling my eyes, barely. "One drink."

"It must have been a pretty strong one."

I raised the corners of my mouth in a smile that wasn't really happy but wasn't angry either.

The sheriff let it pass. "What happened in the bar, Ms. Warren?"

"Nothing. I was just asking a few questions and the next thing I knew a beer was flying through the air."

"A bottle or a glass?"

I was happy to enlighten him. "Neither. It was just the beer itself, sloshing down some guy's back."

"And you didn't slosh it?"

I shook my head. I was free and clear.

"Nor did you see who sloshed it?"

That question was a little trickier. I shook my head again, only this time it was more like a Stevie Wonder nod.

Mateo's eyes narrowed. "Who were you talking to?"

"One of the waitresses. I don't know her name." Even if I did, I wouldn't repeat it. I was already on her bad side without reporting her to the police.

Mateo wasn't about to let me off the hook. "And what exactly were you asking?"

At this point I'd reached my limit of skirting around the truth, so I confessed. "If she knew how often Marlene and Dean, ah . . ." I hesitated, unsure of how to phrase it. Mateo leaned forward with both eyebrows raised, waiting for me to continue. "If she knew how often they hooked up at the bar."

"Are you kidding me? You're spreading gossip about a dead woman?"

I scrunched my nose and shook my head. He was about to figure out the rest.

"Let me guess. You asked the blond waitress who's about your age and wears a lot of hair spray with a uniform about two sizes too small for her shape?"

I happily evaded, "That describes more than half the female population of Texas, let alone Hazel Rock."

Mateo pursued the truth. "She has a tattoo between her breasts of two leaves on a stem with two cherries."

"I didn't see any cherries."

His face turned smug. "But you did see the stem."

"I saw two leaves—"

"Her name is Sugar."

"Seriously? I thought Dean was just laying it on thick." Recognizing my mistake, I quickly added, "I didn't know she loved Dean."

"Of course you didn't know. You're not an investigator. You don't know the facts and you're mucking up my case as we speak."

"I understand that this is your case—"

"Who's in the bookstore?"

His change of topic caught me off guard. "What?"

"Who's in The Barn right now?" he demanded.

"No one—why?" I turned to look in the direction of the store.

"Does anyone have permission to be in The Barn?"

At first I thought of my dad but dismissed it immediately when I saw the glow of a flashlight in the upstairs windows. Dad wouldn't use a flashlight. Then I thought of Scott Duncan, who knew where my dad kept the key. But he was inside the bar.

Mateo's sense of urgency grew. "Charli?"

"No one should be inside the store."

The sheriff got on his radio and asked for backup from the officers in the bar. When he opened his car door, I got out of the passenger side at the same time, but he stopped me before I could follow.

"Give me your keys." I hesitated, and Mateo's mood changed. He wasn't irritated or angry, but it was obvious he meant business and he was in charge. "Charli, give me your keys."

"I can go with you," I insisted as rain pelted my face.

Mateo was having none of it. "A woman died in The Barn a couple of days ago. I'd like to prevent that from occurring again." He paused. "I promise I won't shoot Bobby Ray. Now give me your keys and stay here."

He was right of course. I needed to let him do his job. He was trained to deal with thieves and murderers. I, on the other hand, wasn't equipped to deal with any criminals. Unless of course you want to include undisciplined five-year-olds in that category.

I dug into my purse and handed my keys over to Mateo. "The bigger one is for the side door."

He nodded. "Thank you." Then he pointed to the wooden planks on the porch next to Scarlet and spoke to my friend. "Keep her here."

"Mateo Espinosa, what are you up to now?" Scarlet demanded.

"Just keep her here!" Mateo ran toward The Book Barn Princess.

Thirty seconds later, the female deputy exited the bar, talking into the mic on her shoulder.

"Someone's in the bookstore," I said and pointed toward the light on the second floor of The Barn. She just nodded her acknowledgment as she took off through the muddy street after Mateo.

As soon as the deputy was gone, Scarlet asked, "Are you sure that's not Bobby Ray in The Barn?"

"Why would Daddy be walking around with a flashlight?"

"Because the sheriff wants to arrest him for murder?"

I changed the subject before my fears and doubts led to the same stupid mistakes they had in the past. The last thing I wanted to think about was the possibility of Mateo shooting my dad. I had to trust both men to stay true to their word. "Did my dad ever say there was a problem with the well at The Barn?"

"Why do you ask?" Scarlet said.

"Because Dean said he heard I was having problems with the well," I explained.

"That's weird. Joe told me he'd heard the same thing."

"So is it true?"

"If your daddy was having problems with the well, it would have been found during the sale of The Barn and recorded somewhere in the paperwork. Maybe you should check with Yellow Jacket Realty."

Just then the lights flicked on in the second story of the barn. The shades were still drawn and all we could see were shadows. Scarlet and I looked at each other and out at the downpour that wasn't about to quit anytime soon and took off running for The Barn. As we approached the side door, we heard loud voices coming from within. Actually, just one loud voice. The pitch was high, but I didn't think it was coming from the female deputy.

Out of breath, with my heart pounding in my throat, I opened the door to see Mateo and his deputy escorting a smaller man down the wide steps from the second story.

My breath caught as the man with his hands behind his back began yelling. "I didn't do anything wrong! I've got a right to be here!"

"I don't think you have the right to take anything," Mateo replied.

"I wasn't taking anything!" The man's voice was undeniably recognizable, despite the fact that his face was turned away from me, and the feeling of betrayal seeped into my blood once again.

I'd been a fool to believe him.

Chapter Twenty-four

The sheriff and his deputy had seen Scarlet and me approach, and although neither one looked happy about it, they didn't tell us to stay away either. Marlene's ex, however, was completely taken by surprise.

"Princess!" It didn't take him long to recover and use our agreement to his advantage. "Tell him you let me visit anytime I want."

He was the only person who hadn't run through the rain, and as much as I really hated him at that moment, I couldn't lie. "It's true, Sheriff. I allowed him to come and go as he pleased while he grieved for Marlene."

Mr. Duncan was nodding his head in agreement a little too fast. His enthusiasm reeked of deceit. "That's exactly what I was doing . . . grieving."

"He was stuffing a couple of books into his satchel when we found him." Mateo held up a brown weathered leather bag that I'd seen Mr. Duncan carry on many occasions, including when I first found him in the loft of The Barn.

"They're mine! I brought them with me tonight." Mr. Duncan's eyes were wide and pleading.

Scarlet stepped forward and asked, "What books are they?"

"*The African Game Trails* volumes one and two. Do they belong to the store?" Mateo looked like he already knew the answer.

"I'm not sure. They could . . ." I said.

Scarlet waved her hand in the air to shut me up. "Written by President Theodore Roosevelt?" she asked Mateo.

"'That's correct. They're leather bound—" Mateo started to reply.

"And in a case. Both volumes are signed copies," Scarlet interjected.

"Signed?" I looked at Scarlet and then back at Mateo for confirmation.

"I haven't looked at them that closely yet," he replied.

"They're mine, I tell you!" Mr. Duncan insisted.

"They belong to Bobby Ray and Charli," said Scarlet.

"Take him to the station and let Detective Youngblood know I'll be there shortly." Mateo released his prisoner's arm and nodded at his deputy.

"Sure thing, Sheriff." This time the deputy took the covered walk most of the way as she led Mr. Duncan down toward the bar, where her car was parked. I really wanted him to get as wet as we were, but he was only exposed to a few drops.

Mateo waited for the deputy to secure Mr. Duncan in the front seat of her patrol car before he said, "Can we go inside, ladies?" He moved to the door of The Book Barn Princess and held it open for us. Scarlet went in first and I followed.

"I'll make us some tea," I suggested. I really didn't want to smell like a whiskey distillery while talking to Mateo.

"I thought the well went bad?" Mateo asked.

"Who told you that?" Scarlet and I responded in unison.

Mateo looked back and forth between us as if we were crazy women. "Cade asked me if I thought you'd allow him to help you out because the water tested positive for arsenic."

"Arsenic?" I said.

All I could think about was the tall glass of ice water I'd had before heading out to the bar. "I've been drinking the water. Would whiskey negate the poison? How long does it take?" I cleared my suddenly scratchy throat. "Surely Daddy would have told me . . ."

Mateo's head snapped up from the pad of paper he'd pulled from his shirt pocket. "You've been communicating with Bobby Ray?"

"No." Long and drawn out, my answer sound like a lie on a roller-coaster ride.

"Does Charli need to see a doctor?" Scarlet asked.

Mateo turned to Scarlet. "I don't know. It wouldn't hurt." Then he started interrogating her. "Have you been communicating with Bobby Rae?"

Scarlet shook her head and began methodically inspecting every book on the shelf in front of her.

He rubbed his hand over his face, no doubt tired of us pushing all his buttons. "Why don't we have a seat in the tearoom, have a bottle of water, and talk about what's really going on? You know, communicate on an *adult* level?"

Scarlet's hands went to her hips, and I realized she did that a lot when she talked to the sheriff. "Mateo Espinosa, I know you're not accusing us of acting childish."

"If the boot fits, Ms. Jenkins." He held out his hand, allowing us to lead the way.

By the time we sat down with a bottle of water, I was feeling marginally better until Princess joined us.

Mateo was poised with his pad to take notes. "Tell me about the books."

This time I had no problem telling the truth. "I don't know anything about them. I've never seen them before."

"I have," Scarlet piped up. "About a month ago Bobby Ray told me I could take as many of the books upstairs as I wanted to repurpose into something useful. Princess—"

Mateo eyes strayed in my direction.

"Sorry, I meant the four-legged Princess," said Scarlet.

We all looked down at the rodent, who was currently begging for a handout. Sitting up on her hind legs, she was performing her dog routine again. I gave her half a cookie from the plate on the table next to us, which I had neglected to clear at the end of the day. She sniffed it, took it between her paws, and then shoved it in her mouth before waddling away.

Scarlet continued. "Princess had started going upstairs and chewing on some of the old books. None of the books from upstairs were selling, so Bobby Ray said I could have as many as I wanted. I took a couple boxes full of the hardbacks, some chewed up and some others that were in pretty good shape. When I got back to the salon and started sorting through the books, I realized *The African Game Trails* weren't written by just any old author, but by Theodore Roosevelt— *the* Theodore Roosevelt. The twenty-sixth president of the United States. And when I opened it up, I saw it was signed. I immediately brought them back to Bobby Ray. They had to be worth something."

Mateo put the leather satchel on the table and pulled out two really old leather-bound books that, despite their age and the dust covering them, looked to be in collector's condition. "Are these the books you were talking about?" he asked.

"Yes, sir. Without a doubt those are the books I brought back to Bobby Ray."

"What did he do with them after you brought them back?"

"What do you mean?"

"Did he put them on the shelf for sale? Could Scott have purchased them from Bobby Ray?"

Scarlet shook her head. "Oh, no. Bobby recognized them immediately. He said he'd forgotten all about them and didn't mean for them to get mixed up with the books that were for sale. He and Marlene were talking about them when I left for an appointment."

"You didn't hear any of their conversation?"

"I know Marlene wanted to sell them, but Bobby Ray was adamant that they weren't for sale. He said they weren't his, that they belonged to his princess."

"The armadillo?"

Scarlet smiled. "I'm pretty sure in this case he meant his daughter, Charli."

They both looked at me, but I didn't know what to say. I'd never seen the books before in my life, and if they'd belonged to my mom, she would have shown me. I had the books she valued in my apartment in Colorado. But the most financially valuable books she'd left me were *Dick and Jane* readers from her childhood that were only worth a couple hundred dollars.

I shook my head. "If they were meant for me, he never told me about them."

"Who's to say there isn't more than one set? Maybe Duncan had his own set?" Mateo asked.

Scarlet started shaking her head again before he even finished the question. "There's no way there are two signed sets of *The African Game Trails* in Hazel Rock, Texas. Besides, these were a limited edition, set number one hundred and thirteen out of five hundred."

Mateo carefully opened the book, showing more care than I thought a cop would, and read the copyright page. Then he asked, "How did you know it was the one hundred and thirteenth edition?"

"My birthday is January thirteenth. It's pretty easy to remember."

Mateo nodded, closed the book, and put it back in the satchel. Then it was my turn to be questioned.

I gulped.

"What was Scott talking about when he said he had a right to be here?" he asked.

I sighed, thankful his question was about Mr. Duncan and not my dad. "I caught him in The Barn after-hours two nights ago."

The sheriff's jaw tightened. "And you didn't call the police?"

"I would have, but he was upset. He said he was reminiscing about Marlene—that coming to the store helped."

"The man broke into the store and you didn't report the damage? Nor did you see a reason to tell me about it tonight when I saw the flashlight in The Barn?"

"We went into the Tool Shed right behind Mr. Duncan. Why would I think he was in the bookstore? And he didn't break in. He knew where my dad kept the key under the flowerpot. That's why I didn't call. I figured my dad must have given him permission to come in after-hours. I mean, it seems like everyone has a key to this place."

It was Scarlet's turn to lecture me. "Aubrey, Cade, and I are the only ones who have a key. And your dad never kept a key outside— you should have known that."

"I haven't talked to him in years. How was I supposed to know that? There's a key under the pot at his house!" Unfortunately, my outburst opened a can of worms.

"So you haven't talked to him since you've been back?" Mateo asked.

"No," I lied.

"You wouldn't impede my investigation, would you, Charli?"

"Nope. Not in a million years." But that didn't mean I wouldn't do everything I could to protect the man I loved.

Chapter Twenty-five

I woke up to a voice mail dinging on my phone. It was Dean, telling me he'd left a red Honda Insight parked in front of The Book Barn Princess for me to use. The keys were under the mat and I could stop by to pay him when I returned the car.

Freedom felt pretty good.

I rolled out of bed with a smile on my face—then found out I'd made a big mistake when I'd decided to wash my hair with my daddy's shampoo. I didn't have any conditioner, so I'd done a flat twist with it damp, hoping beyond intelligence that my curls would look all right in the morning.

They didn't. In fact, they didn't even look like curls. I looked more like a hippie with a fried-out afro than a woman with twenty-first-century curls. I threw on some clothes, ran outside, stopped at the cute little four-door hybrid parked in front of the store, and grabbed the keys just in case someone thought a Honda would make the perfect joyride. Then I ran across the street in a panic and rushed in the door of Beaus and Beauties to face a stunned crowd.

Everyone froze at my arrival. Joellen jerked the brush of polish across Aubrey's nails.

"Joellen!" Aubrey yelled, then followed her best friend's gaze to my hair. Her mouth fell open.

Mary dropped the foil in her hand, and I watched it float to the ground unnoticed by everyone but me. I really wished I could be that four-by-four piece of aluminum paper.

Mary grinned. "Honey child, if there was a disco ball and some mirrors, I'd think I'd been time warped back to the seventies."

I threw my hands in the air. "Help!"

Scarlet turned off the hair dryer, leaving Reba Sue's long blond hair covering her face, which I immediately recognized as a tactical move. She knew the woman saw me as competition for Cade's attention and would have turned her cell phone in my direction and taken a photo as soon as she got one look at me.

Cade would run in the opposite direction, if he wasn't already. I told myself that's what I wanted, so who cared? Unfortunately, I did.

"Is that Hazel Rock's princess needing assistance . . . again?" Reba Sue's tone was less than friendly as she started to pull her head up.

Scarlet shoved her head back down. "Don't move, Reba Sue. I think you may have lice. I'm going to get a better lamp to see."

Reba Sue shrieked. "Lice? OMG. I knew I shouldn't have gone to his fishing cabin!"

Scarlet grabbed my arm and yanked me toward the back room, yelling over her shoulder to Reba Sue as we went through the doorway, "You're in luck, I've got the perfect product."

"You know better than to use the wrong product on your hair," Scarlet scolded as she pushed me down in the shampoo chair. "I ordered some products for you the other day and they came in in this morning's shipment. You should have asked."

"I didn't want to bother you." It seemed like that's all I ever did.

Scarlet ran her fingers through my hair, testing the dryness. "Having to look at this rat's nest bothers me. I just hope you haven't damaged it beyond repair."

I may have whimpered. My dad and I had gone through this after my mom's death. Neither one of us had a clue that the special shampoo my mom bought was specifically for our ethnicity. We just thought it was girlie shampoo, and because it wasn't available at the nearest department store, we bought what we could.

I ended up with a buzz cut that made me look like a boy going through a prepubescent growth spurt. The kids at school thought I was a new kid and a few started calling me Chuck. Luckily, it didn't stick.

Thank God, but I didn't want to be called Chuck ever again.

Scarlet massaged conditioner into sections of my hair to make it more manageable to work with and began to finger comb out all of the tangles. When she did that, I breathed a sigh of relief.

I was in heaven.

"Scarlet!" Reba Sue yelled from her chair up front. Her voice sounded like her head was still between her legs. I giggled. I couldn't help it.

"I can't find the light. Hang on! Let me check in the storeroom!" Scarlet called back. She tapped me on the side of my head. "Behave."

"Yes, ma'am."

"I bought this to try—I've heard wonderful things about it, and you can get it cheaper at Country Mart than the price I have to sell it at," Scarlet said as she leaned down close to my ear. "Please don't tell anyone."

I smiled, crossed my heart, made a motion of locking my lips, and put the imaginary key down the front of my T-shirt, which said *All About Those Books*. Scarlet had my undying devotion at that point.

Cade walked into the back room and everything changed. "I'd like to know what that key goes to," he said.

His voice did things to me. I'd been relaxed and enjoying my new friendship more than I'd thought possible. Now I was all tense and tingly, his innuendo making my body feel flushed. I was glad my head was in a sink and other people were present.

I opened my eyes and looked into his heavenly hazel eyes, which looked more blue than green or gray today. Geez, I needed to get a grip. "How are things going, Mayor?" I asked, my tone more cynical than it should be.

Yet he still smiled. He was the perfect politician. A politician who kissed a girl and then turned to another. And he'd spread some pretty vicious lies to the sheriff about the well water at The Barn. I planned on getting answers . . . today.

"Good. I was just wondering if you and Scarlet were planning on having any of those book art classes you mentioned?"

"You're going to join us?" Somehow I couldn't see Cade making crafts. Scarlet couldn't either. She paused in the middle of applying a deep conditioner that smelled like macadamia nuts and looked back at Cade.

"My mom wants to take a class. Said it would do her good to get out."

Fuzz buckets. That was the last thing I'd expected to hear. Scarlet had the same reaction as I did. She turned back to me and pretended to be too busy with my hair. I closed my eyes and winced, as if she'd pulled my hair a little too roughly. That made her pull it for real and I winced again.

"Come on, she's not that bad," Cade tried to convince us. But we both knew better. They didn't call his mom P.S.A. Calloway for nothing. P.S.A. were her initials, as her name at birth was Penelope Southwark Allerton. But her nickname came from the public service announcements she gave everywhere she went. Each time, it had something to do with her husband's campaign or her son's football career.

In fact, when she was given the honor of announcing the homecoming court at a school assembly, she'd stopped right after the announcement of my homecoming princess nomination and given a P.S.A. for family planning.

I had nearly died of embarrassment while Cade hid his face, but the shaking of his shoulders proved he was laughing along with his football buddies. His dad and Coach had looked more than a little irritated.

When Scarlet and I didn't answer, Cade said, "It would mean the world to me."

Scarlet gave in first. She had the least to lose. "We're having one tomorrow night."

"We are?" I asked.

She nodded and said, "We're going to make pumpkins and Christmas trees."

I gave in and went with it. "The class will start at six-thirty. That'll give me time to close the shop and grab a bite to eat."

I peeked out my left eye. Cade kissed Scarlet on the cheek. I wasn't jealous. Much.

"You told me you were looking for a light."

I rolled my eyes up toward the doorway and saw Reba Sue, her long hair parted down the middle like a curtain you didn't want to pull all the way open. She was upside down from my vantage point, but I could tell she wasn't happy, even if she was trying to hide it from Cade.

"I forgot I'd left Charli back here to allow a deep moisturizer to set in her hair."

"What kind of light do you need? I can find it for you," Cade volunteered.

For a moment fear flashed in Reba Sue's eyes. The last thing she wanted was for Cade to know she might have lice.

I couldn't stop myself. "Scarlet thought—"

My new best friend yanked on my hair as she twisted two strands together. "That a new treatment would help with her split ends," Scarlet finished.

Reba Sue glared at me, but then turned the charm on for Cade. "Are you still picking me up at seven tomorrow night?"

All that heat I'd been feeling turned to ice.

Cade glanced at me, but I pretended to examine my nails. I really did need a manicure.

"I think I'll have to change it to seven-thirty. My mom needs a ride," he replied.

"Of course." Reba Sue's coy grin turned into a blinding smile.

I cussed in my head for my stupidity and closed my eyes. Cade was spreading lies about my well water and he was dating Reba Sue. There was no heat in a burned-out stove.

"Scarlet, Charli, I'll see you tomorrow at six-thirty." There was something in his voice that I couldn't read. Nor did I want to try.

I kept my eyes shut and replied, "Sure. We'll save your mom a seat."

I heard him walk out and could imagine the looks the other customers gave him. No doubt everyone watched his rear as he walked out of the store. Everyone except me.

"That man has one fine—" Reba Sue started.

"Ego," I interrupted.

"There's nothing wrong with an ego when the rest of the package can back it up," Reba Sue said. I could hear the smile in her voice. It made me want to barf.

I knew exactly what package Reba Sue was referring to, and if she'd seen Cade's package, she was a step ahead of me. Which really put me in a mean mood. "I like to open my presents and keep them a while. I don't want something that's been opened up by a bunch of other women and arrived at my doorstep soiled."

"Cade Calloway is not soiled," Reba Sue said.

"That's enough." Scarlet wrapped my hair in a plastic bag and sat me up straight.

"She started it," Reba Sue accused.

"You rubbed salt in her wounds and you know it," Scarlet replied. She pointed toward the doorway. "Don't argue with me, Reba Sue. Go sit in your chair and wait for me to come out there and finish your hair."

Reba Sue gulped and nodded. "I'll be waiting up front."

Once Reba Sue was out of sight, Scarlet said, "You need to know that tomorrow is the annual fund-raiser for the boosters at the high school."

"Why do I need to know that?" I asked, knowing darn good and well that Scarlet was trying to tell me about Cade's date with Reba Sue.

"They're honoring Cade and Reba Sue for all the work they do. It only makes sense that they go together."

"How nice," I said. Except it was anything but *nice*.

Chapter Twenty-six

By lunchtime I was bored. My hair was in a scarf while it absorbed the wonderful nutrients Scarlet had put on it, and I'd only had two customers to occupy my thoughts. When they weren't there, I thought about bad water and bad dates.

I really hoped Reba Sue and Cade had a bad date.

"Did you hear?"

I looked up from my phone, where I was searching the internet for the telltale signs of arsenic poisoning. Scarlet was doing that full-of-purpose walk that she and she alone had, straight toward the counter. She'd changed since the morning, when she'd been makeup free and looked like the girl next door. Now she looked like the rich girl in town, her hair in that Grace Kelly swoop she wore so well. Her makeup was applied to perfection, with eyeliner stretching out her eyes in the style so prevalent in the sixties and now again, thanks to Adele. She had on a vintage dress that hugged her curves in a soft light blue satin all the way down past her knees, which complemented her light complexion and her red hair. Her heels were nude but as high as a stepladder.

I looked down at the gray *Hooked on Books* T-shirt I'd changed into after getting my hair done. It matched my cutoffs and flip-flops perfectly. A sigh escaped. I needed to do something about my limited wardrobe. "Hear what?" I asked.

The door swished open and I waved at my neighboring business owner. With a quick "Hello," Betty the quilt maker, along with Mary and her daughter Aubrey, made a beeline for the second floor. To her credit, Aubrey looked about as uncomfortable as a chicken in a fox den. There was no way the teenager would ever want to work in The Barn again.

Scarlet started shaking her head. "You're going to see that a lot today."

"See what a lot?"

The door swished open and Franz walked in with his white baker's hat and jacket still on. He waved, then waddled as quickly as he could to the second floor.

"That," Scarlet said. "The newspaper ran an article about Scott Duncan's arrest and how he found literary gold in the loft of The Book Barn Princess. They hinted that there might be more."

The door swished open yet again and Mrs. Phelps, my old English teacher, walked in. Dressed in a suit with a knee-length skirt and a purse that she clutched in front of her, she headed for the stairs, but then stopped and approached the counter, her chunky heels clopping on the floor the entire way. "Hello, dear," she said over the top of her cat-eye glasses.

"Mrs. Phelps, it's so nice to see you."

"Thank you, dear. I've been meaning to come by to ask if you had any old dictionaries or encyclopedia sets you could donate to the school. I'd like my students to be able to have a real reference book on hand instead of just the internet for their final papers. It's an exercise in old fashioned research and when their papers are complete, they must submit a hard copy instead of uploading them. They're lucky I don't make them use typewriters."

I nodded, understanding her desire to have them do off-line research papers. "I've seen several sets, but I'm not sure where they are. Could I box them up and bring them to the school later?"

"Oh, that would be lovely, dear. Thank you. There should already be a box of dictionaries around here that Bobby Ray was saving for me."

"I'll be sure to bring those as well," I assured her.

"Your father would be so proud of you." She scrunched her shoulders and her nose up at the same time and smiled while holding the handle of her purse up to her chest. "I'm just going to have a peek at what's available in the loft."

Scarlet's eyes rolled back in her head.

I grinned. "Help yourself, Mrs. Phelps."

As she walked away, Scarlet whispered, "People think you've got a treasure chest upstairs."

I shrugged. "Let them. It's good for business."

"Well, that's not what I came to tell you. Mateo has Scott Duncan on a seventy-two-hour hold for investigation of theft, right?"

"Yeah, we knew that last night." My response caused Scarlet to wave at me to lower my voice while she gave furtive glances over her shoulder as Vicki and Gwen entered the store. The two women smiled and then slunk their shoulders and headed for the stairway like everyone else.

I was beginning to think the whole town was two rocks short of a box.

Scarlet leaned in farther. "But we didn't know he would be serving a search warrant on Scott's house and that the search warrant also covered evidence linking Scott to Marlene's murder." Her eyes sparkled with excitement.

The sadness of it all, however, was starting to take a toll on me. "Wow" was all I could muster.

She pulled back, forgetting her earlier desire to keep our conversation on the down low. "*Wow*? Is that all you're going to say?"

"What do you want me to say?"

"Maybe you could start with *thank God they're getting closer to catching Marlene's killer.*"

I shrugged. "That's kind of a given."

"But?" Scarlet wasn't about to let it go.

I paused as two more customers entered the store. The two football players, who promptly made their way to the stairs, completely ignored me on their way up to the second floor. If they weren't on their lunch break, they were definitely skipping school . . . to come to the bookstore. Which was even odder, considering they were going to be in a world of hurt if Coach showed up as planned to work on the faucet in the tearoom for me.

"Don't you think it's sad? If Mr. Duncan killed Marlene, that means he probably did it over a book." I pointed out.

"A very valuable book."

"But it's a book!" I walked out from behind the counter and went into the tearoom. Instead of making tea, I grabbed a bottle of water and held it out to Scarlet. She shook her head and continued to look at me. I closed the fridge and opened the bottle, taking a big drink before I answered.

"Don't you think President Roosevelt would rather not have published his book than have it be the cause of an innocent woman's murder?"

I could tell Scarlet wasn't quite on the same page by the way she inspected her nails. "President Roosevelt has been dead for almost a hundred years. I don't think he really much cares."

"But he would care if he knew it when he wrote it. I don't think he would have signed it if he'd known that tiny little signature would become so valuable that someone might kill to get it."

"He was a man. Men don't look at things like that. Especially men of wealth and power. Do you think the mayor would look at it like that?"

"Which one?" J. C. would have signed it a dozen times.

Scarlet rolled her eyes. "We only have one."

"Well, yeah, but when someone says *the mayor*, I tend to think of the senior Calloway."

"What about the young Calloway?" said a masculine voice.

We both jumped. I wobbled on my flip-flops and dropped my bottle of water. Scarlet managed to maintain her balance in her five-inch heels.

"OMW, Cade Calloway! You nearly scared us out of our panties!" she exclaimed.

Cade made his way into the tearoom and grinned. "Now that would be a sight to see."

Scarlet swatted him on the arm and it was my turn to roll my eyes. It was either that or notice how good he looked in a button-down dress shirt and slacks. I grabbed a dish towel from the counter. "What are you doing here?" My question came out harsher than I'd intended, but I'd already seen him once that day and that was more than enough.

"Why are you so mad?" Cade asked.

I indicated the mess in front of me and the man had the audacity to laugh.

He *laughed*.

I threw the towel in his face, which only made him laugh harder.

"Really, Charli," Scarlet said, "that's no way to treat the mayor of our fine town."

"He's not acting like a mayor. He caused this mess by sneaking up on us, so he can clean it." That was what I made my five-year-olds do.

Cade bowed, sweeping his arm out like we were in Regency England, not modern-day Hazel Rock. "I'd be happy to assist."

I picked up my bottle, resisted throwing it at him as well, and put it in the recycle bin. Then I decided to finally confront him about the rumor he was spreading about the water at The Barn. But first I got him a tall glass of ice water for his trouble and set it down firmly on the table in front of him.

"I'll trade you," I suggested, watching his face to see if he would crack under pressure.

"Uh . . . thank you, but I'm not really that thirsty." It was as close to a confession as I needed.

"Don't be ridiculous," I countered. "It's already in the nineties and it's only ten o'clock. I can see the sweat beading on your brow."

Cade looked at the water as if it was going to kill him.

"So it's true," I said.

"Huh?"

I picked up the glass and held it up between us. "You weren't just spreading rumors. The water is contaminated."

Cade eyed the glass. "I did hear that, yes."

I walked over to the sink and dumped the water down the drain. "Why would my daddy let me live here and not tell me the water was contaminated?"

It was Cade's turn to sound irritated. "How would Bobby Ray know about the water when you were the one who received the notice from the health department?"

I blinked, but that didn't change the look of irritation on Cade's face. "I didn't receive any notice."

"That's not what I heard," he accused.

"Heard from whom?"

Cade's tone was still more accusatory than I cared for. "Are you saying you aren't trying to hide the fact that the report on the well water came back positive for arsenic?"

"I haven't seen any report from the health department since I've been back. In fact, the only time I got the mail was when Reba Sue . . . when Reba Sue brought it in for me."

Scarlet's hand flew to her chest. I'd completely forgotten she was there. "OMW. She wouldn't."

Cade was a little slow with his responses, but he knew he was up the creek with a fork for a paddle. "What?" he asked, looking back and forth between us.

I'd seen that look on his face before. When I was seventeen and he broke up with me because I was bad for his reputation. It was a lie then and Cade Calloway was definitely lying to me now. It was as plain as a gator on a golf course. Reba Sue was the one who told him The Barn's water was contaminated.

The decade fell away, like that rare fog lifting off the river. Cade and I were left standing in the courtyard, water from the fountain trickling in the background. I was looking up into his face, so worried that something was wrong with his mom or dad, or that maybe he'd somehow flunked a test and his grades were going to affect his chances of being recruited by the right teams. My arms looped around his waist and pulled him tight against my body. Wearing only cutoffs and a bikini top, I was sure I could draw him out of his shell. But his arms stayed at his side, his eyes never met mine, and Cade Calloway said the worst thing I'd ever heard:

"Charli, the Tide turned me down. The recruiter called me and said it was because I had a tendency to get mixed up with the wrong people."

I'd laughed. A young, naïve, and foolish girl who didn't understand what he was saying. "That's insane. You're a Calloway. The Tide wouldn't know a good quarterback if he knocked their noses off with a bullet pass for a touchdown."

Knowing Alabama wasn't his first choice, I tried to ease the blow and stood up on my tippy toes to kiss him. He turned away and my lips met his cheek. At that moment my stomach turned. I knew rejection by the Tide would sting his ego, but this was bigger than that. What he said next shattered everything I'd ever thought love would be.

"I can't see you anymore. I can't get caught skinny-dipping, I can't be found sleeping in my car because I drank too much with my girlfriend to drive us home, I can't get you out of jail for trespassing on county property. Every bit of trouble I've been in was because I dated the wrong type of girl."

I dropped my arms from his waist. He still wouldn't look at me. His fingers raked through his dark curls as he turned away.

"You're making that up. Why are you li—" I started.

That was all I got out before he turned to me and yelled, "This is my career! My dream! Football is my life . . . not you!" He walked away with purposeful steps toward the vintage Camaro parked in the street. His parting words spilling tears down my cheeks. "Good-bye, Charli Rae."

I'd watched him leave in a cloud of dust as he spun the tires on his car, eager to get away from me. It was the first time in my life I hadn't fought for what I wanted. What I believed in.

I shook my head and returned to the present. Now I faced Cade on behalf of the girl I used to be. "You've never been able to lie to me, Cade Calloway. Reba Sue started the rumor about the water in The Barn being bad, didn't she?"

Cade didn't say a word.

"And the rats? Was that her as well?"

"I don't know what you want me to say, Charli." Cade's voice was low, dangerous. He could have been mad at Reba Sue. Or me, or the world. I couldn't tell.

One thing was certain, I was madder than a rabid dog at Cade Calloway.

"Ahhh, maybe I should go?" Scarlet eased toward the stall door of the tearoom.

I ignored her, too caught up in the emotions I'd held in check for so many years. "I wasn't the cause of the Tide turning you down. Your parents were. They knew you'd turn tail and run as soon as one recruiter even mentioned my existence."

"Now hold on, Charli Rae. . . ."

But I was on a roll. I poked him in the chest. "That recruiter from the Tide was your second cousin."

"I didn't know that!"

"Initially, no. But you suspected something was up. And when my daddy told you—"

Cade met my anger with a bit of his own. "Bobby Ray told me that I was a bad influence on you the night he took me to get stitches in my head. That I was going to *ruin* your future. That you wouldn't go to college if—"

"If he got you barefoot and pregnant."

None of us had seen or heard the middle-aged man wearing a cowboy hat and boots join us in the tearoom. We all turned to look at the man I'd missed more than I cared to admit.

He took off his hat and ran his hand through hair that wasn't quite as thick as I remembered it. The gray at his temples made me realize how many years I'd missed and would never get back. He held his hat in front of him, his head tilted downward, acknowledging the error of his ways.

His shoulders weren't as straight as they'd been when I'd left. Instead, they were rounded with age catching up to him. Yet he was still an attractive man, still appeared lean and strong in his blue denim shirt and Levi's.

"Daddy?" My voice quivered. I hated this show of weakness when I'd just now gotten my strength back, but it was there.

"I'm glad you're home, Princess."

Little feet scurried across The Barn floor and a squeal echoed through the store. Dad smiled and was about to bend down and pick up his little pink friend when, like a dream ending too soon, we were interrupted.

"Bobby Ray Warren."

Through misty eyes, I saw my daddy's shoulders slump. He patted the little rodent at his feet and then stood up straight. He turned and faced the sheriff standing in the doorway.

"You're under arrest for the murder of Marlene Duncan," Mateo said.

My father nodded his head and held out his wrists without saying a word. For a second I almost read his actions as those of a guilty man. Then I recognized them for what they were: acquiescence. He was giving up without a fight.

I rushed forward, but Cade held me back. "You have Scott Duncan in custody for her murder!" I yelled.

Mateo clinked the cuffs on my dad's wrists with a look of sorrow on his face. "I have Scott Duncan in custody for criminal trespass and felony theft."

"But you served a search warrant on Scott's house." I yanked myself out of Cade's grip.

"Charli, Scott didn't do it," my father said.

Cade moved forward, his voice stern with warning. "Don't say another word, Bobby Ray."

"I'm not going to let an innocent man go to jail for the murder of the woman he loved—" my father started to stay.

Cade stopped him. "Bobby Ray—"

"As my friend, let me have my piece." My father straightened his shoulders and sealed his fate. "Scott Duncan was in Dallas trying to broker a deal for the sale of volumes one and two of Teddy Roosevelt's *African Game Trails* on the day Marlene was murdered. I'd left them out on the counter and Aubrey put them in a box of old books up in the loft. Marlene and I were in the process of searching for them and we sent Scott to meet with the buyer in Dallas with a different book to buy us more time. He left The Barn before I did the morning she died."

"But Mr. Duncan was never on the video from Scarlet's shop," I said. "He must have tricked you and—"

Dad interrupted again. "If you're talking about having a video of the front door from Scarlet's place, it won't show the side door. We hadn't opened The Barn yet. Scott went out the side door and I locked it after he left."

"Let's go, Bobby Ray." Mateo led my father toward the side door of The Barn. At some point the customers had come down from the second floor. Now they stood lined up, watching the sheriff lead my father out of the store. If it wasn't for them, I'm not sure I wouldn't have jumped on Mateo's back. Instead, humiliation and fear slapped me in the face. People from town were standing inside our Barn, eating up the gossip like a bass swallowing a whole school of juicy minnows.

"What are you looking at?" I screamed.

Cade grabbed my arm and tried to stop me. "Charli—"

But I yanked my arm away and stalked over to them, ready to lose every bit of ground I'd gained with the community that stood silently watching.

"Princess."

I froze. He'd given me the name at birth. And when he used it, it meant something completely different. It was full of love and kindness. Wonder and awe.

None of which I deserved at the moment.

I turned to my daddy, tears streaming down my face.

"It'll be all right. Everything works out in the end."

We stood there for a moment. Reliving the past. The good years. No, the great years with my mom. The hard years without her. And the healing years with just the two of us. And then the empty years we'd wasted . . . over mistakes we couldn't take back.

"I love you, Daddy." I wasn't sure, because I was blinded by my own tears, but I thought he was crying as well.

The crack in his voice told me I was right. "I love you more, Princess. I love you more."

Mateo put his hand on my dad's shoulder and my father turned away and walked out the door. Princess squealed, a sad, pathetic sound.

This time my daddy was the one who didn't look back, and both of his princesses were left in the dust.

Chapter Twenty-seven

I rubbed my eyes with the heels of my hands, knowing I'd given the crowd around me the show of a lifetime.

The hand on my back caused me to jump. Sugar, the waitress from the bar who'd aimed the beer at my face, stood in front of me with tears in her eyes. Her hair wasn't big. In fact, it had a cowboy hat covering it and her makeup wasn't heavy. Her one crooked white tooth made her seem friendly. Her outfit looked similar to mine, except her T-shirt said O.Mg—a nerdy take on the chemical properties of oxygen and magnesium. I wanted to laugh, but I knew if I started, I might lose control and never stop.

"Everything is going to work out, just like Bobby Ray said," she assured me.

I sniffed and took a tissue that magically appeared in front of me. I looked up into the eyes of Mary and her daughter Aubrey.

"She's right." The hairdresser's voice sounded like more gravel had been added to the mix since that morning at Scarlet's beauty salon.

I saw the big antique mailbox for my daddy's defense fund was being passed through the crowd. Person after person dug in their pockets, wallets, and purses and added to the fund. My brow wrinkled and I knew I was on the verge of losing it again.

They weren't here to get the latest gossip or gawk and make fun. They'd been shocked into silence when Mateo put the cuffs on my daddy—and I'd yelled at them.

"I'm sorry," I croaked.

Scarlet, appropriately enough, was the first one to comment. "Sawl-right." I couldn't help but smile. Everyone laughed.

Cade made his way through the crowd. "I'll go see what I can do for Bobby Ray," he said.

I hated to say it, but my dad needed an attorney, and there was only one in town. "Don't you think we should get your daddy involved?" I asked.

Cade grinned. "No need."

"But..."

"I'm an attorney, Princess."

"You are?"

"You don't think the town would be stupid enough to vote for him if he wasn't, do you?" This time it was Coach Purcell adding to the dialogue. I had no idea when he'd arrived, but I honestly didn't care. These people were my dad's friends—my friends.

I hesitated, and another laugh rose through the crowd.

I sniffed and smiled. "No, sir, I don't. But I want to come with you," I insisted.

Cade shook his head. "Bobby Ray is on a seventy-two-hour hold. The only visitor he's entitled to see is his attorney."

I swallowed down the lump threatening to strangle me. Cade rubbed my biceps, his smile barely tipping up the corners of his mouth. "He's going to be okay. I'll let you know what's going on."

I nodded and he turned and went out the door.

The rest of the day I rang sales behind the counter. Scarlet brought cookies from the bakery and Sugar stayed to serve and sell bottled drinks in the tearoom. I'll admit, I watched her closely. The last thing I needed was a drink to be thrown on one of my customers, but to my relief, Sugar behaved.

Somehow word spread throughout the day and it was like the entire county came out to support the store and my dad. Although most of them searched through the used books on the second floor like it was a treasure hunt, they still bought one or more books and deposited generous donations in my dad's defense fund.

By the time The Barn closed, I was exhausted and ready for bed. I still hadn't heard from Cade and was more than a little on edge. I locked up the front door and balanced the register. We'd made almost four hundred dollars in sales and I'd emptied the defense fund jar twice throughout the day, stuffing the money in a grocery bag under the counter. I grabbed the bag of money I had yet to count and made my way to the back room. I planned to stash the money until I could deposit it in the bank in the morning. As I opened the curtain, something scurried in front of me and hit my feet. I yelped and tripped, falling into a stack of boxes. I was down on the floor before I could blink.

Princess came over and twitched her nose in my face.

"Fuzz buckets! You're the biggest rat in the state of Texas, Princess." She nudged my hand and walked over to scoot around the money I'd scattered all over the floor.

But I had my mind on other things. Mostly that I was in the spot Marlene had died. And partly I was thinking about cooties—the dead body kind.

I rolled away, knocking the teetering boxes over on top of me, trapping me on the spot even more. I struggled to stand up and, in doing so, moved the last box away from the shelving unit and found myself looking directly at the store's safe. The one I'd been trying to locate for days.

I pushed the last box aside and hopped to my feet. Brushing imaginary or real germs off my body, I pushed aside books, boxes, and money with my feet and cleared a path to the safe's door.

"Why in the world would Daddy put it in here?" I asked no one in particular.

Princess scurried away, no doubt ready to go out for the night through her pet door in the back of The Barn.

Turning my attention to the safe, I tried the combination I still remembered from my youth, mostly because it was my birthday and my mom's combined. The safe opened on the first try. The contents, however, had me stumped.

The safe was a sizable lockbox, three feet tall and three feet wide. It sat at least as deep and stuck out from the shelves. It would have taken forever to move, even if my dad used the three-wheeler. And yet, it appeared as if he'd wanted to hide it the way he'd had boxes upon boxes of books stacked around it to keep it hidden from view.

All of that effort to hide even more books inside. It didn't make sense.

Until I got down on my knees and took a closer look. They weren't just any books. Like the two Scott Duncan had taken, these books were old—and also authored by Teddy Roosevelt. Leather bound with rich gold lettering, the first book I removed took my breath away when I opened it. Although it was thin, *The Strenuous*

Life was a collection of essays written by the President about how to have a successful political and personal life. And it was dedicated to the president's son, Quentin Roosevelt, who'd died in France during the first World War. There, in clear but slightly faded ink below the dedication was the signature of the twenty-sixth president of the United States. I couldn't believe my eyes.

I moved on to the next book and found a fourth book by Roosevelt, entitled *Big Game Hunting in the Rockies*. The topic didn't interest me in the least, the photographs even less, but the inscription to a Mary Alice Bradshaw, offering her his kindest regards, was signed again with that signature I was beginning to recognize: Theodore Roosevelt.

"How in the world did you get these books, Daddy?"

Obviously, he didn't answer. I finished pulling out several more books, all by presidents, all first or limited editions, and all signed. Just looking at them made my heart palpitate.

The curtain swished open and I nearly jumped out of my skin.

"Geez Louise, Cade. You should know better than to scare me like that."

A smile turned up the corners of his mouth, but then they flatlined when he saw the books in my hands. "What are you doing with all the dead presidents?"

"What?"

He wasn't the least bit put out. Instead, he repeated his question. "I'm going to ask you again. What are you doing with my father's dead presidents collection?"

"They're not all dead."

"They were before he added the one by Carter."

I looked at the books. Abraham Lincoln, John F. Kennedy, Richard Nixon, and Jimmy Carter were there with Theodore Roosevelt. "Anyone looking over my shoulder would know that," I argued. Poorly.

"*A Strenuous Life* is dedicated to Roosevelt's son. *Big Game Hunting* is dedicated to Mary Alice Bradshaw. Abraham Lincoln's is simply signed and John F. Kennedy's and Jimmy Carter's are signed 'to my mother.' Nixon's is signed 'to my father.'"

"I get it. You've seen these before." I put everything down carefully on the floor and stood up.

"I haven't just seen them. They're part of my parents' estate. So could you please explain to me why you have them?" Cade folded his arms across his chest.

I decided it was time to come clean. He was after all my father's attorney. "They were in my dad's safe."

Cade nodded. "The Roosevelts, Nixon, and Carter."

"And both Bushes and Obama," I added, pointing to the other three books on the floor.

"Nothing from Harrison or Washington?"

"George Washington?" I said incredulously.

Cade's voice was steady. "The one and only."

I shook my head, wondering what I would have done if I'd seen George Washington's signature.

Cade looked troubled. "At least he didn't take the most expensive ones."

I wasn't sure I'd heard him correctly. "Excuse me?"

"Look, I've known your dad for many years. I know he's not capable of murder. But I know my dad just as well—even better when it comes to finances. And I can tell you, J. C. Calloway Senior is not capable of giving up anything worth that amount of money. Not to someone he likes, let alone a man he barely speaks to."

It was my turn to cross my arms and tighten my jaw. "What exactly are you saying, Cade Calloway?"

He stopped pacing and looked me straight in the eye. "I'm saying that you're in possession of stolen property."

"You know this for a fact?"

"My father would have told me if he'd sold his collection. And I seriously doubt he'd use The Book Barn Princess as a broker to sell them. Let me take them back to my father and it will stay between the two of us."

"Wait . . ." I held my hands out to stop him from coming closer. Cade listened while I tried to figure out things that just weren't adding up.

"What if Marlene took these?" I asked.

"How?"

Frustrated, I raised my voice an octave. "I don't know. The same way you think my daddy did?"

"Okay, what if?" Cade waited for me to come up with an answer.

I snapped my fingers and smiled. "Scott Duncan was caught taking books out of The Barn last night. What if he was working with Marlene and the two of them stole them from your parents? Then, after Marlene died, Mr. Duncan was trying to get all the books back?"

Cade hesitated, thinking about what I'd said. "What books did Scott take?"

"*The African Game Trails* by Theodore Roosevelt, volumes one and two. Marlene was also cheating on my dad with Mr. Duncan," I added.

Apparently, that was something Cade hadn't heard before. "What makes you say that?"

"Scarlet heard talk at the beauty shop."

"We know firsthand how false gossip can spread in this town."

"Except I verified some of it with Dean McAlister."

"Dean?"

"Yeah. The gossip was that Marlene was cheating on my daddy with Dean, Mr. Duncan, and Mike Thompson."

Cade was surprised by my revelation but had trouble with one name in particular. The same name I couldn't wrap my head around.

"Mike Thompson? Come on . . ." he said.

"He has the best hair in town and, according to Joe, he sings like a dream."

"I suppose." Cade still looked skeptical.

"Anyway, Dean said Marlene was like him: unable to commit to one person. So what if Mr. Duncan stole the books and Marlene was hiding them here at the store? But then my daddy found out about the two of them conducting more than business and made Marlene return the books. That would tick Mr. Duncan off enough that he just might kill Marlene and take the books for himself."

Cade was shaking his head before I finished.

"What?"

"You're reaching mighty far, Charli. There's no evidence—"

"There's no evidence against my daddy either," I argued. I stopped when I saw the expression on his face. "What aren't you telling me?"

"There is evidence against Bobby Ray."

"What? The fact that he was the last one to see her alive? That doesn't mean anything."

"There are four sets of DNA on the belt that was wrapped around Marlene's neck. Hers, yours, your daddy's, and a fourth belonging to an unidentified person."

"But that's it! It's Mr. Duncan's."

Cade shook his head. "I suspect it's my DNA."

"How could your DNA . . ." I remembered the night in his car, when he'd wrapped up my hands. It obviously showed on my face.

He smiled sadly. "Yeah, I liked to play with your belt."

"You liked to take my belt off," I argued. "But that was over ten years ago."

"A simple swab will tell."

"But you're representing my father. You didn't volunteer to give a DNA sample, did you?"

"No, but it's only a matter of time before Mateo asks for it. And once he does, I won't be able to represent Bobby Ray anymore."

"So you're telling me if I tell Mateo about these books . . ."

"It's potentially further motive for your dad to kill Marlene."

It was exactly what I didn't want to hear. "Aren't you obligated to tell Mateo about it?" I asked.

"Eventually, I'll have to."

And there it was. The truth was standing between us like a mine-field ready to explode, but the only thing that would be damaged was my heart and the life of a man who wasn't even there.

Chapter Twenty-eight

I awoke to Princess in my face. For a moment I thought I was in the swamps of south Texas with an alligator ready to swallow me whole. I almost knocked her off the bed.

"Fuzz buckets, Princess. You nearly scared the living daylights out of me."

I squinted, noticing the sun hadn't come up. The only light in the room was from the moon and the alarm clock. Princess twitched her nose and tossed her head, as if she was telling me to follow her, then moseyed down to the end of the bed where I couldn't see her and dropped to the floor with a thud.

There was a second thud that made my eyes nearly pop out of my skull. It'd come from inside the store. I jumped up and grabbed my daddy's baseball bat, which I'd hidden underneath the bed. I looked down, expecting Princess to take the lead as she'd done the last time someone was sneaking around, but this time she seemed to be waiting for me.

"Thanks for nothing," I muttered.

She chattered back and I got the distinct impression she was telling me to be thankful she'd woken me at all.

I had to give her that. "I do appreciate you waking me. I just wish you'd done it before whoever that is arrived."

I grabbed my cell phone and dialed 911 as we walked through the kitchen.

"911, what's your emergency?" asked a deadpan voice on the other line.

"There's a burglar inside The Book Barn Princess at 127 Main Street, Hazel Rock."

"Are you calling from inside the store?"

"No, I'm calling from the adjoining apartment," I whispered. Princess and I were approaching the bookcase in my dad's bedroom when a thud on the other side made her jump straight up in the air.

Irritated, I swung my hand at her, wishing she'd knock it off. She squeaked and toddled off in the opposite direction.

So much for backup.

"Do you have deputies close?" I asked.

"They're at least ten minutes away, at an accident scene on Highway 287."

Another bump in the night made my heart skip. I knew the officers wouldn't get there in time. Whoever was in the store sounded like they were moving toward the stairs at a fast rate.

"They need to get here now, 'cause whoever it is, is leaving."

"Ma'am, do not—"

I clicked off the phone. There was no way that scumbucket was going to get away again. Not in my lifetime.

I slipped the phone down the front of my tank top and cringed as it dropped to the floor. I froze and listened to the silence on the other side of the bookcase. I could picture my burglar standing at the top of the steps, waiting for me to walk away.

"Not a chance, scumbag!" I yelled.

I pushed the bookcase door open. It stopped abruptly and I ran into the wall, smashing my nose with the bat. "Son of a schoolmarm!"

I heard footsteps on the stairs in the bookstore and then someone stumbling and rolling down to the bottom with a splat. I pushed on the bookshelf again, ready to do whatever it took to bring the killer to justice and save my dad. The shelf gave an inch. Not even enough for me to get my fingers through to flip the light switch and see enough to identify the burglar.

I pushed again but got nowhere. Then the bell on the side door of The Barn began to jingle. I turned around and ran through the bedroom and out to the living room. Once I finally got the door open and stepped outside, I heard the gate slam and saw a shadow run in the direction of the river. I flew down the steps. Literally hanging on to the railing with one hand, I was on the ground in three hops. I rounded the railing and ran toward the backyard, my bat ready to whack the SOB straight to detention.

I finally got a glimpse of his shadow and was surprised by his size. He was shorter and rounder than me but was moving like a track star. I picked up my pace but felt as if I'd already run a marathon. Inhaling huge, deep breaths for all I was worth, I swore at that elliptical back in my apartment in Denver that had made me believe I was cut out for this type of activity.

We were behind the quilt shop when I finally heard sirens in the distance. Unfortunately, so did the guy I was chasing. His pace increased as he headed for the privacy fence at the end of the lot. If he made it over the top before I got to him, he'd be home free.

He hit the fence with a leap almost as graceful as a deer in the moonlight. He only made it halfway over the fence, however, and struggled to hoist himself completely over.

I poured every ounce of energy into my gait and was within an arm's length of reaching my goal.

I grabbed his shirt and pulled as he reached the top of the fence. The fence creaked and with a loud crack it came crashing down. So did my suspect.

On top of me. For several minutes I saw stars. I gasped for breath that wasn't there and felt a soft, squishy human being on top of me. He groaned.

I could hear someone yelling my name. A light flashed before my eyes and was gone a moment later. I didn't know if my assailant had a firearm or a knife, but his body was definitely smushing the life right out of me.

I gasped like a fish but didn't succeed in getting anything but a mouthful of hair. Soft, curly hair. Satiny smooth with a scent so rich it smelled like I was dying in a bed of flowers.

Mike Thompson. I felt a sense of satisfaction that I'd figured it out but an even bigger feeling of failure that I was going to die with the secret locked inside me, unable to communicate with anyone.

Mike groaned on top of me.

I promptly bit down on his ear.

He yelped and rolled off. I sucked in air like a dehydrated dog lapping imaginary water in a desert. It wasn't pretty.

A light shone in my eyes, causing me to blink.

"She's alive!" I heard Mateo say.

"Thank God," replied Mike. "I thought she was road pizza."

I pointed at the man who'd broken into my store and said, "Arrest him! He broke into The Barn."

The sheriff didn't hesitate. "Mike, you're under arrest for breaking and entering."

My head flopped back on the ground. As soon as I could breathe, I'd let the sheriff know it was murder, not burglary.

Chapter Twenty-nine

$\mathbf{M}$ike Thompson had an alibi.

Not for the breaking and entering but for Marlene's murder. He'd been recording a country music album when Marlene was killed. Tonight, however, he'd been trying to steal one of the president books because he needed money to finish the record.

When I asked him if he'd ever heard of YouTube, Mateo escorted me back to the bookstore, with Mike in tow, wearing steel bracelets.

"Do you want to press charges?" he asked when we were seated back inside the store.

I looked at my muddy tank top and filthy boxers. Then I looked at the broken window in my door.

"I'll take that as a yes," he said.

"Take that as a hel—"

"An emphatic yes," Scarlet said as she walked in the door looking like a million bucks.

Mateo couldn't help staring at her and I didn't blame him. It was either that or look down at my filthy PJ's again. Which neither of us had any desire to do. I made my way to the counter and grabbed some hand sanitizer from under the register.

"What are you doing up at this hour?" I asked Scarlet.

"I heard the commotion and decided you need this more than I do," she said and set a black and yellow Taser on the counter.

"Put that away," I said, pushing it back toward my friend.

"You either take this or I bring my gun over for you to keep."

"You wouldn't."

She cocked her head and lifted her left eyebrow. "I would."

"We're talking about a gun that's registered, aren't we?" Mateo asked.

"Always, Sheriff. No vigilantes here," Scarlet assured him.

I looked at Mateo, who in turn was studiously studying his notepad, and shoved the Taser under the counter. Then I pursed my lips and growled at Scarlet, who just grinned at me in return. Obviously, I'd lost the argument before she'd crossed the street.

"I'll show you how to use it tomorrow. Just realize that it's charged and fully capable of discharging if you release the safety and pull the trigger," she said.

"You're scaring me."

"The amount of visitors you've had is scaring me."

I couldn't argue with her there.

An hour later Mateo had carted Mike off to the station, Scarlet had gone home, and The Barn was locked up tight, with cardboard covering the window Mike had broken. I'd taken a shower and was back in bed. Princess was the only one who had decided to stay outdoors. I couldn't blame her. There seemed to be fewer predators outside.

I woke up early the next morning despite being up late. My dad's preliminary hearing was set for nine a.m., still two hours away. Instead of pacing back and forth and watching the clock tick off minutes too slowly for my sanity, I went down to the bookstore. First on my agenda was to make a sign stating we would be closed for the day in honor of Marlene Duncan's funeral. Once that was done, I boxed up all the encyclopedias and dictionaries I could find to drop off at the high school for Mrs. Phelps. Then I got started on my last task before leaving. I got the two-wheeler and as many boxes together as I could gather up. Aubrey and Darrin had agreed to load up the memorial items that were left for Marlene at the front door and take them to the cemetery immediately following the ceremony. Unfortunately, the funeral was set for ten-thirty, so my attendance depended on the length of the court proceedings.

A knock on the door made me jump and grab my chest. Coach was on the other side of the glass, holding two eight-foot-tall pieces of lumber. One of these days I'd stop jumping at the littlest things.

"Good morning, Princess," he said when I opened the door.

"Coach, I'm sorry, did we . . ." I started.

"I need to work with my hands today," he explained. "The sheriff told me you needed a new pane of glass and I thought I'd start building this table. It'll help keep me busy."

"I can't stay." I hadn't planned on the second table even being started for several months . . . at least not until after I returned to Denver.

"Do you mind if I stay?" he asked. "I just can't bring myself to go to the funeral."

What could I say? The man had done so much for me, my dad, and The Barn. If he needed to work through his sorrow and frustration, who was I to stop him? "As long as you don't mind being here by yourself and locking up when you leave."

Coach smiled as if I'd just handed him the state championship. "Deal. Don't you worry your pretty little head about it. Your door will be fixed in no time flat."

"Thank you." I didn't want to tell him I could fix it myself, because honestly, finding the time was becoming a real problem.

He patted my arm. "You go about your business and I'll have it fixed in a jiffy."

Guilt made me hesitate. "I have to leave to go to court, and I was planning on going to Marlene's service right after that."

Coach nodded. "I'll lock up when I'm done. Tell your daddy I'm thinking about him."

"Thank you." I hugged the big bear of a man, who turned red as a pomegranate. "Go on, now."

I smiled and headed for the apartment to change, which took all of thirty minutes. Wearing my black dress and a pair of black flats I'd left behind at seventeen because they'd gone out of style ten years ago, I looked in the mirror. My curls had turned out perfectly, but I'd decided to go with a more unadventurous style and wear my hair up in a tight knot at the base of my skull with a crystal comb. I finished the outfit off by tying one of my mom's scarves around my neck.

I couldn't do much more to play the part of loyal, upstanding citizen, daughter of the accused.

When I arrived at the courthouse, the parking lot was full. I parked Dean's Honda on the street and prayed I wouldn't get a ticket. I entered the courthouse, went through the metal detector, and found myself surrounded by the people of Hazel Rock. Coach and Scarlet, who was touching up Marlene's makeup and hair for her funeral, weren't there, but Betty the quilt maker was, along with her always-present sidekick, Franz. Dean winked as he escorted Sugar into the courtroom. She was dressed in a long floral dress that went past her knees but didn't hide her voluptuous shape.

Aubrey and Darrin were holding hands, looking totally freaked out by the proceedings, and Joellen came up and hugged me hello. We made our way to the courtroom as a group. When the doors opened, Cade looked up from his place at the defense table on the left.

I counted my lucky stars he wasn't sitting on the right.

Cade smiled and walked over to the railing that separated the crowd from the attorneys and the defendant. Dressed in a navy blue suit and tie, his white shirt was crisp and clean. It was the first time I'd seen him as a real lawyer.

It was kind of scary to be so grown-up.

"Everything's going to be okay," he said.

I nodded.

"I spoke to your father—"

"How is he? Is he okay?" I interrupted, too scared to wait for him to get to the point.

"He's fine." Cade let his voice carry so the entire courtroom could hear. "Bobby Ray wanted you to know there's nothing wrong with the water at The Book Barn Princess. The inspection came out better than the city water. And there are no pest issues to worry about either."

I smiled, appreciating his subtle way of spreading the word through town. "Thank you," I said.

"And I owe you an apology. It seems my dad gave the president books to your father after all."

"He *gave* them to him?"

"Apparently, my father is getting soft in his old age. He felt bad for running Bobby Ray's only child out of town. He thought the presidents would make it up to him."

"I'm surprised my dad took them," I said.

"He told J. C. he was only taking them to invest in your future. I wish you could have seen the George Washington signature."

"Wait—what? J. C. even gave him his George Washington?"

Cade nodded. "It seems so. Guilt can be a mighty powerful emotion. That's what your dad wanted to take care of before he spoke with Mateo. He sold it yesterday morning."

I was pretty sure it hurt Cade to say that. I couldn't imagine having a real autograph of George Washington's and *selling* it.

But my daddy had and it gave me hope for making his bond.

The door at the side of the courtroom opened and my dad was brought out in an orange jumpsuit.

"I've got to get to work." Cade squeezed my arm and then left to talk to my daddy. I watched him lean over and whisper something in my dad's ear, he nodded, and Cade patted him on the shoulder before sitting down.

I finally caught my dad's eye and he smiled, genuinely happy to see me.

I may have blubbered a bit; seeing him in that position was pretty overwhelming. Cade looked over his shoulder and winced. Betty was beside me with a quilted hankie in no time flat.

"All rise!" the bailiff shouted.

Betty pulled me out of the aisle to stand in the second row with Franz. Everyone rose to their feet as the judge was announced. "The Forty-second District Court of Texas is now in session. Honorable Judge Jacob Sperry presiding. There will be no talking in the court-room. You may be seated."

Everyone started to sit. I stood staring at the white-haired man in the black robe who had more wrinkles than a skinny Shar-Pei.

"Holy crap, I thought you were dead," I blurted out.

The crowd gasped.

Out of my peripheral vision I saw Cade drop his head into the palm of his hand, but I couldn't look away from the bench.

The bailiff took a step in my direction, ready to throw me out of the courtroom.

No one had prepared me for this. I'd really thought the man was dead.

But he wasn't. The judge looked over the top of dark-framed glasses and stared me down.

"I should have known you would return to Texas. Have a seat, Ms. Warren. You're in *my* courtroom now."

I waited for the scripture, but it never came.

Betty grabbed my arm and pulled me down into my seat. The Honorable Jacob Sperry, former sheriff of Coleman County, had my daddy's life in his hands.

He was screwed—thanks to me.

Chapter Thirty

I made it out of court and found the sheriff waiting for me at my car. He was leaning against the driver's door, his arms folded and his legs crossed. He was the epitome of all that was good and lawful, wrapped up in one sexy uniform.

I expected him to give me a ticket for parking illegally, but he told me he'd let it slide.

"Then why are you here?" I asked.

Mateo stood up straight and rubbed the back of his neck; dark circles marred his beautiful eyes. "I wanted you to know that yesterday was the hardest day of my life. I didn't want to arrest Bobby Ray."

"But you did."

He nodded. "I did."

"I understand," I said. Because I did. I'd disciplined numerous five-year-olds who I absolutely adored, in the same manner I treated the little monsters whose behavior made teaching a daily challenge. My personal feelings didn't matter. I did what was right and fair.

The corner of the sheriff's mouth turned up. "It's true," he said.

"What?"

"You are a princess." Mateo walked away, and I couldn't help but admire his swagger.

Everyone made it from the courthouse to the funeral home in time for Marlene's service. It was pretty weird. The same people who had stood by me and supported my father in court were at the funeral mourning the loss of the woman he was accused of killing.

The crowd at the funeral was a little larger, though. Scarlet, who'd understandably missed court, was waiting for me when I arrived. I didn't envy her job in the least.

Mr. Duncan had been released when my father declined to press charges. He sat in the front row, tears streaming down his face, and that funky cactus with the forgiveness sign attached to it taking up the chair next to him. I couldn't help but think I was missing some private joke.

I knew Mr. Duncan had planned on keeping the funds he made off the Roosevelt books for himself. But my dad had let it slide, so I was willing to as well, for the man who had nothing.

I also felt horrible for my daddy. Even though we hadn't had the opportunity to talk, I knew he'd want to be at the funeral something bad, but unlike Mr. Duncan, his bond was set at four hundred thousand, and that wasn't going to happen anytime soon. Our defense fund wasn't close to reaching forty thousand dollars. Cade had said my dad refused to use the money he'd received for George Washington's autographed book and offered to buy the other president books back now that we knew they actually belonged to my family and not his. I told him I wanted to speak to my dad first, which I wouldn't be able to do until later that afternoon.

The service was nice and respectfully done. Marlene didn't have any family, but tears were spilled and a few stories about her were told by the people of Hazel Rock.

No one mentioned her extracurricular activities with Mr. Duncan, Dean, or Mike Thompson. Of the three, Mike was the only one who wasn't present, and I found it ironic that Dean, the least respectable of the bunch, was the only one who hadn't tried to rob me blind.

After the service was over, when most people went to the diner, I decided to go for a drive. Not that I had anywhere to go, just that I wanted time to think without being interrupted or pressured. The town had had a little growth since I'd left, but for the most part it looked like home. The high school and the water tower brought back memories that made me smile. The tough ones were beginning to fade behind all the warmth the town had shown me since I returned and I realized sometimes the memories you have from childhood can be tainted by an immature brain. At seventeen I probably couldn't see the whole picture clearly.

I headed back to the bookstore with plans to work through some of the things that were bothering me about Marlene's death—kind of like what Coach was doing in the loft. When I arrived at The Book Barn Princess, all the flowers, balloons, stuffed animals, and crosses left in Marlene's memory were gone from the front door. It looked rather vacant and I decided a permanent plaque in her memory was warranted.

I entered through the side door because that was the only key I had and heard Coach hammering away on the second table for our book art classes. The man had been a godsend since I'd decided to revamp the store into a profitable business.

I dropped my purse on the counter and walked up to the loft to see how his mourning was progressing. He was bent over as he attached the last brace for the legs.

"Wow. That's gonna be awesome, Coach."

He stood up and beamed with pride. "Woodworking has gotten me through some rough years."

I immediately felt bad for the vacation hours he was taking to fix the store. "I promise you, when this is over, I'll pay you for every hour you've put in."

He waved me off and laughed. "This is what we do in Hazel Rock."

"But you missed the service for Marlene . . ."

His eyes grew sad and he turned away. "I could do more good here. No one needed me there."

I understood. Funerals weren't for everyone, yet I still felt bad that he had worked through the morning. "You've gotta be getting tired. What with practice and games, teaching in the afternoon and working here in the morning and on the weekends, how are you still going?"

Coach got that philosophical look on his face, the one teachers wear when they're going to impart a serious life lesson. It was a look I had yet to master, but I never had the attention of my five-year-old students long enough for it to be effective anyway.

"I was raised to give my all. So I do," he said as he slid his hammer into his tool belt. "Grab the other end, will you?"

I did as he asked and we flipped the table over and stood it up. It was beautiful.

"I don't know what to say." My voice cracked and I laughed to cover it up. The top of the table matched the first one he'd made and was as smooth as a baby's bottom. It seemed wrong for me to take so much from him, even if he was willing to give it.

"What about your wife—how does she feel about you spending so much time over here helping me out?" I asked.

He looked up at me as he was running his hand across the seam in the table I could barely see. "My wife left me three years ago."

I cringed. Scarlet hadn't told me that. Granted, I should have realized I'd yet to meet her or see her out in public, but still, it felt as if I was missing a lot of information about the people in town. Information I would have known had I stayed. "I'm sorry."

He shook his head and snorted. "Don't be. She hated football."

I couldn't help but laugh.

"Yeah, she loved basketball," he continued. "I'd like to blame it on being young and dumb like you and the mayor were, but we were older and took it one step further."

I wanted to say he was wrong, Cade and I hadn't been young and dumb, yet part of me saw some truth in his comment. The other part . . . well, I didn't really want to listen to the other part.

"You didn't say how court went," he said.

I turned away and headed for the two boxes against the wall. "His bond was set for four hundred thousand. We've got a lot of work to do to raise the rest of the money. These tables will help tremendously."

But a part of me didn't think we ever could. I sighed and got to work. "I'm going to take a couple boxes of books over to the high school, so I won't be opening the store right away."

"Do you need some help?" Coach asked.

"If you could carry one downstairs for me that would be great." I handed the top box to my angel in overalls and grabbed the second one for myself. We headed for the stairs, and as I took the first step, my shoe slipped off the back of my heel. I grabbed the railing and shifted the box but felt the cardboard give. The bottom of the box buckled and my attempt to reposition it only made it worse. Grabbing for the edges, I missed a flap and watched helplessly as all the dictionaries and encyclopedias spilled out. They tumbled all the way down to the bottom of the stairs.

When the last one thunked on the floor, Coach said, "That could be you down there if you'd tried to carry both of these boxes."

I thought about that for a moment and couldn't stop the image of Marlene flashing in my head. If I'd fallen, I would have ended up in a similar position.

"Come on. I'll help you pick them up," Coach said.

We made it down to the first floor and began stacking the books.

Most of them looked okay, but a couple had been damaged during their rough descent.

"Are these all dictionaries and encyclopedias?" Coach asked.

"Yeah. Ms. Phelps wanted some for the English students to use. She's tired of the kids only using definitions and information they find online. She thought it would do them good, and no one is going to buy them, so I told her we'd donate the lot to the school." I started on my second stack.

Coach nodded. "Most of our kids don't even know what an encyclopedia is."

"It's my contribution to the kids for helping with the store. Although I think they'd rather have pizza." I put what I thought was the last book on the stack, then saw a folder on the ground over near the register.

Coached patted me on the arm. "Your daddy would be proud, Princess."

"I hope I can make him proud." I stood up, amazed to realize that I wanted to make him proud of not only my accomplishments but of me as a person.

Aware that Coach had worked up a sweat and was still helping me, I asked, "Can I get you something to drink?"

"A tall glass of water would be great." Coach stood up, put his hands on his lower back, and moaned as he stretched.

I cringed at the noises his back made. "You got it. Coming right up."

I went to the tearoom, got two glasses of ice and filled them with water from the tap before I returned to the coach, who was straightening the books in one of the boxes.

I walked over and picked up the clear plastic binder that had made its way behind the counter.

"Everything all right over there?" he asked.

"It's fine. This folder must have come out of the box." I held up the binder, which had the top edge chewed off, possibly by one of those rumored rats The Barn had, but more likely the damage was done by an armadillo. The title on the cover page, however, was still legible. I read it aloud: "*The Socio-Economic Growth of Hazel Rock, Texas, and the Real Estate Market of 2016.* Geez, does it get any more boring than that?"

I had lost interest at *Socio-Economic*, but I flipped it open anyway just in case the header wasn't destroyed on all the pages. The title and the author's name weren't present on any of them. Princess had done a number on it.

"Princess, did you do this?" I asked.

She peeked out of her bed and looked at me as if she was wondering who else could have done it, then looked at Coach. My money was still on her.

Then I remembered Aubrey's term paper. "Shoot, I bet this is it."

"This is what?" Coach asked.

"This is the term paper Aubrey couldn't find." I looked up at Coach, glad that I could finally do something for someone else.

His face looked pale as he stared at the document in my hand.

"Coach, are you all right?"

"What makes you ask that?"

"You're looking a little on the fish-belly white side of pale. Do you need to sit down?"

He ignored my question and held out his hand. "Let me see that."

I handed the folder over. "Do you recognize it? Is it Aubrey's?" I asked as I looked under the counter for a new box to put the books in.

Coach thumbed through the pages, so engrossed he failed to acknowledge my question. I cleared my throat and rephrased it.

"Do you know who it belongs to?" I asked while maneuvering an old adding machine and a paper cutter out of the way so I could pull out the last box I had.

"Can't say as I do. But I'll take it by the office at school when I leave here," he offered.

"That's not necessary. I'll drop it off with the books." I held out my hand, but he closed the binder and pulled it back out of my reach.

"It's really no trouble." Coach looked me straight in the eye, almost daring me to challenge him. Then he took a drink of his water. I didn't know why, but something didn't feel right.

Shaking it off, I told Coach, "You worry about your players. I have to go to the office anyway. It makes more sense that I drop it off. If it's Aubrey's paper, it's due today. The last thing Princess and I need to be responsible for is Aubrey failing English."

I reached out and grabbed hold of the folder, but Coach wouldn't let go. We had a moment of tugging back and forth before our eyes met.

"Coach?"

"I can't let you take it, Charli."

"Aubrey may need this. Or what if it belongs to one of your players?" I thought that would make him understand the expediency.

"Why would you think it belonged to one of my players?" Coach set down his glass of water.

"They were in the loft complaining about their papers..." That's when it hit me. That little nudge I'd felt when I brought back our drinks. "You're drinking the water," I said.

"So?" He smiled, but it wasn't friendly and that nudge started growing into a push.

I let go of the folder. It wasn't worth that look in his eyes. "When did you find out the water was okay to drink?" I asked.

"It's never been bad," he answered.

"I don't understand. Why didn't you say something? You were here and told us to go out and buy more water—" Then I realized Reba Sue may have told Cade, but it was Coach who'd brought up the need for bottled water while everyone was at The Barn. "You're the one who started talking about the well water. Why wouldn't you just tell everyone it was okay to drink?"

He shook his head, rolled the plastic binder containing the term paper up, and put it in the back pocket of his overalls. "Charli, Charli, Charli. People trust me. So if I tell Reba Sue the water is bad, I certainly can't turn around and tell everyone else it's good."

"Why would you tell her or anyone else the water at The Barn was bad in the first place?" I was at a complete loss.

"Because Reba Sue can't help herself. She likes to gossip. Now, be grateful for what I've done for you." He waved his arm out, encompassing the entire Barn. He'd transformed it—twice, the second time completely free of charge. "Leave it be," Coach said and turned to walk away.

I'd never been able to hold my tongue. Unfortunately, I couldn't do it now either. "You hurt our reputation. I haven't been able to serve anything out of the tearoom because of the rumor you started." I stopped and thought about the other rumor. "Did you tell everyone we had a rat problem too?"

Coach froze for a moment and then he turned around and stalked toward me.

"I've always thought you had half a brain," he said.

"I've got a full brain," I retorted, secretly reaching for the Taser under the counter.

He cocked his head. He didn't believe me. Fine. I don't know why I asked the next question, but I did. "You killed Marlene, didn't you?"

He laughed. I was getting tired of men laughing at my ideas and wanted to tase him just for the heck of it. Instead, I took a step back, the Taser hidden from his view as he reached the counter.

"Why?" I asked.

"You of all people should know that when someone gets in the way of the game you take them out of the picture." Coach pulled the hammer from his utility belt and swung it at my head.

I screeched. A man I trusted—who'd helped repair my shop and donated countless hours all out of the goodness of his heart—was trying to kill me.

"Coach, we're friends. You've been helping me—" I ducked again as he swung the hammer like a backhand in tennis. He nearly knocked himself over with the force behind his miss.

"I helped you because I needed time to find this paper. If you hadn't had so damned many customers, I wouldn't have had to work so hard." He grunted and swung again, catching the light above the register before bringing the hammer down to crash into my mom's antique register. "Yet no matter how many rumors I started, the customers kept coming!"

My eyes nearly popped out of my head with disbelief as the drawer exploded. Coins spilled over the floor. "But you've done so much!"

"And I asked for one tiny little favor in return." He pulled back his weapon, catching several register keys and yanking them from the brass machine.

"What do you want from me?" I screamed.

"You're just like her. No matter how I phrase it, you're too stupid to let it go." The hammer connected with the wooden counter with a deadly thud. His glass of water shattered on the floor.

It was my window to escape. I ran from behind the counter but forgot the stack of books. I tripped and fell, sprawling across the wet concrete. I rolled over and aimed the stun gun, but then realized I was soaking wet. Could I electrocute myself? There was water all around me. My dress and hands were soaked. I wasn't quite desperate enough to try it. Yet.

Coach was breathing heavily, his face red with rage.

"Why do you want that term paper so badly?" I asked as I scooted backward, trying to distract him as I made my way to the stairs.

"It's the whole reason I had to kill Marlene!" he bellowed, and I couldn't help it, I hoped he'd give himself a heart attack.

"Why would you kill her over Aubrey's chewed-up term paper?" I scooted up the second step of the stairs, aiming the gun at him but realizing the first step had water on it from my clothing.

"It's not Aubrey's paper. It's Darrin's, and Marlene knew it was plagiarized." His next sentence came out with a grunt. "She threatened to expose my boy."

I wasn't sure what he was talking about and I honestly didn't care. His reasoning for murder seemed insane. "Why would she care?"

"Because with the sale of The Barn to Country Mart, she could show this town she was better for it than the Calloways ever were. She'd regain the business they lost."

"What?"

Coach laughed, the noise sounding manic instead of humorous. "You didn't know? Country Mart was going to turn The Barn into a mini Country Mart. Cade was against it. Marlene told me if I didn't turn my back on Cade and openly support her in the next mayoral race, she would expose Darrin and ruin his career."

I knew Coach was loyal to his players, but to kill for a mayoral race or the college career of a kid who'd cheated? Who would do that? Coach continued to advance with the hammer in the air, sanity completely missing from his expression. I tried to stall his pursuit. "How did the paper get here?"

"Dumb kid left it inside a book he brought to the bookstore and Marlene found it."

"So you killed her for your player's paper?"

"I killed her for being unreasonable. All she had to do was give me that damned paper."

"She didn't have the paper," Aubrey said from the side door.

Neither one of us had noticed the young girl walk in. Coach growled, thoroughly ticked off that another person had inserted their presence into the whole mess.

"What do you mean, she didn't have the paper? Of course she did. She said she did!" Coach yelled.

But Aubrey just shook her head. "I found it and hid it in the box of dictionaries. I told Marlene about it but wouldn't give it to her. I was scared and didn't know what to do. Darrin said he was sorry. . . ." A tear ran down Aubrey's face. "I helped him write a new paper. I had no idea . . . I'm sorry."

"There's nothing to be sorry about, but I think it's time you leave," I told her.

"She's not going anywhere!" Coach screamed, his complexion nearing purple.

"Why do you care about Darrin's future so much?" I asked as I flipped the safety off the stun gun.

Aubrey answered for him. "He asked me to push Darrin to go to the University of East Texas. The sports director offered Coach the head coaching position if he brought Darrin there." Her face nearly crumpled with guilt. "I pushed Darrin to East Texas because it would keep him close to home." Another tear ran down her face.

I knew her tears well. Knew what it was like to love and lose over a game of football. Even Coach was beginning to understand how bad a loss could feel—and he was willing to kill to turn it around.

"And I thought you understood the importance of the game." He sneered at Aubrey. Coach made his move, but it wasn't toward me, and I made mine.

Before he could take his second step in Aubrey's direction, I aimed the little red dot of the laser light in the middle of his chest and pulled the trigger. The prongs flew out of the front of the weapon with surprising speed and struck Coach just above his overalls. His eyes rounded, and for a moment I thought it hadn't worked.

Then I heard the charge entering his body, but he didn't move. He stood frozen with the hammer held above his head, his eyes moving between me and Aubrey at top speed.

Coach began to scream.

Really scream—high-pitched and warbling. It was worse than a birthday party filled with a bunch of ten-year-old girls. It hurt my ears. Made me think twice about using the Taser and then, God forbid, wondered if a prong had struck him . . . in his manhood.

I wasn't removing that prong.

"Run!" I yelled at the young girl, who seemed as frozen as Coach. She didn't hesitate. Aubrey ran out the door. For a moment I panicked that she wouldn't get help and Coach would turn on me and kill me where I stood.

Instead, he fell over like a tree.

My mind yelled, *Timber!* I grimaced as he hit the concrete floor. The hammer bounced out of his reach and I couldn't have been happier. He shook and continued to scream, finally making words out of the noise.

"STTTTT . . . . OOOOOOPPPPPPPPPP!"

I let go of the trigger. And heard him take a deep breath.

So far so good. He started to sit up.

"Don't you move!" I bellowed. Coach ignored me and I zapped him again.

This time his screaming bounced off the rafters, and I wondered if I'd somehow increased the voltage. Was I killing him? Did it matter?

I wasn't sure what the answer was to either of those questions, so I let go of the trigger. "You move and I'll hit you again!"

Despite my warning, Coach lumbered toward me and I tased him again as Mateo ran through the door. I think Coach was mighty happy to see him.

Chapter Thirty-one

My statement to Detective Youngblood was completely different this time. Although I expected to be escorted to the interrogation room, where I'd be read my Miranda rights for literally tasing the crap out of Coach, we avoided that sterile environment completely. Instead, we went straight to his cubicle and chatted like old friends. We talked about family, and when I asked about the photo on his desk of the woman surrounded by five kids, he beamed with pride. His wife of ten years had been his childhood sweetheart.

The way he opened up kind of surprised me, and when he offered a snack from his cookie jar, I was too afraid not to accept, lest I jinx my new friendship.

I ate two of his wife's gourmet oatmeal cranberry cookies, which were sweetened with chunks of white chocolate, and accepted a soda over a cup of coffee. I figured I may as well take them while I could, just in case I ended up on the other side of the jail doors once again. I even used the restroom in anticipation of my interview going south. But it was all for naught.

When I asked if the sheriff would be joining us, Detective Youngblood advised that Coach refused to talk to anyone but Mateo, so I probably wouldn't see the sheriff for the rest of the day.

We talked for well over an hour, both personal and professional. Only once being interrupted by another detective who asked to speak to Youngblood in the hall. When he returned, we finished my statement and I signed the nine-page document.

"When will you be returning to Denver?" he asked.

"Denver?" I hadn't thought about going home, but suddenly it looked like I'd better make plans.

"Yeah. The DA will want to know how to reach you."

"I guess I'll be here a couple days." I thought of my job. If I didn't return on Monday, I'd be looking for a new one. "I'll probably head back on Sunday." Which felt way too soon.

"Okay. Sounds good. I'll let her know." Detective Youngblood put my statement inside a manila folder, and I knew he was getting ready to escort me out. But something still nagged at me about the case.

"Why didn't they find Coach's DNA on the belt?" I asked.

"There's still that unknown DNA we need to find a match for." Detective Youngblood leaned back in his chair and took a sip of his coffee. He peered over his cup as if he was waiting to see if I'd give a truthful answer.

Confessing was harder than I thought. "I think I may know whose DNA you should test."

"Oh?" He set down his cup and folded his hands across his belly. He wasn't a big man, but you could tell his cookie jar was taking a toll on the buttons of his shirt. He waited for me to respond.

Pushing through the heat that was warming my face, I told him the truth. "It probably belongs to my high school boyfriend. He . . . he liked to play with my belt."

Detective Youngblood's smile told me he knew exactly what type of playing I was talking about. His dark brown eyes twinkled, and I saw just how attractive he could be.

"The mayor gave a DNA sample about a half hour ago. That's why Detective Wilson interrupted your statement. It turns out Coach had on his work gloves, which would account for the slivers of wood we found on the belt and the victim." He stood up, letting me know it was time to go.

"The mayor was here?" I hadn't heard his voice, but I was glad Cade had shown up.

"Yup. He heard about the arrest and came down right away."

"Oh." We walked toward the front of the office, passing two other detectives in identical cubicles along the way.

"I'll have a uniform take you home."

"Is the mayor still here by any chance?" I asked, hoping to thank him for everything.

"No, he left a while ago."

"And my dad—will he be released?"

"The sheriff and the mayor spoke to the judge and got your dad

214 · *Kym Roberts*

released as soon as Coach started confessing. The mayor took your father to Marlene Duncan's gravesite."

I nodded, disappointed that I couldn't be the one to take him home, but I knew it was probably for the best.

We walked upfront to where a uniformed officer waited. I shook Detective Youngblood's hand. "Thank you for everything. If you bring your kids by The Book Barn Princess before Sunday, I'll be sure to give them a tour of our new kids' sections. They'll love it."

"I just may do that." Detective Youngblood turned and disappeared through the door and I walked out a free woman, despite the uniformed escort.

I couldn't help but think of the sheriff when the officer opened the passenger door. He was young and stiff and reminded me a lot of what I thought his boss would have been like at twenty-one. Polite, brisk, and buff, ready to conquer the world.

I was extremely grateful he didn't put the palm of his hand on the top of my head as I bent over to get in the front seat.

The drive to the bookstore was quick and uneventful. The sun had disappeared into the horizon and I was surprised to see that it was after eight o'clock according to the dashboard clock. Cookies and soda weren't exactly dinner, but by the time we made it to Hazel Rock, the diner was closed and I was in no mood to cook.

I thanked the deputy for the ride and walked across the stone pavers of the courtyard. The Book Barn Princess was dark; only the exterior light above my mom's gate was on. The gate creaked softly like a welcome home as I went through while frogs serenaded me from down by the river.

I let myself in the apartment, half-expecting, half-hoping my dad would be there along with Princess. They weren't. The place was quiet and lonely. I waited up for a while, wondering if he would come home, but by nine-thirty it was obvious he wasn't. I called my cousin Jamal and told him the entire story. He said, "*Get. Out,*" at least ten times before we hung up with the promise to talk again the next day. Disappointed my dad wasn't coming home and exhausted beyond belief, I did the only thing I could think of and went straight to bed.

The next morning, I woke up to the bright rays of the sun reflecting off the mirror on the armoire and striking me in the face. Squinting, I rolled over and looked at the alarm clock.

Nine-fifteen. The bookstore should have opened fifteen minutes ago.

I jumped out of bed, grabbed my last pair of clean cutoffs and a T-shirt that still had the bookstore price tag under the arm, and ran for the shower. Five minutes later I was dressed, with body cream soaking in my skin and my curls loose around my face. I looked in the mirror to see if I looked somewhat presentable and decided I really liked the message on my T-shirt: *Leave the Drama on the Pages*. It was the perfect mind-set for a day like today.

I grabbed my keys and ran for the door. Locking it behind me, I took the steps several at a time and realized for the first time that morning that it felt really good to be alive. Especially when I looked up and saw my mom's sign had been rehung. I ran and jumped up to tap Eve's gate with my fingertips, "Good morning, Mom," I whispered.

Going through the gate, I paused and thought of Marlene. Only my dad knew if she was planning to steal the books out from underneath his nose, and I got the feeling he'd never tell—never dampen the town's love for a woman who'd taken another path.

Feeling my mood darken a bit, I unlocked the side door and was greeted by Princess squeaking at my feet.

"Well, there you are. I was wondering where you went off to last night," I said to the little rodent standing on her hind legs with her ears twitching at top speed.

"Good morning, Princess." His deep, musical voice made me jump straight up in the air. The little armadillo at my feet did the same. She, however, was frightened by my squeak and not by the man I'd always loved. The man who'd sacrificed so much for my success and gotten so little in return.

He was behind the counter, sitting in his leather chair with a book spread open in his hands. He was wearing a plaid shirt with the sleeves rolled up that looked like every other one I'd seen him wear in my childhood. So many years had passed, but in his eyes I saw the younger man I'd depended on every day of my life.

"Daddy . . ." I smiled. "We're home."

If you enjoyed FATAL FICTION, be sure not to miss the next book
in Kym Roberts's
Book Barn Mystery series
A REFERENCE TO MURDER
A Lyrical e-book on sale May 2017!

Chapter One

My time was up.

Literally. The clock struck three o'clock and the class was over. Thank God.

Sure it had been fun, but it'd been a long day and I was ready to call it quits. The students were in a good mood. The gossip had been friendly with no tinge of envy or meanness. It was the type of comradery a teacher dreams about with her students.

Not that it ever happened in my Kindergarten classes. But this particular class was full of men and women well beyond the age of five or six. My current students ranged from eighteen to eighty-seven and they had come together on a common ground to create something they could all enjoy—wall clocks made of repurposed books.

My best friend Scarlet and I had started teaching the classes at my family book store, The Book Barn Princess, a few months back when I'd made the decision to return and put down roots in my hometown of Hazel Rock, Texas. It's kind of a long story, but after more than a decade away from home I came back to sell the family business and ended up bridging a gap between my estranged dad and me. Now, we were working out all the kinks years of misunderstandings had caused.

"We need to wind it up, ladies and gentlemen." I smiled as they groaned at my clock humor.

Scarlet joined in. "Time flies when you're having fun."

"Big time," replied Betty.

"Maybe we could turn back the hands of time," my oldest student Jessie replied.

My dad decided to chime in. "You can't beat the clock."

Our sparring was interrupted by the entrance of two incredibly good looking men. One was a staple in our town; the other was new to the circuit and had been turning heads for the past two days. He joined in without missing a tick or a tock.

"Darn, I'd been hoping to kill some time with y'all," added rodeo star Dalton Hibbs. His blond hair glistened under the fluorescent lights. His deep blue eyes made every woman in the room drown in their cool depths. He had what it took to melt the coldest of hearts, and I had to admit, even though he wasn't my type, he gave me warm fuzzies when he winked in my direction.

But it was Scarlet who was completely smitten, tongue tied, and utterly lost when his gaze captured hers. And at that moment I knew she was in trouble. Big trouble. But I didn't know how much that look would cost her. If I had, I would have shoved her in the closet, locked the door, and thrown the key in the middle of the desert. Instead, I stupidly smiled and watched her fall.

Three career paths resonated for **Kym Roberts** during her early childhood: detective, investigative reporter, and . . . nun. Being a nun, however, dropped by the wayside when she became aware of boys; they were the spice of life she couldn't deny. In high school her path was forged when she took her first job at a dry cleaner's and met every cop in town, especially the lone female police officer in patrol. From that point on, there was no stopping Kym's pursuit of a career in law enforcement. Kym followed her dream and became a detective who fulfilled her desire to be an investigative reporter with one extra perk—a badge. Promoted to sergeant, Kym spent the majority of her career in SVU. She retired from the job reluctantly when her husband dragged her kicking and screaming to another state, but writing continued to call her name.

Visit her on the web at kymroberts.com.